PRAISE FOR *INSTAMOM*

"Instamom is a delightfully cheeky rom-com about women's choices that fall outside of the norm, the vulnerabilities of modern love, and having the courage to change how you show up in the world—all in the complicated age of Instagram. Kit Kidding is a heroine you'll think of often as you scroll through your social media feeds!"

—Ashley Audrain, *New York Times* bestselling author of *The Push*

"Fun, romantic and thought-provoking, *Instamom* explores a woman's journey to discover what she needs as opposed to what she always thought she wanted. Chantel Guertin's characters are so endearing and compelling, and the story is full of joy, hope and inspiration. A perfect escape read that will also empower you to reach for your dreams."

—Samantha M. Bailey, #1 national bestselling author of *Woman on the Edge*

"Chantel Guertin's *Instamom* is the #InstaFun rom-com you need right now: witty and spirited, with a modern love story that satisfies thanks to a charming meet-cute and timely insights. Pitch-perfect, sexy and smart! #LovedIt."

—Karma Brown, bestselling author of *Recipe for a Perfect Wife*

"Instamom reads like a love letter to my soul, a laugh-out-loud funny, sexy, moving novel about love and family that is as smart as it is delightful, and doesn't shy away from unpacking the fascinating complexities of modern women's lives."

—Kerry Clare, author of *Waiting for a Star to Fall*

"Witty and compelling, this is a modern story about unexpected connections and adapting priorities. Kit's growth as she learns how to let more into her life while staying true to herself is expertly crafted. A delight!"

—Farah Heron, author of *Accidentally Engaged*

"There's a provocative question at the heart of this charming rom-com from Chantel Guertin: What if the social media brand you've built—one that celebrates personal growth and empowerment—prevents you from growing yourself? This is the dilemma faced by Kit Kidding, charismatic online promoter of the child-free life, when she falls for an irresistible single dad and has to decide whether to risk her carefully curated life. Guertin's insider observations on the influencer lifestyle are sharp and funny, and will leave you rooting for Kit . . . and wondering if you should delete your social media accounts."

—Kate Hilton, author of *Better Luck Next Time*

"Chantel Guertin shines in this witty and tender rom-com that amplifies the pressures women face navigating career, relationships, motherhood . . . and, of course, social media. All with a delightful cast of side characters, and some seriously swoony hot-chef vibes, this is a book I wish someone would have handed to me in my twenties."

—Jean Meltzer, author of *The Matzah Ball*

"*Instamom*, Chantel Guertin's terrific romantic comedy of oh-so-modern manners, takes us beyond expected tropes and deftly skewers the outdated expectations and assumptions that continue to limit our 21st-century lives, among them the undying conundrum of career versus motherhood—but she does so with wit and warmth and verve. Delicious and compulsively readable!"

—Jennifer Robson, bestselling author of *The Gown*

"*Instamom* has it all: a heroine you'll wish you were friends with, a male lead you'll want to date, and a cast of characters that make this smart, refreshing story about love and life choices truly shine. Chantel Guertin made me laugh, she made me swoon, she made me obsessively turn pages—but she also made me think deeply about how our pasts shape our futures, and how change takes courage. Perfect for fans of Sally Thorne and Emily Henry, this is the book you'll be telling all your friends to read next!"

—Marissa Stapley, bestselling author of *Lucky*

Instamom

Instamom

A NOVEL

CHANTEL GUERTIN

KENSINGTON
PUBLISHING CORP.

www.kensingtonbooks.com

ISBN-13: 978-1-4967-3536-2 (ebook)
ISBN-10: 1-4967-3536-6 (ebook)

ISBN-13: 978-1-4967-3535-5
ISBN-10: 1-4967-3535-8
First Kensington Trade Paperback Printing: July 2021

10 9 8 7 6 5 4 3 2 1

Printed in the United States of America

For Chris

If you order a latte but you don't
post it to Instagram, did you
really order a latte?
#butfirstcoffee #happinessis

No one's life is as perfect as
their Instagram feed
—anonymous

one

I finish the chapter of the book I'm reading, then reluctantly bring myself back to reality. Getting up from the bench where I'm sitting, soaking up the last drops of spring sunshine before the sun sets, I slip the book into my purse and start walking toward the nearby hotel.

Come on, Kit. Let's do this. One more event to go and that'll make twenty influencer events this week—possibly an all-time record, but everyone knows spring is a busy time for openings, launches, collaborations. And the invitation for the Beachdazer event promises I'll have a "beachy good time." Right now, my idea of a good time is going home, kicking off the world's most uncomfortable heels I reserve solely for these events, changing into my favorite pj's, pouring myself a large glass of wine and finishing off this novel. But it's fine. It's Friday (#Friyay!), and while these launches don't pay, they pay *off* in campaigns. All I'm expected to do is smile, laugh, drink a cocktail, snap a bunch of photos and share them with my followers. It's not exactly comparable to having an open-heart surgery to perform before calling it a week, I remind myself.

My phone buzzes.

Where r u?

Feloise, my agent. Likely seeing other influencers posting to their social channels, and worried I'm skipping the event.

I snap an upwards shot of Hotel 6ix, the hot fifty-story hotel-slash-residences that shot up at the waterfront seemingly overnight, and send it to her, resisting the urge to roll my eyes because sure, Feloise has been riding me a bit lately, but she's just doing her job, and it's the reason she's so sought-after. Plus, I chose this career, this life. I have no one to blame but myself. And so I Superwoman pose in my white T-shirt, black cigarette pants and silver heels and tell myself that I've got this. Head held high, smile plastered on, I push through the massive glass double doors, flipping my shoulder-length brown hair over my shoulder.

Inside Hotel 6ix, the lobby is a cavernous space of dark wood, cold metal and shiny tile. Off to the left is the row of junior publicists, lined up in order of ascending height like neat Russian dolls, clipboards in hand, bleached teeth gleaming, hair in beachy waves. They're dressed head-to-toe in beach-inspired outfits: white sundresses, sunglasses on their heads, beach bags hooked into the crooks of their arms.

"Hi, Kit!" one of the publicists says to me in her singsong voice. "You made it!" I rack my brain for her name, then remember it's Emaline as she checks me off her list. Emaline leads me to the mirrored bank of elevators and we ride up to the fortieth floor, filling the air with small talk until the elevator doors open into a massive room that feels spacious and airy, with floor-to-ceiling windows that give a near–360-degree view of the Toronto skyline: the CN Tower, the OVO Centre where the Raptors practice basketball and the islands, which are a favorite escape for everyone but me on hot summer days. I've been in this room for three other events already but I still love this view of the city. But back to the event space: it's been completely transformed into a beachside resort and even though I've seen a million space make-overs, I'm impressed: several windows have overlays so you can stand in front of them and look like you're on the beach in Bali, Thailand, Australia; the floor is covered in a light layer of sand, and lounge chairs, beach umbrellas and beach balls are scattered throughout. "You can pick out your beach bag here," Emaline says, leading me over to a lineup of straw baskets with tassels, striped canvas totes, bright bags with neon handles. The bags are all adorned with inspirational puns such as *Shell Yeah!* and *Seas the Day!* I choose one—an outfit-matching black-and-white striped tote that says *Avoid Pier Pressure* and peek inside to see that it's filled with beach essentials—flip-flops, a beach towel, sunglasses, a sunhat, and the *pièce de résistance*, the Beachdazer curling iron. It's generous, for sure, and my twenty-year-old self would've ridden this freebie high for days, but sometimes, it's hard not to think about how, if I really needed a new curling iron (or beach towel or sunglasses, for that matter), I could easily buy the item in less time than I'll be spending at this event. And the towel wouldn't have the Beachdazer imprint on it.

"Aren't the cabanas amazing?" Emaline waves an arm to the far wall where half a dozen brightly colored *fronts* of cabanas have been created. They're not real—you can't go in them, they're just for show. For the 'gram. To give influencers the ability to choose the appropriate backdrop to fit their Instagram grid. But they look real. And if those don't work, there's an entire white-washed wall near one of the huge windows letting in natural light—ideal for those who can't afford to have their own lights, tripods or photographers in tow. Or can't be bothered. "If you need to change, there are washrooms by the elevators. Once you're ready, you can head over to one of the hair stations to get your hair 'Beachdazed'"—she shoves her clipboard under her arm so she can air-quote—"and then help yourself to food and drink, have a *great* time and take lots of pictures, obviously. I can't wait to see your final look!" She claps excitedly, then hands me a square pink card. "Here are the event hashtags, so you don't forget." I look down at the card: #lifesabeachdazer #rideabeachdazer #beachhairdontcare.

Emaline excuses herself and starts her spiel from the top with a woman who's just entered the room behind me, a large black bag slung over her shoulder, a photographer—in his early twenties, thin, stylish—trailing behind her. Possibly a photography grad, though probably her boyfriend. Potentially both.

I scan the room, debating whether to prioritize beachy waves or a bourbon on the rocks, and take in the usual influencers. @NoNoJoJo is standing on the "beach" with a beach ball. Her whole schtick is that she doesn't use any filters or editing—she does, however, have a professional photographer, and at this moment, a whole slew of lighting accessories. Her photographer snaps away while she tosses a beach ball, laughs and catches it. Toss, laugh, catch. Toss, laugh, catch. When she's satisfied, she moves on to one of the beach chairs, pops on a pair of sunglasses and picks up her pink cocktail, twirling the drink umbrella in one hand, pretending to sip the drink through the striped paper straw. Meanwhile, @PugMama is trying to coerce her pug into sitting pretty on one of those massive blow-up flamingos that's on top of a blue floor that's supposed to look like water. The pug is not interested and @PugMama looks stressed. I root around in my oversized Balenciaga bag, remembering that earlier today I was at the opening for a pet café and spa in Yorkville, and we got a gift bag. Sure enough, there's a dog treat. I make my way over to @PugMama and hand her the nail polish–shaped dog treat. She looks at it, then at me, then throws her arms around me dramatically and showers me with thanks before getting back to her shoot.

That's exactly how these events go. There are rarely any boring speeches, or presentations about how a product works anymore—that aspect of events died out about five years ago. That info will all arrive in our inboxes after the event, along with the next steps in our contract how to post about actually *using* the curling iron. For now, all the brand cares about are the photos we take: that the tens of thousands of dollars they've spent on making this event look picture-perfect will result in perfect pictures on our grids—making our followers jealous that they didn't spend their Friday night in the same way, and convincing them that getting a Beachdazer iron will make their lives better.

And so, we eat pretty food, drink sugary cocktails, chat to other influencers and make sure we get *the best photo possible*. A bad photo isn't just a bad photo: a bad photo gets low engagement. Low engagement means you can't charge as much for campaigns. And if engagement gets low enough, brands drop you from their rosters . . . and so on and so on, until we're unable to make our livings as influencers. Most of us got our followers before the algorithm changed. Now, you've got to constantly weed out the bots to make sure your following is legit. Because while brands say they don't care that much about "number of followers," they really do. And getting new followers is a slow race. Turtle instead of hare. Brands are being pickier, followers even more so. Autumn (@LoveAutumn) leans toward me from the next chair. "You got the Crystal Clear junket, right?" she asks and I shake my head.

"Oh shoot, sorry. I just figured you were one of the five on the list. They're taking us to Fogo Island for two nights." Her mouth drops open. "Can you believe it? But it's not like you can't go on your own, right?"

We both laugh and throw back our drinks, because we both know that no one goes to these hot spots *on their own*. And besides, that's not the point. Sure, anyone *can* stay at the Instagrammable Fogo Island Inn, *if* they have $2K a night to throw at a room at the only hotel on the remote island in the Atlantic that takes a full day of planes, cars and ferries to get to. It's not about that. It's about *not* having to pay. Getting the junket invites is an unspoken competition between influencers, and while I tell myself I don't care, that this isn't my main event like it is for some of the others in the room, that a free trip doesn't actually pay the bills, it still feels like an insult not to be one of the chosen few. And yet, my schedule for the coming months is already packed. The last thing I can squeeze in is a multi-day press junket. Especially when I still need to perfect my Women in Business speech, for my *real* job.

An hour later, my shoulder-length, normally straight brown hair is in big waves and I'm looking around for the ideal place to set up my camera when someone taps me on the shoulder. I turn to see a guy, dressed in black, with a camera around his neck. "Do you mind . . . ?" He holds up his camera.

"Of course." I brush a strand of hair away from my face. These events also have their own photographers, so that the publicists can create a post-party report. "Where should I stand?"

I turn a few degrees toward the windows to reduce shadows and flash my teeth in the smile I've perfected in thousands of similar photos at thousands of similar PR events.

But the photographer is looking past me. I turn, and there she is: @LegallyBrunette. Brown hair, coffee eyes, flawless brown skin, Balaya is 5'11" and model-thin. She's in law school but has made it quite clear that if she hits a million followers by the time she's called to the bar she'll give up law for the influencer life. "It's my passion," I remember reading in *The Cut* a few months ago, an article that apparently garnered her another 300,000 followers. The thing is, I believe her. I believe she *loves* getting dressed up and having her picture taken. Like right now. She loves every minute of this.

I slink to the right, embarrassed, as @LegallyBrunette moves into place, hips out, lips pursed. I look around the room, wondering how much longer I need to be here until I can sneak away.

"Oh come on, it can't be *that* taxing to be here," a voice says and I turn to find myself looking into the greenest eyes I've ever seen. Chiseled face, bit of five o'clock shadow, brown, swoopy Roger Federer hair. He's tall, broad, and he's making the tray full of food he's holding with one hand seem like it's as light as a dime.

"Excuse me?"

"Aren't you supposed to be looking like you're having a fin-tastic day? Laughing. Smiling. That sort of thing. You can do better."

"I *was* smiling, until you decided to tell me how I'm supposed to be acting." Why am I even talking to this guy?

"Ehhhhh—you were *pretending* to smile but really, your eyes say your mind is elsewhere. You know you're supposed to love being here, that this is supposed to be so much fun, but you're not feeling it. And you're sort of feeling bad about yourself because you're not more into it, that you can't muster up the excitement that the others have for being here, getting their hair done and their pictures taken, free drinks, amazing food, and calling it work. But mostly you're feeling a bit washed up—excuse the pun. And it's all coming out in your Resting Beach Face." He laughs. "They should put *that* on one of those beach bags you're all getting."

My mouth hangs open. Why do the best-looking guys also have to be the biggest assholes? I'm about to lay into him but he grins and says: "I'm teasing you. You have a very pretty face, you just look like you don't want to be here."

"First of all, I don't need you analyzing what I look like because it's none of your business. And second, you're a *man* at an influencer event for a curling iron. How desperate are you?"

"That"—he points a finger at me—"was sexist. But I'm going to let it slide because unlike you, I'm not an aging influencer. Insta-atheist, actually. I'm also the reason you can't stop eating the canapés. I'm the caterer for this thing. So there." He smiles, his green eyes twinkling.

"Wow," I say, fanning myself with my hand. "You must be *some* caterer to land this job." He looks confused. "Catering an all-female press event where no one even touches the food. You know those could be inedible and no one would know, right?" His eyes narrow and I smirk, and walk away, but my heart's pounding. And my stomach is growling. But no way am I touching anything that jerk made.

Lucy, the head of the PR firm hired to run this event, walks up to me. "Whale hello there." She grins. I put my glass down on the high-top table beside me because Lucy doesn't just air kiss me like the other publicists, she gives me an actual hug. We've known each other since we were both starting out in media and she's one of my favorite people.

"Thanks for coming—I know you hate these things. It means a lot."

"Are you squidding me? I'm having a beachy great time." We both laugh and I silently curse the caterer.

"I know, it's a bit much, but the client seems happy."

I shrug and smile. Lucy and I work with some of the same accounts, like Fresh Food Fast, which sends its customers all the ingredients they need to create home-cooked meals. Everything comes in pre-measured bundles and is packaged in attractive sustainable recycled cardboard that makes you feel you're saving the Earth simply by eating the food. Or, at least, that's the intention. Fresh Food Fast is my single biggest client and Lucy keeps me on their good side, so it's important I support her on her other clients, too.

"Remind me I have a great opportunity to send you. It's a mini-spa getaway for Mother's Day. We're letting guests bring daughters or mothers, so you can bring . . ." She catches herself. "Oh shit, I'm such an ass. I'm so sorry."

I shake my head. "It's fine, Luce." I put a hand on her arm. "Don't worry about it."

She sighs. "Anyway, I want you to meet someone," Lucy says, looking around. She disappears for a moment, then returns, her arm looped through someone else's.

And there's the chef, *again*, with his dimple, grinning at me.

"This is Will MacGregor," she says. "He's the chef I hired for the event. Have you tried the food? It's incredible. Will, this is Kit Kidding, one of our key influencers."

She looks at me expectantly. This isn't the first time Lucy's tried to set me up with someone. It's not that she doesn't know a hot guy when she sees one, and I'm grateful she thinks of me first. But I'm not sure I'll ever get involved with a guy again. I sometimes think I'll be happier being single forever.

"We've met," I say curtly. My stomach grumbles, loudly.

Another PR rep touches Lucy's arm and she holds up a finger. "Excuse me," she says before walking away. "You two should chat—Will's not on Instagram." Her eyes are wide as she turns to Will. "Maybe Kit could help you out with that." She smiles and pats him on the shoulder.

"Fat chance," I say once she's out of ear shot.

"Fine with me. I don't need help. Aren't you a little old to be an influencer?" Will says, his eyes smiling.

"Aren't you a bit too much of an asshole to be a chef?"

"I think chefs are *supposed* to be assholes," he laughs. "And I'm not saying you're old, per se. You're quite cute." He doesn't look me up and down, as I expect him to. Instead, his eyes are fixed on mine, and I can't seem to avert my gaze. He continues. "But aren't influencers in their teens and twenties, living at home with their parents, taking selfies all day in their bedrooms?"

"Where do you get your information—*Dateline*, Grandpa?" I retort, but I've lost my edge. "You do realize that a chef without an Insta account is a bad business move, right? One of the top categories on Insta is food porn."

"Wow, already talking dirty to me." He raises his eyebrows, his eyes boring into mine. My heart pounds. Shit.

"How did Lucy even *find* you? Kijiji?" There, I'm back.

"Real life," he says. "You should try it sometime. Oh wait, but if you can't take a picture and post it then did it really happen?"

His eyes are still shining, and his dimple is giving him away. My breath catches and before I can stop myself, I'm flirting back.

"I don't know, why don't we find out." I hand him my phone. "Make yourself useful and take my picture so I can get out of here, and back to *my* real life." I walk away from him, heading toward the blue cabana, praying he's following me. I turn, and there he is, sauntering toward me. I hold the pose I've refined over the years, and as Will looks at me through my phone, I find myself taking him in. His muscular arms, strong jaw, tanned skin. Oh boy.

"Grab that Frisbee and toss it in the air or something," Will says. When I make a face he throws his hands up. "What? I thought part of my job as Instagram boyfriend was to give you direction."

"Just take the picture." I pose a few more times, reluctantly grabbing the Frisbee because it's actually not a terrible idea to be doing something with my hands. A few minutes later, Will hands my phone over. "There. I got three or four pics. I'm sure one will be fine."

"*Three or four?!*" I grab my phone.

He chuckles. "Relax. There's about a hundred, give or take a thousand."

"Great, well, thanks. Now I've gotta go. See you around, Will MacGregor."

He nods, his lush lips together. "See you around, Kit."

I make my way to the exit, say my goodbyes to the publicists, who are handing out cards with the event hashtags in case we've somehow lost the first one, and get into the elevator just as the doors are closing. I exhale, letting my entire body relax. It's really too bad I'm not interested in dating right now, because that guy was hot. Even if he was a cocky asshole.

Making my way through the lobby, I flip open the Uber app and as I'm entering my address a text pops up from a number I don't recognize.

Have a real drink with me. Meet you in the lobby bar in five minutes.

My heart pounds and I stare at the message. How? When? Is this really meant for me?

I click on the message and see that there's a message from *me* to whoever the sender is. It says *Hey Hot Stuff.* Seriously?!

I stare at my phone, then flip it over to make sure it really is mine. The case is a picture of a set of French doors, stacks and stacks of books on the floor. Yep, it's my phone.

But I did not send that text—I squint at the message—three minutes ago.

"Pretty good party trick, huh?" I look up to see Will standing in front of me.

"How did you . . . ?"

He shrugs. "Come on." He holds up a box. "I brought you some of my canapés. I figured you were probably starving. That's usually what it means when someone's stomach's grumbling." He chuckles. "Though I do admire your determination in not caving in to the temptation of my canapés just because you don't like me."

"Give me those," I say, grabbing the box. "And thank you."

"You're welcome." He smooths a wave of shiny, thick hair across his face with his left hand. No ring. I follow him into the lobby bar to two stools at the bar, and immediately open the box. The bartender is drying a martini shaker with a tea towel. "What can I get you two?"

"Bourbon on the rocks," I say between mouthfuls. Will raises an eyebrow. "No girlie drinks for you, huh? I like your style. I'll have the same."

The bartender nods. "One tab?"

"No," I say at the same time as Will says "Sure." He looks at me.

"I buy my own drinks," I say. *And do my own taxes and fix my own problems,* I think to myself.

"I wasn't implying I was going to buy yours. I just thought, the least you could do was buy me a drink after I took your million-dollar photo up there. And brought you snacks."

I roll my eyes. "Fine, one bill." I pop some sort of fried dumpling in my mouth. It's delicious.

A moment later the bartender slides our drinks toward us and we pick up our glasses. Before I can take a sip, Will clinks his with mine, then brings it to his lips. "So, have you posted the photo yet? Have you gotten a million likes? That's the game, right?"

"Not a game. And did you just ask me for a drink so you could verbally harass me or was there some other reason?"

Will shrugs. "That was pretty much it. You're just so easy to tease."

I slap him on the arm. "And you're so easy to slap." My hand feels like it's on fire. He flexes. "It's the guns. Can't miss 'em."

"Do you practice these cheesy lines in front of a mirror before you leave the house?"

And this goes on, this thrilling banter, for quite a while. When his knee touches mine, it's electric. Like a current running through me. We order more drinks and I wait for those tiny surges, sometimes making them happen, a hand here, a knee there, innocent but intoxicating, until the bartender announces last call.

I stand and grab my bags. Will stands too. "This was fun."

"Maybe for you." Now I'm teasing him, but there's a part of me that doesn't want the night to end. I hate to admit that I'm having a lot more fun than I would be if I were in my empty apartment . . .

"You wanna see the view from my room?" he asks.

"Is it better than the view from the event space on the penthouse floor?" I say, but I'm intrigued. If he has a room, he's not from the city. Which means that this could be a one-time thing and I'd never have to see him again. One and done. Exactly how I like things in my life right now. No commitments, no emotional attachment. This is my year to focus on my career—nothing else.

He shakes his head. "No, I'd say the view's worse. But I have mixed nuts in the mini bar. Do you want to see my nuts?" He tries to keep a straight face but when I laugh, so does he. "Ahh, see? I knew it. You wanna see my nuts. C'mon, let's go."

And then I'm nodding, and Will's taking my hand and leading me to the elevator and then up, up, up we go, our bodies close, the air thick. Will slides his arm to my back, his fingertips working their way up to my neck. His touch feels so right, sending tingles up and down my entire body, as though he's touching me everywhere. I want to slow this moment down, to savor it and the feeling of anticipation of what's to come.

Eventually there's a ping, and the elevator doors open and he grasps my hand again and pulls me out of the elevator and down the hallway, fumbling in his pocket for his key card and tapping it against the door before pushing it open and pulling me inside.

He kicks the door closed and I turn, and push him against the door, determined to be in charge, and take a step closer to him. His hands move to my hips and my hands run over his arms. He pulls me closer and tries to kiss me but I move my lips to his ear, my teeth nibbling at his earlobe. He moans, and squeezes my hip bones. My hands move to his toned chest. Four or five buttons down his fitted dress shirt he stops my progress and pulls off the whole thing and it's his turn to kiss and bite his way down my neck. His chest is tanned and muscular, a hint of hair creating a line down his abs, disappearing beneath the waistband. I take off my white T-shirt, remembering that I am wearing a very practical, nude T-shirt bra. For a flash, I'm self-conscious, but that feeling fades as he takes a step closer to me, running his fingers up my back. Then he's undoing the clasp on my bra with a practiced pinch. He lassos it around a finger and lets it fly across the room and I laugh.

"Oh you like my moves, huh?"

"I'm not sure yet," I say, as he moves me over to the bed, and I sit down at the edge as he bends down, his lips picking up where they left off on my neck, his tongue making a line between my breasts, down my stomach, to the top of my pants. He unzips my pants and I shimmy out of them, kicking off my heels in the process.

"Can I keep going?" he asks, looking up at me. I push his head back down and he gently nudges me back, so that I'm lying on the bed. He spreads my legs with his hands, and moves his face into the V, his lips moving more quickly. I moan. I can't help myself.

"Hang on," he says, and before he walks away I take in his whole body.

"How are you so fit when you're a chef? Aren't you supposed to be flabby from eating too much butter and cheese?" I call after him, laying back on the bed and staring at the ceiling.

"Uhhh . . ." There's shuffling in the bathroom.

"Weren't you bragging about what a good chef you are?" I tease.

"Why are we talking about my culinary skills?" he calls back.

"You should be asking me if I'm good at sex."

I can feel my face heating up, but keep my voice confident, like this—whatever we're doing—is something I do all the time. "Alright. Are you good at sex?"

"You'll have to see." He emerges from the bathroom holding a shiny square packet. "This probably makes it seem like I was planning to have sex tonight but just for the record, I happen to always have a condom in my toiletry bag. It's been there forever."

"Forever?"

His brow furrows. "Well, not forever. Wait, let me actually make sure about that." He squints at the packet then pumps his fist. "Still good. Phew."

He rips it open, and slips the condom on, and my whole body warms with a yearning to feel my body on his. Then things go from slo-mo to time-lapse and I'm pushing him onto his back and climbing on top of him, reaching for him and maneuvering us so I can lower myself on top. We move in sync, my back arched, his hands on my hips, and then he's rolling me over and he's on top, and we're back at it again, his hands beside my shoulders, as though he's doing push-ups on top of me. It all feels better than I remember sex ever feeling and I'm climaxing and a second later he lets loose too, and then we're collapsing onto our backs, completely out of breath.

#

"I was not expecting *that*," Will says, his eyes smiling, his dimple ever-present in approval. We're still lying in the massive hotel bed twenty minutes later and he's looking into my eyes, intensely. He strokes my hair. I smile up at him. This feels so easy and comfortable, like I've known him forever, not a few hours. How is that possible? He leans over and kisses me on the lips. It's soft and tender with just enough weight. He pulls me into the crook of his arm and it feels so good. Too good. Pulling the sheet around me, I sit up.

"I have to go," I say.

"No, you don't," he says, the surprise evident in his voice. "Stay. We'll get room service in the morning. Anything you want. Waffles, whipped cream, the works."

"Can't," I say. "I've got something early in the morning."

Will watches me in silence as I gather my clothes. My back to him, I pull my clothes on, all too aware of his eyes on me. Dressed, I turn and kiss him quickly. "This was fun. See you later," I say, though they're empty words. I know I'll never see him again. I look around, see my purse and beach bag on the chair by the window, grab them and then get the hell out of there.

two

Nothing better than an early morning run, amiright?
Just ran along the boardwalk, feel like I'm on vacation
in the city! Running is one of the best ways to boost
your creativity! Happy #weekend everyone! #workout
#fitnessmotivation

I'm not actually running. I'm in bed, in my pajamas, thinking about my night with Will, how good we were together, how easy it was to be with him. Will I ever see him again? I post the picture Feloise took of me a few weeks ago. I wasn't even on a run. I was just dressing the part—wearing a new pair of shiny running tights, tank top and shoes—and jogging slowly back and forth until Feloise got a crisp pic. Fitness pics do great on the 'gram, and Feloise is trying to get me a big fitness-brand contract. The client likes me, according to Feloise, but feels my grid isn't showing as much #fitnessmotivation as they'd like to see, if they were to seriously consider partnering with me.

My account hasn't shown a lot of fitness lately because going for a bike ride or doing a yoga class feels like one of the few times I can justify self-care without having to snap a selfie. But living alone is a lot more expensive than I ever anticipated, and it's hard to turn down paying work. And that's exactly what my Instagram account is, I have to remind myself whenever it doesn't feel that fun. It's work. A job. It just looks like real life.

My phone buzzes and my heart pounds until I remember that I completely blew Will off and there's no chance in hell he'll be calling me after the way I bolted out of his hotel room. Which is exactly how I want it, I remind myself. Even if that was the best sex I've had since things were good with Eric. Maybe *before* Eric, actually. But just the thought of Eric, of five years wasted . . . I look around my teensy apartment, how the breakup has set me back to my post-university days. Never again. This time I'm doing things on my own. No commitments. No dependency. No relationships.

My phone's still buzzing and I'm jolted back to reality.

It's Feloise.

"I just posted the running pic," I say before she can ask. She's been harping on me to post it for weeks now and I've been putting it off—mostly on account of the fact that I don't actually run.

"The Fresh Food Fast people are not happy," she says.

"What do you mean? My pics are always great."

"But you never cook the food."

A pang of embarrassment shoots through me, as it does whenever I fail at anything domestic. I think about my mother and how she was good at absolutely everything: cooking, knitting, sewing. Why didn't I get any of those domestic traits?

"So?"

"So, you're doing sponcon with a brand whose sole purpose is to provide people with all the ingredients they need to *cook at home*. You need to cook the food, Kit."

"But I don't cook. I told you that when we were signing the deal and you assured me it was going to be fine."

Feloise sighs. "Yes, and they understand that. That's why their PR agency is sending somebody over to cook the meals for you. All you have to do is stage the shots. You can at least do that, can't you?"

I make a face at the phone.

"The chef will be there the day after you get back. I'll send you the calendar invite."

I hang up and immediately forget about Fresh Food Fast as my thoughts go back to Will. He's probably already on his way back to wherever he lives. I flip over to the text he sent me last night and then realize something significant: his number is local.

#

That afternoon I'm on a plane to Milwaukee, to the North American Women in Business conference—one of my favorite events of the year—where I'm not just posing for selfies, but giving the motivational speech I've been working on for weeks. That's my real passion. Not being an Instagram influencer, but influencing women with my book—*Kid-Free Forever*—on the many merits and joys of choosing a child-free life. The release of the book spawned dozens of No Kidding groups across the

US and Canada, groups where women can get together to talk about their careers, their goals, anything—anything, that is, except children. I had no idea how much the idea would take off, but more and more groups are popping up everywhere. Women seem desperate for a safe place where they can talk, guilt-free, about their desire, and decision, to remain child-free.

I'm settled into my seat, reviewing my talk, when my phone pings.

The other night was fun. You free for dinner this week—Thursday?

My whole body tingles. There's something I find so attractive about him—despite initially being turned off by his arrogance. I like that he seems old-fashioned, writing texts in full sentences, as though it's an email, and that he's decisive, asking me to a specific activity on a certain day, rather than most guys, who are so vague you're not sure if they want to see you this century or next—or if they even care either way. Would it be so bad to see Will again? What's the big deal? But I know I can't. Because it's there—that unsettling feeling I get in my stomach whenever someone feels like they might be *more* than a short-lived fling. And right now, I can't let myself go down that path—can't let myself fall for someone who will inevitably tell me that they're so relieved *not* to hear my maternal clock ticking, then ghost me for the same reason. Because that's what happens every time. So for now, until I figure out a foolproof method to avoid heartbreak, I need to stick to guys whose names I can barely remember—or don't take up more than a millisecond of thought per day. And right now, Will's on dangerous ground.

I close the messages and slip my phone in my purse and pull out my book.

#

I check into the hotel, text Gloria and Xiu, two of my best friends who are also attending the conference, to let them know I've arrived, unpack, and run through the talk that I'm giving this evening at the opening dinner. I quickly get dressed and head down to the lobby bar. Several women from the local No Kidding chapter greet me as I enter the dark, amber-hued space.

"We've been following you on Instagram for years," says one. Another tells me she's been a fan since I had my No Kidding blog on BuzzFeed. That seems like a lifetime ago—my whole "dating when you know you don't want children" schtick. The woman is about my age, and introduces herself as Arietta Smythe—and it's a name I recognize.

"Oh, I love your work," I tell her. "I order your day planner every year."

Arietta creates inspirational agendas for working women, which means she's filtered out the family-focused reminders that seem endemic to any female-aimed day planner. Sundays are no longer for meal-planning, but for replying to the hundred emails you've let slide over the week.

Gloria and Xiu find me and we quickly catch up. Xiu's quieter than usual, but I figure she's just tired, since she puts in eighty-hour weeks and probably more, this week, just to be here. Gloria makes up for her, though, rattling on about the latest house she sold—while on the flight here. "Laneway apartments are goldmines for me," she says. "You should consider it."

I shake my head. "I want a garage."

"I know, but for your price range . . ." She gives me a look, like she knows best, and maybe she *does* know real estate but I know what I need. Gloria's the only one who knows I'm looking for a garage, but she doesn't know the reason why.

A woman close to us is on her phone and is sounding more and more agitated. "It's *one* weekend, Miles. You just have to figure it out. You're the other parent, remember?"

Gloria laughs. "I love our child-free life, don't you two?" And I exhale, because I really, really do.

Just then, one of the meetup organizers materializes to ask whether we've snapped a pic in front of the event backdrop that's emblazoned with the #womeninbiz hashtag, and after a quick detour to get that out of the way, we follow the crowd into the ballroom where we'll be having dinner. I make a plan to meet up with Xiu and Gloria later, back in the bar, then make my way to the head table, where I'm seated next to the one-armed female surfer whose memoir I devoured six months before. Since *devoured* is probably not the best word choice for a memoir about surviving a shark attack, I instead tell her I couldn't put the book down. She's also read my book, and asks me if I plan to write another. "My publisher is hoping I'll write a follow-up—you know, five years later . . ." She makes a face and I nod. "Mine, too." That's the thing—while both our books may be bestsellers, they're not timeless classics that'll continue to sell at the same rate for years to come. And many of the women in the audience probably already have my book. Soon, these conference organizers won't purchase the book as part of my contract. While I loved writing *Kid-Free Forever*, it took me a really long time, and that was before Instagram campaigns started taking up so much of my energy. And with everything else I want to be doing, writing another book just isn't on my radar right now.

Out of the corner of my eye I catch the meetup organizer, a petite woman of about forty, short blond bob, calf-length wrap dress, nude heels, make her way onto the stage. She taps the mic with her nail and asks for silence at the lectern. We all turn to listen.

She introduces herself, welcomes us and then walks through the high points of my bio. To hear my story like that, it sounds very impressive, even to me. Except really, in the post-internet publishing market, even a bestselling book doesn't provide much to live on. Although what it *does* provide is a solid social media following. And with that, the constant requests from brands to partner with you to monetize your audience.

The applause signals it's my turn to take the mic. I stand, turn to the crowd, and wave to the hundreds of women in the room. I've given a version of this talk many times over the years, but this is definitely the largest crowd. This Women in Business weekend has drawn more than two thousand attendees and the dinner is completely sold out. And everyone's getting a copy of *Kid-Free Forever*.

These are my people. My women. My friends. Or at least, the child-free-by-choice ones. The ones who don't agree with me will probably slip out to the bar or to use the restroom while I give my little motivational speech.

"Hello ladies!" I say into the mic. "Who else is *so glad* they've made it here? To this convention, for this weekend, to be surrounded by thousands of inspiring women who are just like you. You're hard-working, you're independent. You're strong! You're savvy! Maybe you're child-free like me"—I pause in advance for the imminent applause, cheers and whoops of agreement—"and maybe you're not, but for this weekend, you're all here, which means you've made yourselves the priority. And I am so happy to see so many familiar faces out there—and so many new ones who I hope to meet this weekend. Because we're women, we're amazing and we're here to make our careers better, to make ourselves better, to make our lives better! Together!"

The crowd applauds, and I beam.

#

The following morning, lanyard on, I take my seat at the first session of the day. A Bosnian refugee talks about her journey to becoming an AI professor. A widow of a capo in the Sinaloa drug cartel tells us how she's established an educational charity. I sit in on a lecture about how the invention of the bicycle triggered an early wave of Victorian-era feminism. By the time lunch rolls around I feel so inspired I could take on the world.

The afternoon sees everything break up into one of three different streams. I'm on the Child-free by Choice panel. The room is small, but packed. Even women who have children tend to attend panels on the topic—because for many, having children doesn't mean putting their careers aside. Though it also means the talks can get a bit controversial. Nothing I can't handle, though.

"Do you look down on women who choose to have children?" comes the inevitable question toward the end. The question's directed at me, as the movement's nominal head.

"Of course not," I say. "I don't look down on anybody. Child-free by choice is a very personal decision. And each one of us has to define, in our own way, how we came to it. I can't speak for anyone but myself, but what I want women to know is that their contribution to society goes well beyond their capacity for procreation. Having the *ability* to create life doesn't make it an *obligation*. I just don't see why this single biological capacity should allow anyone else—men or women—to make assumptions about me, or other women, for the simple fact I happen to have a uterus. Pursuing a child-free lifestyle stands as a rejection of those assumptions. The powerful women who identify as child-free are combatting the idea that women *have* to be mothers and are creating a new template for female identity. We're expanding minds. And expanding minds is hard work."

"What about your own mother? What do you think about her, then?" someone else asks as a follow-up.

My jaw clenches. "My mother has nothing to do with this. Next question."

#

The next day I'm standing in line at airport security, waiting for my carry-on to go through the X-ray machine, when a TSA officer confronts me. "Is this yours?" He's patting a small blue suitcase in front of him.

Uh-oh. "Umm, yes?"

"I'm going to have to ask you to meet me at the end of the line," he says, his voice cold and formal.

The officer is about my age, with dark-chocolate skin and piercing brown eyes. Full lips. Broad shoulders. I smile at him sweetly, but he doesn't budge, and I suddenly feel very nervous.

"Where are you headed?"

"Toronto."

He nods.

I stare as he pulls on a pair of black plastic gloves and unzips my bag.

Thankfully my clothes are folded neatly and my underwear is well hidden. But then he starts rooting around. His hands disappear into the bag and out comes the first of my gifts.

Earlier today, we were bussed to an old Harley Davidson factory in the outskirts of Milwaukee that now produces vibrators for a company run entirely by women. We were given the grand tour, which concluded with all of us receiving several of their top-sellers as parting gifts. We all got a good laugh, but now that my bag is open under the harsh fluorescent light, it's beyond me why I had to accept them all.

"What's this?" he asks.

"The Softail Slim," I say, staring at the combination of chrome and rubber in his hand. We'd learned about the benefits of its deep rumble. I decide not to elaborate.

He sets it on the table next to my bag.

Next comes the Fat Boy. It's bright pink and rubbery and wobbly in his hand. That goes alongside the Softail Slim. Then comes the Low Rider (it goes low and slow) and the Road King (it will take you places).

I can feel the lineup of people behind me. Men, women. Children. The elderly. They're all watching the officer remove the last of the devices—the Electra Glide, which comes with a little nub designed to—well, it doesn't matter. My face is burning. Could I just abandon my bag right here and now? Is there anything in the suitcase I *really* need? Then I remind myself there is really nothing to be embarrassed about. I take a deep breath, square my shoulders and look the officer in the eyes.

"Is that it?" he asks. His formality has dropped and now he's smirking.

"That's it," I reply firmly.

"You know," he says, putting the vibrators back into my suitcase and zipping it shut, "with a little lipstick, you could easily find a man to do all this, right?"

three

The next day, I can't stop thinking about that TSA jerk. And the more I think of it, the more furious I become. As if I need a man to explain to me how to find pleasure, or even to get pleasure. He just assumed I was heterosexual. I could have been gay. Asexual. Questioning. It was none of his business. I don't need some uptight asshole telling me how I should be living my life. This is just another example of why I don't get involved with men anymore. Sex, OK. Anything deeper, no way. The problem is that I seem to think too much about sex—because I won't let myself have anything more. Like, why did my first reaction to this jerk have to be admiration at his deep brown eyes? Why couldn't I see the jerk that hid behind them?

The intercom buzzes. Fionn, aka the Kind Concierge (my building has two full-time concierges and Fionn is the older, kinder, grandfatherly one), tells me the Fresh Food Fast chef is in the lobby. "And he's got a big box of food so you better let him up before I convince him to cook *me* lunch." He belly laughs and I smile. A few minutes later I open the door to my apartment and nearly drop my phone.

"You?" I say. "*You're* the chef?"

"At your service," Will says, the ends of his mouth slowly curling up, his dimple forming. "They didn't tell you it was me?"

I'm going to kill Lucy.

Will's wearing worn jeans and a gray, fitted T-shirt that shows off his toned arms, his muscles flexed to support a large cardboard box balanced on top of the green Fresh Food Fast box. My mind goes back to that night at the hotel. I try to push the thoughts away but his body brushes mine as he steps into my apartment, and all the feels are all too real once again.

He sets the boxes on the island in my kitchen.

"So *you're* the influencer who can't cook, huh?" He grins. "I shoulda guessed."

"What was it you called yourself? An Insta-atheist?" I jab him in the ribs.

"Yep, but this is your deal, not mine. I don't care what sort of photos you take or post. My job is to make this"—he pats the cardboard box—"look like a five-star meal. Though I don't get it: if you don't like to cook, why would you agree to work with a meal kit delivery?"

I fold my arms across my chest. "That's really none of your business."

"I see . . . you'll do anything for a buck. I get it." Will shrugs, then turns to admire my view—a condo, another condo, a construction crane for a condo, and a small slice of the lake—and I find myself admiring him, and letting him get away with the comment.

"So, it looks like we're stuck with each other," he says, turning around to face me, a smile wide across his face. "It could be worse."

"As long as we keep this professional," I say. "You do your thing"—I wave my hand over the box—"and I'll do mine." I hold up my phone.

His green eyes are on mine. "Whatever you say, Boss." And with surprising efficiency, he unpacks: several large knives, a chopping block, tea towels. Like a culinary magician.

"Wow, you came prepared," I say, sitting on a stool. *You came prepared*? My witty repartee gene seems to have taken a sick day. Maybe we shouldn't talk.

"I like to use my own equipment."

The line is so obvious that I don't even respond. I just stare. He flushes.

"No, seriously, you should see some of the things I find in cupboards when I'm catering in people's homes."

Oh no. My mind goes instantly to the books. I forgot all about the books.

"So let me get this straight," Will says, as he opens the Fresh Food Fast box. "Normally you get all this food—for free. And you get paid to cook it, by using these very, very easy-to-follow instructions." He holds up the large bi-fold card with its colorful photos. "But you've never actually cooked it?"

I nod.

"But . . . then how do you eat the food?"

"I don't."

He looks at me, those green eyes wide. His face is clean-shaven today, and I can't help but wonder how clean-shaven would feel. That smooth, soft skin on my hands, on my cheek, between my legs . . . *Stop it, Kit!* Could I be any *less* professional?

"You know one in nine people go to bed hungry every day, right? I just did a *pro bono* event for one of the food banks downtown. So wasteful. How can you just throw out all this food?"

"I don't *throw it out*," I tell him, offended. "I give it to people who like to cook, or to the homeless shelter down the street." Truthfully, I've only done that once, and although they were grateful, I realized a food box that serves a gourmet meal for two isn't exactly the kind of donations they're seeking. He's right, of course. My face reddens. But if Will notices, he lets it slide.

"I think I forgot a sieve," he mutters to himself, head down.

Before I can stop him, he opens a cupboard. He sees the books. He closes the cupboard door and opens another. More books. And another. He leans down to open a cupboard under the island. I can't see the open cupboard, but I know what he sees. Books. Will straightens and looks at me.

I shrug. "This place is short on bookshelves. Just improvise, would you?"

He points a finger at me. "Uh-uh. You're cooking with me. You're not just going to sit there looking pretty, distracting me." He raises an eyebrow, gives me a long look, then turns and opens the oven door. "For fuck's sake," he says. "This is a fire hazard!"

"Not if you never turn the oven on," I point out. My thoughts go to my mother. She was such a good cook, and baker too. The oven was always on, the smell of muffins or cookies wafting through the house whenever I got home from school. Often, I'd grab whatever it was before heading up to my room, to talk on the phone with my friends. Why didn't I stay downstairs with Mom more often? If only I'd known how little time I'd have with her.

From the storage space in the oven he retrieves *The Joy of Cooking* and a volume from the Barefoot Contessa series I've never cracked.

I come around to the other side of the island and start pulling out the other cookbooks packed into the space.

"You have cookbooks *in your oven*—but you don't cook."

"And biographies in the upper cupboards, romance in the lower ones . . ." I stack the books on the island and avoid his gaze. He probably thinks I'm kidding, but I'm very organized when it comes to my books. He turns one of them over in his hand. "Huh. I love these Harry Bosch novels," he says, and I see he's holding *The Black Echo*, Michael Connelly's first novel. "I haven't read this one."

"Hmm, that shouldn't be in there. Definitely not a cookbook. Crime is in the closet." Along with all the boxes of my mom's old books, which I still can't bring myself to sort through. I heave a heavy stack of hardcovers onto my desk. "I guess I'm going to have to figure out where to put these, if using my oven is going to be a regular thing." Of course I know what I'm ultimately going to do with the books, but that's the long-term career goal, and definitely not something I'm about to share with Will when he's part of the now-career. If Feloise ever found out I was considering a career change . . . well, she can't find out. Besides, I barely know Will. Not even my closest friends know my plans.

"You could put some floating shelves up over there," he says, pointing to the empty wall by the sliding door to my balcony.

"Uh-huh," I say noncommittally.

"They're pretty easy to put up."

Every time I think about doing anything permanent to this apartment, I get a sickening feeling in the pit of my stomach. Like I'm giving in, giving up, on the dream. "I rent, so . . ."

"They're easy to take down, though, too," he says. "If you pick them out, I don't mind putting them up for you next time I'm here."

"I could do it myself, if I wanted to," I say defensively. Will carries a stack of books over to the desk and I watch him, wondering how it's possible that I feel so comfortable with him.

"I didn't say you couldn't." He taps the top of the stack of books. "So have you *read* all these?"

"Most of them. And that's one of Connelly's best," I say. "My dad got me into the series. I'm no book snob. A good read is a good read. Borrow it if you like."

"Thanks." He puts the book on the island. "So you've *never* used this oven?"

I shrug.

"And the rest of these cupboards are also filled with books, so, you don't have *any* kitchen tools? No spatulas? Whisks? Do you even have dishes?"

"I told you. I'm not much of a cook. And I broke up with my boyfriend, so . . ."

"He got all the dishes and you didn't know where to buy more? There are stores for that, you know." He grins and I rip off a strip of paper towel, ball it up and throw it at his head. He ducks and I laugh.

"Also, it feels like clutter. I like the aesthetic of a clean countertop."

Will runs his hand over the smooth countertop, stepping toward me. "Oh yeah?" The corners of his lips turn upwards.

"Don't get any ideas." I shove the Fresh Food Fast box toward him.

The Meanderers come on the speakers and Will points in the air. "Love them."

"Me too. They're supposedly coming to the amphitheater later in the summer," I say. I make a mental note to check when tickets go on sale.

"There's something about seeing a show outside that just feels like you're really experiencing summer, you know? Bring a picnic, some ciders, a book for the lull between the opener and the main event . . ."

My stomach flips as I picture myself, on a soft blanket, lying next to him, staring at the sky, listening to the Meanderers' twangy music fill the air.

No. I'm not committing to anyone—I'm an independent woman. Flings only. At least for another year. Which was *supposed* to be what that thing with Will was the other night.

"So do you always sleep in hotels?"

"Never, actually. But Hotel 6ix is trying to convince me to be their in-house chef. So it was a perk. And it worked out, I'd say." He gives me a long look that makes me feel faint.

"Alright, let's get started," Will says. "Lack of cooking utensils aside, this kitchen is pretty insane."

"It looks great in photos," I say, and he rolls his eyes and turns the tap on, running his hands under the water.

"No!" I say, flipping the tap off, realizing the faucet is positioned over the right basin of the double sink. "You can't use the tap on that side."

Will raises his eyebrows. "Why not?"

"There's something wrong with the drain on that side, water leaks out and—"

"Let me guess. You have books under here." He grabs a dish towel and dries his hands, then bends down to open the doors.

I lean down too and he passes me the books, which I move into the bedroom. "You might be right about me needing bookshelves," I call.

When I return, Will's lying on the floor, his head and shoulders under the sink, his torso and legs splayed across the kitchen floor. "Do you have a wrench?" he asks and I grab my toolbox from the closet.

I pass the wrench to him and he takes it, putting both arms above his head. His T-shirt rides up and knowing he can't see me, I let my gaze linger a fraction of a second longer than I probably should on his taut, muscular stomach. A trail of hair leads from his belly button to the top of his jeans. My pulse quickens just as Will slides out.

"That should do it," he says, standing.

"Thanks." I turn away to hide the heat I'm sure is showing in my cheeks.

"Here." He hands me the instructions. "You read these and I'm going to offer assistance if you need it." He puts the wrench back in the toolbox and closes the lid then washes his hands.

"Fine." I open the instructions and read Step 1. "Assemble all ingredients on a counter or work area." I line the vegetables up like they're on death row, which, I suppose, they are. "Done."

Next Will shows me the proper way to slice an onion, which reminds me of being a kid, sitting at the kitchen counter doing my homework while Mom cooked dinner. Her love of cooking is probably why Dad has no idea how to cook, even now.

I hand Will my cutting board and he scrapes the onion into the wok, then hands the cutting board and a red pepper back to me. "Here, cut this."

I place the pepper on the cutting board and am about to make the first cut when Will whistles.

"What?" I pause, knife mid-air.

"You're just going to lay into it like that?" He shakes his head. "No, no, no, no, no."

"There's a right way to cut a pepper?"

"No, there's an *only* way." I think he's going to come around behind me like Patrick Swayze in *Ghost* and I hope I remembered to put on antiperspirant. Instead he holds up his knife.

"Are you watching?"

I hold up mine, just like him, and then he points at the pepper. "Like this." He holds the pepper upright and then cuts a circle around the top. "Like you're carving a pumpkin. You know how to carve a pumpkin, right?"

I make a face.

"Stop it."

"What? It's so much effort. And the guts get everywhere. I mostly just . . ."

"Pay other people to do it for you?" he teases.

"Only once." I smile.

Will opens up the bag he brought and pulls out a block of butter. "Off the record, you should always use butter, even when a recipe calls for oil. Or, most of the time. Definitely for sautéing onions. But not for stir-frys." He cuts a massive slab of butter from the block and drops it into the wok.

"See? This is why cooking is not for me. Too many rules, too many exceptions."

Will hands me a wooden spoon and instructs me to sauté the onions. I'm stirring them around in the pan for a bit when my phone dings. I put the spoon down and scroll through my phone for the app I use to plan out my Instagram content. I load today's scheduled post: a photo of me wearing a two-piece linen outfit I was gifted at the launch of a new boutique that opens this week in the Meatpacking District in Manhattan, as well as a bunch of Instagram stories promoting their spring collection, photos of me walking around the store that I took when I was in New York a few weeks ago. I copy and paste the hashtags.

"OK so the onions are going to burn. You realize cooking requires *all* your focus, right?"

"I'm working," I say, staring at the screen.

"I don't get it," Will says, peering over my shoulder. "We're doing this for your Instagram, but you're posting other pics at the same time of you . . . shopping."

"Exactly."

"So when are you going to post pics of this spread?"

"Sometime next week. Pending the client's approval." The flood of comments and emojis are already starting to come in on my post:

Gorgeous!

Soooo pretty!

Oooh, must check out!

😊😊😊😊

"And you went to this store . . ."

"A few weeks ago."

He shakes his head.

"What? You can't take photos of yourself shopping in a store when it's *actually* open. There would be random people in the shots, the racks would be a mess. Instagram nightmare!" I joke. "And then there's the grid—you want to make it look aesthetically pleasing, so I lay it all out ahead of time to make sure it all works as pieces of a bigger puzzle before posting."

He shakes his head. "That's ridiculous. Sorry, but it really is."

"Laugh all you want, but don't you think you'd be more successful if you had a social presence?"

Will flips a spatula. "I *do* have a social presence. In real life. I see people in the flesh when I host cooking classes, or do a presentation at FoodiExpo every year. If everyone were to just start staying in, living through their phone, big conventions like FoodiExpo would flop. I look forward to it every year—and tons of other small food events. The chance to talk to people." Will slaps the spatula down on the counter. "Food is more than just something we need, it's this common interest, and our relationship with food can tell us so much about ourselves. Even if you don't like to cook, you probably like the idea of being invited over for dinner—it's not even the meal itself, it's the gateway to deepen a relationship. You're sitting around a table, a few bottles in, sated from the meal, relaxed. You have those great conversations, you know what I mean?"

I nod, knowing exactly what he means, but never having thought about it quite that way before.

"Even these food boxes. They're a dime a dozen, and yeah, brilliant idea—capitalizing on people who don't want to cook— but why do people buy them? Sure, it's partly because they don't have time to shop or don't want to be bothered to find a recipe or risk it not turning out, but I think it's more than that. There's something about a meal—something you made with your hands" —he holds his hands out, palms up, for emphasis—"and then sit down to enjoy that's bigger than what you can get by ordering a pizza. It means you're spending time with your family, your kids, you're taking time to connect . . . that's because of food. And you really get that when you make it yourself. That's what I love, those connections." He pauses, grabbing a dish towel and wiping the counter, then looks back at me, his eyes meeting mine. "And people say social media is a way to connect with people when you can't see them, but I don't think it is. It's seeing a curated picture here or there, thinking you know the person because you see that they had a baby or read that they got a new job, but you don't know more about it—why did they change jobs, is the commute stressful or a bit of me-time, how are those sleepless nights affecting their mental health? You only get that when you speak to someone." He shrugs. "That's what I think. But I know it's not popular opinion. It's a lot easier to Like a photo than to pick up the phone or meet someone for a walk." He tosses the dish towel beside the sink.

I take a sip of water. "I get what you're saying," I say. "And you have a point, for sure. These people who see my posts, they're not my friends. Or some of them are, but those are the ones I do see in person. For me, social media is a job, nothing more. It's an extension of the talks I give, the interviews I do—to inspire and connect. But the reality is that work isn't always guaranteed, or full time. And this stuff—despite being a pain in the ass, and fake—it's pretty easy. And maybe someone sees my sponsored post, buys the box and invites a few friends over for dinner because it feels more achievable than having to meal-plan and grocery shop. Or maybe they end up having dinner with their kids rather than going through the drive-thru on the way to some sports practice. But they wouldn't have known about this"—I splay my hands out—"without promotion. So sure, maybe we connect better in person, but that doesn't mean social media can't play a role in inspiring us *to* get together."

Will raises his eyebrows, then nods. "Good point." He hands me a spatula.

"Thank you," I say curtly, my hand brushing his as I grasp the wooden handle and my body feels tingly, despite my being mildly annoyed by Will's speech.

But as we work in tandem, the conversation flows easily from topic to topic and I find myself moving in slow motion when it comes to actually cooking the meal—not wanting it to end. How is it possible to feel so comfortable with someone I just met a few days ago—someone who initially bugged the hell out of me? One minute he's teasing me and the next minute we're serious, focused on the food, and then we're joking around and then we're talking about childhood friends. It's just all so effortless—and foreign, really. The only other person I feel this comfortable with, so *myself* with, is my sister, Izzy. And that's not even taking into consideration the heart palpitations I get every time I even look at Will—without him noticing, of course.

Eventually, he opens the oven to remove the roast.

"Alright, I think we have ourselves a meal."

As Will plates the food, I think back to Eric. How we rarely cooked together and, by the end, barely even ate together. Eric worked later and later hours and I started going to more and more evening events. If we ate a meal together, it was always at a restaurant, usually with clients.

Will's voice interrupts my thoughts. "You seem troubled. Don't worry, the food doesn't bite. Anymore."

I make a face. "Gross."

"Alright—well, I was saying it's your turn to plate."

"Me? But you're doing such a good job."

"You plate one and I'll take pictures while you do it. Otherwise how are you going to trick your users into believing you did this all on your own?"

"They're called followers," I say, taking the plate. I carefully arrange sliced meat and veggies while he snaps away. My plate doesn't look quite as good as his, but it's not that bad. I look at his photos. "Your hidden talent is photography," I tell him. "See why you should be on Instagram?"

"So my clients can think that I make dishes from a delivery service? That's a recipe for disaster. But thanks for the compliment. I actually quite enjoy taking pics, even if I'm usually the only one to see them."

I put the camera at the far end of the counter.

"So, now what?" I say. "Want to try it out—see if it's even any good? I think I have a beer in here, if you're interested."

"Tempting, for sure, but it's the middle of the afternoon and I already ate lunch."

"Oh, sure," I say, looking away so I don't show my disappointment. I grab a dish towel and wipe at the counter, trying to figure out what's next. But a moment later Will takes the towel from me. I turn toward him and his green eyes are on mine, and he steps toward me.

"I've got a better idea," he says, and I lean against the counter, feeling weak.

"Oh yeah?"

"Oh yeah." His hands move to my waist, and then up my body to my face, his breath hot on my lips. I press my lips on his as he lifts me onto the counter. He puts himself between my legs and slips his hands under my shirt, his fingertips dancing on my bare skin, giving me shivers. I lean into him, kissing him more intensely.

And then a phone buzzes. Will pulls away and reaches into his pocket.

"Shit. It's already three-fifteen?" he says, stopping the alarm. When he looks at me his eyes are wide.

"What? That's when you turn into a pumpkin?" I tease, pulling him closer.

He runs a hand through those Federer waves.

"No, that's when I have to leave to pick up my daughter from school. Otherwise I'll be late. I hate being late for her. And not *just* because she makes me buy her a donut as penance."

I grip the edge of the counter, my heart pounding. *Daughter?* No. I obviously heard him wrong. He can't have a daughter—not after the night we spent together and now this afternoon. Surely this is something that would've come up before now. Was I just not listening or was he purposely not saying something? But I'm always listening. So that something like this doesn't happen.

He's bustling around, grabbing things he brought, and I avoid his gaze, bending down to pick up the box on the floor. I hand it to him and am making my way to the door to unlock it when he holds up the Bosch book. "You sure I can borrow this?"

"It's yours," I say as he rushes out of my apartment.

It's not like I can ever see him again. This time, I mean it.

four

"So you've been childless for how many years now?" asks Byron, the host of the #BreakingTheRules podcast. It's the following day and I'm in a podcast studio, twenty floors up in a glass building on Bay, connected through the headphones to Byron, who's in another studio somewhere in LA.

"Child-*free*," I correct him. "There's a difference. 'Childless' refers to someone who isn't *able* to have children. 'Child-free' is the term used to describe someone who doesn't *want* children. And just to be clear, it could be a woman *or* a man. But the issue I have around having children has to do with the pressure and stereotypes we place on women that they are supposed to have children. That it's their duty—and that if they don't want them, if they choose other aspects of their lives to take precedence, that they're somehow damaged goods, or wrong."

He clears his throat. "Right. So then, how long have you been child-*free*?"

"My entire life," I say wanting to roll my eyes. "But I made the conscious decision in my twenties. I knew that to be happy and fulfilled, I didn't need to define myself as a 'mother.' That raising children would not be one of the ways I chose to spend my time."

"And have you drawn a lot of flack for this over the years?" he asks.

"Of course. The general understanding is that women are put on this planet to reproduce."

"Well, in fairness, men can't do it alone."

"I get that," I say. "But there are lots of women who *want* to have children. And countries where birth control still isn't a choice or readily available. Children are being born at a rate that is ensuring civilization will continue for much longer than our planet will even sustain us. And there are women who do not want to have children. And they're no lesser women, no lesser humans. All I'm asking is that if a woman chooses her work to be her life's focus, or her hobbies, or even her relationships with a spouse, or other family members or friends, that we don't condemn her. Growing up, I had a wonderful great-aunt. And you know, part of the reason I suspect she was so selfless, so kind, so fun, and spent so much time with me?" I don't wait for an answer. "Because she didn't have kids." I could stop there, but I don't. "If a man was highly successful and didn't make time to cook, deciding instead to order takeout every night to save time and energy since eating is merely a necessity for survival, no one would judge him. But if a woman does the same thing, somehow she's less of a woman, less of a human."

"Well now you're talking about household chores," Byron teases. "Are we going to get into whose turn it is to clean the toilet?"

I bite my tongue before I can say anything that I'll regret being broadcast to hundreds of thousands of the podcast's listeners.

After the interview ends, I head out onto the street, call Feloise for the zillionth time since Will left yesterday. She's yet to pick up—or reply to any of my texts. I slip my phone in my pocket and look up, just in time to avoid running right into her.

"I got your messages. All of them, annoyingly. I spoke to Lucy earlier—she says the client *loves* the new pics. And that chef is hot."

"Tell me about it," I moan. "Not that that's relevant. But wait—how do you know what he looks like? Did I send a pic of him by mistake?"

"Mm-hmm. By mistake?" she teases. "Although that's the kind of mistake you can make over and over."

I definitely lingered over the photos of Will when I was going through the pics—before deleting them, or so I thought. It wasn't just a sexual thing—though I don't think I've ever been more attracted to someone. Even Eric. But it was more than that. How easy it was to talk to him, how much we had in common—except, now I know there's so much, or one major thing, we don't. The deal breaker. I keep wavering between disappointment, shock and anger.

Feloise snaps her fingers. "Oh, they also want you to throw a 'girls' night in' where you serve the food boxes. I told them you could do it for one of your No Kidding dinners."

I shake my head. "I don't have the space to host. And we always meet at a restaurant," I tell her. "You would know that if you ever came to one of the meetings."

"The last thing I need is to re-live the whole reason I don't have kids to a bunch of strangers."

"They're not going to ask you. The whole point of the group isn't to sit around talking about why we don't have children.

It's to be a safe place to talk about all the other things in life that women care about, period." That isn't exactly true, because the point of the No Kidding groups is child-free women supporting child-free women, and that does sometimes mean we talk about living an unmaternal, unpopular life by choice. And maybe the group isn't the right one for Feloise, given what she's gone through, but I often think if only she would experience the camaraderie of a supportive group of like-minded women, maybe she would consider finding her own group. Or at least going to therapy. "And I bet you'd get a few new business leads," I add, in a last-ditch effort to entice her.

"Oh Honey, the way you've been killing it lately, I don't need anyone else. But well, I suppose a vacation property wouldn't be the worst thing ever. I'll think about it. Now back to that guy. Is he single?"

"Don't know, don't care. But if we aren't seeing him in my pics anyway, can't they send someone else?"

"Nope," she calls over her shoulder, already walking away. "You're stuck with him. So I guess you're going to have to deal."

Of course I can deal with it. This is my job—nothing more.

five

I'm inside the new pop-up shop for Bed in a Box, surrounded by a full camera crew of eight, shooting a piece for a new mattress that splits down the middle to individualize the comfort level. The "ask" in PR terms is six Instastories, but the firm doesn't want me to shoot them myself so they've hired a film crew instead. So as the mattress guy explains how the mattress works, the trio of assistants bustle around me, setting up lighting and testing out the best angles to shoot. Then they hand me the script, which I memorize. What I'm about to say isn't even true, but I remind myself they're paying me a lot of money to do this, and that I'm basically an actress. And so I ask myself, What would Reese Witherspoon do? (The answer: Reese Witherspoon would not take on this bad commercial job.) Years ago, I loved sharing new finds with followers on Instagram. It felt like a way to connect with people outside my core friend group who shared my interests. It came at the right time, too, as most of my friends were starting to have kids, and I was feeling disconnected from them.

"Hi guys," I say to the camera with a wave. "As many of you know, I broke up with my boyfriend last year and now I live on my own. When I was looking for a new bed, the first brand I thought of was Bed in a Box. I love the convenience. All I had to do was order the mattress online and it arrived"—I snap my fingers—"just like that. I didn't have to worry about delivery or set up. If you're a single woman, you know what I mean. Now Bed in a Box has taken things to the next level by letting you customize both sides of your mattress. So if you and your partner are sleeping in separate rooms because you can't stand to sleep together, this may be for you. I'm not saying it would've saved my relationship, but who knows, it might save yours."

I cringe inwardly as the publicists clap and tell me how great I'm doing. I'm asked to repeat my lines another dozen or so times, just to make sure we've got the *authenticity* right. And then we move on to five different variations. I talk about how, with my steamy sex life (in not so many words), it's nice to sleep on a bed I love, and how I don't need a man to help me move furniture.

It's after two when we wrap, and as part of my contract, I get to keep the mattress.

"Do you have someone to help you get this into your car?" the publicist asks as the camera crew packs away their equipment.

"Oh, they're not delivering it? Isn't that part of the appeal of a Bed in a Box purchase?" I don't have a car. I don't even have a driver's license. But that's not something I proudly reveal.

"But it's out of the box," she says, rooting around in her purse and then pulling out her phone. She looks at it, as though focusing on our conversation is too boring to keep her undivided attention.

"Well, can they put it back in the box? And then deliver it?" The irony that I'm asking for help with the very product I just finished raving about because it *doesn't* require a man to move it is not lost on me.

She shakes her head and leans closer. "That's the thing," she whispers. "They come out of the box, but they don't go back in." She holds up her phone. "I've got to take this. Good luck with the mattress!"

The mattress weighs a ton. I pull it through the door and lean it up against the brick wall of the store then pull out my phone. When the Uber driver arrives with his SUV ten minutes later he says he won't take the mattress. "Liability reasons," he says. He drives off and I'm standing with my back against the mattress trying to decide what to do when I hear a voice beside me.

"Don't tell me you gave up the glamorous Instagram life to sell mattresses on the side of the road."

I swivel, preparing to give my best death glare to a stranger and find myself looking right into Will MacGregor's green eyes. My breath catches. Of the more than four million people in the city, I have to run into him?

I roll my eyes. "No, I did not," I huff, feeling embarrassed.

"Looks like you could use some help."

Being out of alternatives, I nod. "Yes. Please."

"You got it." He lifts up the bottom end of the mattress and I struggle to hold on to the other end. We make our way down the sidewalk and stop at a red light.

"Where's your car?" I puff.

"Two more blocks. You can do it."

Of course I can *do* it. I hoist my side higher. When we approach a black pickup truck Will takes hold of the mattress, and heaves it into the back of the truck on his own.

"You can just drop me off, I'll get the concierge to help me bring it up," I say as we drive to my place. "I'm sure you have things to do. Or your daughter to pick up." This is more a reminder for myself than for him. *Don't get involved, Kit.*

"Are you OK?" he asks, glancing over at me.

I look out the window. "Yep."

He pulls up in front of my building and I hop out and go around to the back. "I'll climb in and help lift it out to you?" I say, pulling down the back flap on the cab.

I lift the mattress, noticing some slabs of wood underneath.

"Those are um . . . I was just getting rid of stuff in the basement and found these old shelves I wasn't using, and I threw them in the back of my truck just for . . . next time I uh . . . anyway, I thought, if you wanted them . . ." His face is flushed. Did he plan to bring these over to me? "I know you said you could do it yourself."

"Well, since they're right here . . ." I smile, my eyes meeting his.

"Great. I'll bring them in after we get the mattress up." We maneuver the mattress through the double doors and then, after a five-minute debate with Ivan the Grumpy Concierge about not having booked the service elevator, we get the mattress up to the thirty-ninth floor. Then Will goes back down for the bookshelves and I do a quick run around the apartment to tidy up, but then study my armful of things and quickly toss everything about again. Why am I trying to impress him? It's better if he thinks I'm a slob.

Will returns with the bookshelves and looks around. "Did you redo your apartment?"

I fan my hand. "It's my June look. I call it my White Period."

"Wait a sec. You bought an entire new set of furniture? For June? Maybe I *should* be rethinking my career."

"Rented," I say. I explain the campaign I have with Stay-a-While. In exchange for Instagram promotion, I have a free subscription, which means I can swap out my furniture as many times as I want for the next year.

"Why would anyone want to keep changing their furniture?" Will asks, putting the shelves down by the blank wall. "Furniture is supposed to make you feel at home. Comfortable, comforted. It's supposed to be familiar. Do you have a cordless drill, by chance?"

"Actually, yes," I say, going to the closet and grabbing the cordless drill bag. I hand it to Will, who looks surprised.

"I was kidding, you know."

"And I told you I could do it myself."

Will opens the bag and I look around the cold, white space. Comfortable is not an adjective I would use to describe my apartment at this moment. "You know, I do it—the furniture—for the illusion. So it looks like I have a bigger place," I say. Will just stares at me so I explain. "A lot of my influencer competition is women who live in sprawling homes in the Midwest. On Instagram, no one considers that rent on a one-bedroom apartment can be as much as a mortgage on a four-thousand-square-foot home in the 'burbs."

Will just sort of shakes his head, then says, "OK. But why would a *normal person* rent furniture?"

So I give him the spiel about trying out different styles before committing to costly renovations. How it's great for roommates and college students. And also for short-term rental units. Even if I wasn't being paid, I would still think it's a great business model.

"Would they take a couch back if it was stained with markers and ketchup? Because this might be the solution to all my problems." Will laughs. I don't. I'm not going to pretend that I think it's so cute that he's got a daughter who makes a mess when I'm still bitter.

He finishes screwing hooks into the studs in the wall and bends down to lift up the first shelf, then slides it onto the hooks. He makes sure it's secure, then takes a step back. "What do you think?"

The shelf actually looks great, and I'm excited to put books on it. "Thanks," I say as he starts to secure hooks for the second shelf.

"You know this was all my plan to make sure you get your books out of your oven. The last thing I want is a hot firefighter showing up here and taking my place."

My face heats up and I turn to the fridge and open it, letting the cool air blast onto my skin. "You want some water?"

He positions the second shelf on the hooks, then puts the drill back in the bag and zips it closed. "Sure."

I pour him a glass and hand it to him. He's wiping the sweat off his forehead with his shirt, his taut stomach showing.

"You should go before you get a ticket. I can handle the rest from here."

He smirks. "Oh, come on. Let me help you get the mattresses swapped out." And so we go into my bedroom and take the sheets off my bed, and lift the old mattress off. "More books, huh? I'm not sure why I'm surprised," Will says, looking through the slats of the bed frame.

"Yep. Mysteries."

"What do you want to do with this?" he asks, tapping my old mattress.

"I think we can just take it to the dumpster out back."

"Great. Cuz it looks pretty uncomfortable."

"Oh, and you're a mattress expert?" I tease, walking out of my bedroom to get the new mattress.

"I like to think so," he calls after me. "But you know what kind of mattress I've never tried?" I grab the new mattress by one end, turning to face Will, who's grinning at me. "A Bed in a Box mattress." We bring it into the bedroom and position it onto my bed frame. Then he leaps across the mattress so he's on the same side as me. A line of perspiration has formed above his upper lip, and all I want to do is taste the salt. He moves closer but I force myself to put my hand on his chest. "Uh-uh. You have to go," I say.

"Playing hard to get? I like it." He takes a step closer, but I hold him back more firmly.

"Really. I can't . . ." I know I should just tell him. Tell him why it would never work out between us. He's going to find out eventually, if we're forced to keep working together. Even though he doesn't have social media, it's surprising he hasn't done a search on me and seen it all—my book, my website, the pages and pages of search results that show me being quoted about being child-free. But he hasn't, I guess. And I don't bring it up because people who have kids get all weird when they learn what I do, and we're just cooking food—nothing more. He doesn't need to know about the rest. And so I turn, heading out of the bedroom. "I've got—I've got this thing in twenty minutes. You have to leave."

six

"Let's start with good news," I say as the waiter pours wine in our glasses. We're in the private dining room in the basement of an Italian restaurant at our monthly No Kidding meetup dinner.

"Can I go first?" Casey asks, then tells us she got a personal best on her hundred-mile ride through the Rockies last week. "And thanks to you ladies supporting me, I raised enough money for my niece's school so they can all have their own recorders for music class. My sister is *thrilled.*" We all laugh. "And now you'll have to go to the Christmas concert," one of the other women jokes.

Casey shrugs. "At least she'll still want her cool Aunt Casey to come to a Christmas concert. Who knows how many more years it'll be like that. She's already borrowing my jeans and rolling her eyes."

"We should think about supporting a school as a collective," I say, looking around to see how this resonates with the dozen women at the table. One of the misconceptions I'm always battling as a champion for the child-free is that those who don't want kids don't *like* kids. "I know one of our mandates is *not* to talk about kids, but file this under fundraising and good PR."

"What are you thinking?" someone asks.

"A woman I know goes to Ghana to bring supplies to schools there. Maybe I'll do a little research and share some suggestions at the next meeting. See what everyone thinks."

The waiter returns with a few charcuterie boards for the table, and we continue with good news and hot tips—promotions, vacation destinations and book recommendations. Then Xiu speaks up.

"Jed doesn't want to get a vasectomy," she announces as she takes a piece of bread from the basket being passed around. She hands the basket to me and I wonder when this came up— Xiu didn't mention anything about it to Gloria or me when we were in Milwaukee, though she did say she was glad for the girls' weekend. I figured she meant because she'd been so slammed with work lately. Now, a dozen sets of eyes are on her as she smooths a small strand of hair behind her ear. The rest of her shiny black hair is twisted into a neat bun at the nape of her neck. Feloise elbows me. "I thought you said . . ." she whispers loudly. I top up her wine glass and avoid eye contact.

"Obviously this is extremely annoying because we have talked, *at length*, about not having kids. I love our life the way it is, and they're not in the plan, for us, not ever, so why does he need semen shooting out of his dick?" Xiu sips her wine, her lipstick miraculously staying put.

"Semen still . . . shoots out after a vasectomy," Casey says. "There's just no sperm."

"Whatever."

Xiu must really be upset, because she never talks about her personal life with the group. She goes on to say that she went for a Pap recently and her doctor was worried about her estrogen levels being higher than normal. "My sister died of breast cancer when she was thirty-five, and I'm turning thirty-five next year. If that isn't enough of a scare . . ." She trails off. I've never seen Xiu looking so distraught. She gulps her wine. Everyone offers support in one way or another, but my mind drifts to my own mom. Thirty-five. Mom was thirty-five, too, when the diagnosis came. When I was a kid, thirty-five seemed so old. But now, as I creep closer and closer to that same age myself, I know exactly where Xiu is coming from. I reassure her that Jed probably needs a few weeks to come around to the idea, but Xiu turns back into the fiery litigator that we all know.

"I need a plan."

"Book him the appointment, girl," Gloria says, flipping her long, skinny braids over her shoulder. Oh dear. I know this group. We all have strong personalities and opinions to go with them. This is going to get messy.

"And then what? Drug him and make him show up?" Xiu is skeptical but interested.

"Tell him it's a physical. Once he's there, what's he going to do?"

"Tell him you'll divorce him if he doesn't get it done."

I clink my glass to try to quiet the group, but everyone ignores me. Then Xiu speaks: "There's more. He said, 'What if something happens to you?'" Xiu looks angry. "I thought he meant, what if I get sick and he realizes that without me, and without kids, he would have no memory of me, so he wants to keep the door open, like we're in some sort of Nicholas Sparks movie. But I'm kind of touched, I guess, and so I'm like 'Honey, that's so sweet that you would want my memory to live on in some tiny version of us. But I'm not going to get sick and die anytime soon. Don't even think that.' But he's looking at me like I'm completely insane. And then he says, 'What are you talking about? I meant, What if you die and I meet another woman and she wants to have kids?' I honestly thought he was joking." She wrings her hands in her napkin. "But he wasn't. He wants to hedge his bets. In case I *die*."

"He was thinking with his cock, obviously," says Emma, the woman on the other side of me. "I'm sure he didn't mean it." A waiter enters the room and picks up the water jug, but pauses, recognizing the intensity in the room. He looks to me and I nod. He continues to make the rounds as Xiu goes on: "I told him that if he felt like there was someone else out there that he might want to have kids with, he should find her. Don't let my being alive stand in the way." Xiu looks at us. "Why would I want to be with someone who's waiting for me to die so he can have kids with someone else?" I glance over at Feloise, to see how she's doing. She's head-down, engrossed in her phone.

"I'm sure that's not what he meant," someone pipes up. At this point every one of us is trying to make Xiu feel better. Xiu looks at me.

"Kit, what do you think? Isn't this what happened to you?"

I smile wanly. "Well, not exactly . . ." I say. I can feel Feloise's eyes boring into the side of my head.

A few years before we broke up, Eric and I had talked about a vasectomy and he had refused. Eric was strongly against elective surgery. He wouldn't even get laser eye surgery—even though he could barely see without glasses, and was apparently, according to his optometrist, a perfect candidate for the procedure. I didn't push him, even though I thought, if we were both in agreement that we never wanted kids, wouldn't it be simpler to do away with other forms of birth control? But how would I have felt if he insisted I get my tubes tied? Still, maybe deep down I knew the real reason he was so opposed to a vasectomy was that he wasn't sure about kids—or me. Maybe if I'd pressed him to get a vasectomy, we would have broken up long before we did.

"I think it's good Jed is being honest with you," I tell Xiu. "And he isn't saying he doesn't want to be with you. He's just being weird about a vasectomy—which is normal. I think Eric always wanted kids—and thought at some point I'd change my mind. When he realized that wasn't going to happen, he decided that having kids was more important than being with me. It's definitely a tough situation," I say sympathetically.

Xiu shakes her head. "It's the principle of the thing. Now I know he's waiting for me to die, or for us to break up, so he can go off with another woman and have kids." Xiu throws down her napkin. "I've lost my appetite. Someone else please monopolize the conversation—and can I get more wine?" One of the many bottles of red on the table gets passed down to Xiu, while Gloria looks down the table. "So Feloise, when did you know you didn't want kids?"

"Feloise has *always* known," I jump in. "And anyway, Fel's just here to check us out—see if we're her kind of people. Let's not give her the fifth degree. And maybe we can change the topic *off* kids."

"No, it's fine," Feloise says, downing her wine and clearing her throat. Her face is expressionless. "I actually did want kids," she starts. The air feels thick. The room is still, as everyone hangs on her every word. She continues: "Always. I just assumed I would. I had it all mapped out, the career, husband, the house with enough bedrooms, a yard, all of it. But it was miscarriage after miscarriage. Four years. Tests, prodding, poking. We almost gave up, and then, it took. Who knows why, but you hear stories like it all the time. I was pregnant. Seven months in. And then," her voice catches and for a split second I don't think she'll go on. I reach for her hand, but she pushes it away. "And then I wasn't. Just like that. I lost the baby and any chance of ever getting pregnant again." She looks around the room, her eyes filled with tears. "I'm not child-free by choice like all of you," she says bitterly. "I just pretend to be now. So people don't feel sorry for me. I don't need anyone's pity." At that, she breaks down and I reach to wrap my arms around her but she shoves back her chair and stands. "This was a mistake." She's already rushing out of the room.

seven

I'm on the phone with Feloise the following morning discussing a lunch 'n' learn speakers' series I want her to pitch me for when Dr. Anjii's office nurse, Nena, calls my name. "Shoot, I've gotta go. But hey, I just want to say sorry again about last night—" I still feel so bad about inviting Feloise to the group. I truly can't imagine how hard it must be to want something so badly and know there's nothing you can do to have that. It makes me feel lucky—and motivated to take action on the things I really want out of my life that I've been putting off.

"We're good." Feloise is back to her no-nonsense self. "Like I said, I was PMSing. Nothing more. I don't need therapy. I'm fine. Besides, could I work 24/7 if I had kids? No. And neither could you—which is why you're my superstar client. Now go."

I hang up and hurry over to Nena. "Sorry about that."

She shakes her head but smiles. "Are you always working?"

"Pretty much." Nena hands me a gown and then shuts the door behind her so I can change. A moment later Dr. Anjii enters and sits in the chair by the computer and turns to me. "How are you, Kit?" she asks. The fact that she always remembers to call me Kit, and not Katherine, endears her to me.

"Any changes to your life since I last saw you?" she asks, glancing over the clipboard in her hand. "Last time you were here you were taking a multivitamin. Would that still be accurate?"

I can't remember *ever* taking a multivitamin.

"Scratch the multivitamin and add a breakup."

She turns to me, her forehead creasing, but I tell her I'm fine. "It's been over a year." She tells me it's more important than ever to be taking a multivitamin. *More important than ever?* Do single women need more vitamins? Does it stave off the adoption of cats and dying alone?

"It keeps the doctor away better than apples," she says. "Calcium would be a good supplement too. And iron. Is your period regular?"

"Ish. Maybe I'm in menopause?" My sister, Izzy, is always talking about menopause as though it's a bad thing, like it's the final step before death. But I say: bring it on. If you're not going to have kids, why worry about a period? But maybe periods are better than hot flashes?

She scribbles on my sheet. "You're still quite young to be in menopause, or even peri-menopause. But you should monitor your menstruation cycle. Keep track on your phone. It's pretty easy. How's your stress level?" she asks.

"OK."

"And money. Can you make ends meet?"

"Yes."

"What about your eating habits?"

"All the food groups. Usually."

"Drinking?"

"A glass or two," I guess.

"A week?"

Yikes. "A day?" I say. "But not every day. Definitely not on Mondays."

"Hmmm. And how about your mental health?"

I consider telling her that sometimes, I get scared. That thirty-five is coming up and ... my thoughts go to Mom. What if my time is almost up? A few weeks ago, over cocktails with the gals, the topic of milestone birthdays came up and I felt myself listening rather than brainstorming bucket-list places to go for my fortieth. Because sometimes, I worry I'm not even going to make it to my fortieth. But instead of sharing this thought now, with Dr. Anjii, I say nothing. She's not a therapist. "It's fine. I'm good. Busy."

"Are you sexually active?"

Again, I stop to consider my answer. "I'm not dating anyone, but I have sex sometimes." I think about Will. And how I'm definitely not going to have sex with him again.

"You use protection, right?"

"Always."

She puts my file down and leans closer.

"Have you given any thought to freezing your eggs?"

"Freezing my eggs?" I repeat.

"You're thirty-three. I know last time you were here we discussed this, and you said you and your boyfriend weren't planning on having kids, but if you're not in a relationship right now, it could take a year or two before you meet someone you want to have children with—if you're thinking you want the option. Or you may decide you want to have a child alone. Freezing your eggs reduces the chance of the eggs being too old and tired."

"I thought you said I was young."

"Young for menopause. Old for bearing children the natural way."

"Well, I don't want to be a mother," I say, steeling myself for Dr. Anjii's protests. I know how this conversation goes, because I've had it hundreds of times, whenever I've said I don't want kids to those who have them. First there are the raised eyebrows. Then, the questions. "Are you not *able* to have children?" or "Do you hate children?" Of course my doctor is not going to say these things, but I suspect she'll use the third option: "You'll change your mind." As though at thirty-three it's not possible that I can be set in my own mind, to know how I want the rest of my life to play out.

I wait for Dr. Anjii to say something, but she doesn't. She simply nods and tells me to lie down on my back for my physical. I do, then sit back up. "Why didn't you challenge me there?" Her back is to me, and she turns around.

"Pardon?"

"Why didn't you say 'Are you sure?' or something?"

She pulls on a pair of gloves and interlaces her fingers together. "It's not my place."

I lie back down and stare up at the ceiling, at a *New Yorker* cartoon of two jailbirds in striped jumpsuits. One has removed the bricks in the wall to escape. The other is lying on his cot, a book in hand. *No thanks*, he says. *Reading is my escape.* I smile.

Dr. Anjii inspects my breasts, and tells me to exhale while counting to five. Knowing my family history, she must recognize this makes me anxious, because she counts with me.

Twenty minutes later, she hangs her stethoscope around her neck, announcing that we're done. "We should have the test results within a few days. No news is good news but if you're worried about anything or you haven't heard from us, you can always call and ask for me, OK?" Before I change out of my gown, I snap a selfie, thinking I can share it as a reminder to others to make time for their own physicals. Feloise hates when I post anything that's not fun on my feed, but what's the point of having a platform if I can't use it to help others? That's part of the whole reason I started my Instagram account—to be real. And even though, in the past year or so, the pendulum's swung the other way, to the paid promos, I've got to channel the motivation I'm always sharing with others—like in Milwaukee, or at the No Kidding dinners. I Favorite the photo so I don't forget to schedule it later.

#

My phone pings, reminding me that I agreed to meet Thom with an H, for a drink. When one of the No Kidding women suggested I meet her cousin, I jumped at the chance to maybe, hopefully, forget Will by moving on. We're meeting at You've Bean Served, which is the name of his coffee shop. I tell myself that he's a legit business owner, which is nothing like a topknot-wearing male barista. But I can already see that the photo Casey showed me was not quite accurate because he does have long hair. And while it's not pulled back into a man bun, he *is* wearing a tank top. He probably does yoga, too. I'm too judgy—there's nothing wrong with yoga.

Thom with an H is mopping the floor when I arrive at the shop. He looks up when I tap on the glass door. Smiling, he comes over to let me in since the shop closed at six.

"Hi, hi, hi," he says, opening the door wider. "Come in, come in, come in. I'm so glad we could finally get this thing going," he says and puts the mop to the side, then wipes his hands on his shorts. I'm not sure what we're "getting going" but I nod and try to keep an open mind.

He goes behind the bar and asks me what style of coffee he can get me.

"Are you sure you don't want to go somewhere else?" I ask him. "We can get a drink and you won't feel like you're working."

"Oh I just love *bean* here after closing. Bean here." He slaps his leg.

"Punny. Can I get a decaf?"

He makes a face. "You know even decaf has caffeine right? And by attempting to strip the bean of caffeine you're stripping it of its whole *raison d'être*."

"I'm just trying to cut back after noon."

"Well we don't really *do* decaf—like, we don't even have it."

"Alright," I sigh. "I'll have a regular coffee." I force a smile and Thom looks absolutely delighted.

"Great!" He claps his hands together. "So tell me, what kind of coffee have you *bean* craving?"

Breathe, Kit. He's passionate about something. That's a *good* quality. "Any kind."

"We have this new Peruvian."

"I'm sure whatever you're having will be perfect." Can he just brew the damn coffee?

So Thom is a beanist. Plus, even though he's really tall, he reminds me of a golden retriever—he has golden skin and golden hair that flows in waves down to his shoulders. And when he moves it's more like he's lumbering and when he breathes, it's like he's panting.

As Thom goes on—and on and on—about coffee, my mind wanders to Will. What is he doing right now? Is he building Lego with his daughter? Or watching her from the bleachers while she takes her swimming lesson? Or is she with her mother while he's on a date with someone else? I force myself to refocus on Thom. Who is fine. Happy. Loveable. Like a dog. Exactly what I need. I wouldn't even have to walk him. A self-sufficient companion.

Four years later, after the coffee has finally brewed to perfection, we're sitting across from each other on the two chairs Thom has flipped right-side up. The coffee is beautiful. He's done that thing with the foam and a toothpick to create art, but as I look closer, I realize, it's not simply a swirl or a heart.

"Is this . . . *me*?" He's captured the waves of my hair, the collar of my shirt. I look away from the coffee and up at him. He's smiling broadly.

"You like it?"

I nod. It's really impressive. And thoughtful.

"Good, good, good," he's saying.

I snap a photo of my coffee and then ask Thom to take another, of me and the coffee. "I'll post this later," I say, taking a sip. Maybe I was too harsh on Thom with an H. "You're really talented."

"Aw shucks. I'm not going to lie—I practised it a few times, before you got here. Had a look at your Instagram account. You sure do have a lot of photos of yourself on there." I can feel my face heat up. I know that to non-influencers, the number of selfies I post is borderline obnoxious. I'm regretting having asked him to take my photo just now.

"It's not a bad thing," he says quickly. "You're easy to look at."

I clear my throat.

"So, so, so," Thom says, rubbing his hands together, back and forth, back and forth like he's starting a fire between them. "The way I figure it is if this date goes well then for the next date we should get the ol' folks involved. I think at our age the only way to see if a relationship is going to work is to kickstart it. You know? Really giv'r. Be all in."

I'm a bit too stunned to speak.

"Or . . . no? You look frightened. I know you don't want kids," he says, flipping his long, shiny hair over his shoulder. "Again, the Instagram thing. Which is great, because I have a whole plan and I think we could really work well together on that front. I know I know, I move fast but so does life."

My heart is pounding. "I think maybe you're a few cups of coffee ahead of me on this."

But he's not hearing me.

"I think not having kids is the way to go. The earth is over-populated, and I mean, climate change, dude. Who would even want to bring kids into this world? Plus, they're so draining on energy, time, resources, the whole shebang. I figure, we both have good careers, we both make good money, why not spend it help-ing others? Every few months we could go somewhere and do something good—build a house for Habitat for Humanity, help put up a windmill in Africa, all the rebuilding that will need to be done once the flooding starts."

He babbles on, but I find myself actually considering his offer. After graduating college, a few friends and I did a build in

Cuba, but it seemed so showy—like, look at us, doing good on our vacation, when we mostly just goofed off and let others do the hard work. Maybe it's time to try again. For real this time.

"You've really thought this out," I say.

He nods and leans closer. "Sure have. Sure have."

#

The ladies from Clean Slate, the cleaning service I get twice a month in exchange for posts, wake me up with their arrival. I forgot they were coming, which makes me feel guilty. If my mom could see me now, allowing someone else to clean up the mess I made in my own home, I know she would be ashamed of me. And yet, I scramble to get out of my place without showering. A few hours later, I'm still sitting at Jimmy's, drinking *decaf* and trying to get some work done but finding myself distracted by thoughts of Will despite the barrage of texts Thom keeps sending. How is it possible that someone I have no interest in dating is now stopping me from dating other guys? Sure, hooking up with Thom was not the most enticing idea, given his whole panting dog vibe, but he was clearly into me—and was definitely disappointed when I didn't follow him back to his apartment last night, instead choosing to go home alone and curl up in bed with my book. The old me—the two-weeks-ago me, the me before I met Will—would've definitely gone home with Thom. So what is going on?

When I return to my apartment, it's spotless. But the clean lines of the cabinets, the white walls, the structured furniture, it all feels so sterile and empty and cold. My phone dings, telling me it's time to post a photo. I open the app, the explosion of bright colors filling the screen. Today's photo is one of me sitting on a pink velvet couch in front of a wall of fresh florals, at an event for a new pink lipstick that's supposed to look good on everyone. The lipstick does look good on me, but it took me twenty minutes to get it off my lips before bed, and then my lips were chapped for two days afterward. But I really like the PR rep and she's already emailed me three times to remind me that today's the day the lipstick hits beauty counters everywhere in conjunction with #NationalLipstickDay. I hit Share and unleash my bubbly, happy self out into the world. And that hollow feeling in my chest takes hold. Maybe Thom's right. Maybe I should use my extra energy and time to do things that give me a good feeling in my soul. But being a voice for child-free women is my cause, and I know that every speech I give, every event I host, every group I sponsor helps other women. So why doesn't it feel like enough anymore? I know why. Because so much of what I do, like posting lipstick selfies, has nothing to do with that. And if I'm going to be doing stuff that isn't helping others, I want to be focusing on the project I've been putting off for years. And yet, even now, I don't try to tackle it.

Instead, I go to my bedroom closet, pull out *Anne of Green Gables,* which is one of those books I find as comforting as a warm blanket, and flip to one of the dog-eared pages, to read a line I love: *It has been my experience that you can nearly always enjoy things if you make up your mind firmly that you will.* I curl up on the couch. It may be the world's most beautiful couch, all shiny and white, but it's cold and uncomfortable.

eight

I have this memory of Mom. I'm five or six and we're walking down one of the cherry blossom–lined streets in Niagara-on-the-Lake. It's just the two of us—Dad and Izzy were probably at one of Izzy's many practices—and it's a warm and sunny morning. Spring. Mom has my hand and we're looking at houses. Houses with garages. Some garage doors are open, the items inside for sale. Amidst the mostly grown-up things—pots, pans, chairs and tools—there is usually a small children's section, with toys and puzzles and games. Mom tells me I can choose anything—as long as it doesn't cost more than fifty cents.

As I root through a cardboard box filled with myriad plastic toys, Mom asks the owners if they're moving. She asks this question at every house.

"Why do you always ask if they're moving?" I say as we walk back down the driveway.

"Because if we can find the perfect house with the perfect garage, then, there's a chance we could move." And then, she tells me her secret. And then she says that it's now *our* secret. Something we can work on together, just the two of us—if I want to, she says. When I hear the plan, I want to. But we never found the perfect house with the perfect garage. And now she's gone.

And I pushed the memory deep down, where it stayed, buried, for years and years. Until one day, about a year ago, I was looking to replace a light fixture in the guest bathroom. The chandelier I was seeking was a metaphor and I knew it—change the light fixture, change my relationship with Eric. It didn't work, but when I couldn't find the light I was looking for in an antique shop, Izzy had suggested garage sales. I went out that following Saturday, house to house, and though I never found the light I was looking for, it was as though the switch flipped, and a corner of my memory I'd kept dark for years was illuminated.

I've been garage hunting ever since. I don't bother with garage sales. Instead, Gloria sends me links of open houses and I narrow them down to the ones with garages—though it's not just *any* garage. I have something very specific in mind. I'm looking for a detached garage in the back of the home that leads into an alley. So, it really is a garage hunt, not a house hunt. And I'm always looking. The thing is, time is running out. I've been thinking about doing this book garage idea for years. That was Mom's dream, and at some point it became mine. But Mom never got the chance. And now, I keep putting it off, too. I'm only two years younger than Mom was when she died. What am I waiting for?

#

A few hours later, after having popped into a few shops on Queen, I'm crossing the street to cut through Trinity Bellwoods Park when someone calls my name. And there he is, sitting on the stone wall of the entrance, waving to me. I take a deep breath. Will and I still have to work together, after all. I walk over to him and see he's sitting with a girl of about eight or nine. She has a book in one hand, a *pain au chocolat* in the other. She's wearing pink shorts, a tie-dyed shirt, her long brown hair pulled back in a ponytail, held with a velvet scrunchie.

"Hey," he says, standing and walking over to me. He looks unsure for a second, as though gauging my reaction, and I know it's because I haven't replied to his texts. And yet, he leans in to hug me. He smells like sandalwood and coffee. I breathe him in, not letting go. When we break apart, he motions to the girl. "Addie, this is Kit. Kit, this is my favorite daughter, Addie." She rolls her eyes but it's obvious she's flattered by the attention. "It's his favorite joke." She pulls at the edges of her T-shirt to reveal the front, which reads *World's Greatest Daughter*. "Guess who bought me this T-shirt?"

"You act like I made you wear it," Will teases, wrapping an arm around her. She leans into him and laughs, her green eyes—the same shade as Will's—sparkling. She has the same skin tone as Will, too, though hers is spattered with freckles. Even her hair is the same chocolatey brown. I wonder what it must be like to have someone look like you, and to so clearly adore you and for a moment, I have a pang of envy, then dismiss it, reminding myself that "Having a child so you have someone who looks like you" probably ranks high on many Top 10 reasons *not* to have kids lists. As Addie chatters, I wonder how Addie's mother feels about the fact that her daughter looks like a very pretty, girl version of Will, and, likely, not like her? I lean my head to check out the book she's reading, surprised that she's not staring at a phone, though maybe she's too young for a phone. I've never been good with guessing kids' ages. I pull *The Interestings* out of my bag and hold it out to her. "Look at the book I just picked up. It's by the same author." She looks at the cover of the Meg Wolitzer book in her hand—*The Fingertips of Duncan Dorfman*—then back at me.

"You read kids' books?"

I shake my head. "No, mine's for adults. But I really like Meg Wolitzer. What's yours about?"

"These kids who play Scrabble. I have to finish this before Dad will let us go to VR. But it's pretty good. I'm getting some good Scrabble words out of this, so watch out, Dad." She looks at me. "He always wins, but not for long."

"You don't let her win?" I tease. "Harsh."

"Life's harsh." He grins. "That's also why I make her read. Kids who read turn out to be far more successful than those who don't," he says for her benefit. She groans. "Seriously, Dad? Not every second has to be about learning something, you know. We *could* just be getting ice cream."

When he shakes his head, she buries her face in her book and Will nods for me to join him a few steps away.

"Hey, so, um, are we cool? You didn't reply to my texts." His voice has an edge, like he's protecting himself.

I nod, but keep my distance. *Say something*, I tell myself. But what—I'm going to just blurt out how, despite my growing crush on him, there's no way we could ever be a thing? My stomach clenches and I fold my arms over my chest, to stop myself from reaching out to him. There's something magnetic about him— even though it would be so much easier to just tell him I'm not interested, or lie and say I'm in a relationship and that our one-night thing was just a mistake—but I don't.

He studies me for a moment, his green eyes on mine, challenging me to tell him what's going on, but all I want to do is kiss him, and eventually I look away. But he takes a step closer.

"Do you want the rest of this?" Addie calls, breaking us apart. We both turn and Will makes his way back over to the wall, to Addie, and I follow him back even though there's no reason for me to hang around.

Will takes the pastry. "There's no chocolate left in this."

"Why would I leave the chocolate?" she says. "It's the best part. Besides, you're always saying you're trying *not* to eat chocolate." She looks at me. "He keeps the chocolate chips in the freezer because he likes them cold and then he eats handfuls of them while I'm at school." Will points at her, looking slightly embarrassed.

"Hey, you're giving away all my secrets." He turns to me. "It's either cut back on chocolate or exercise more. Maybe that's the benefit of living in an apartment building. If I lived where you do I could take the stairs for exercise."

"Wait, you're the lady Dad likes who lives on the forty-fourth floor?"

"Thirty-ninth," I say. The word "likes" echoes in my head and I meet his eyes. They're locked on mine. I turn back to Addie, knowing my face is red, though shouldn't Will be the one who's embarrassed? "The forty-fourth floor has a gym and hot tub and a place to barbeque if you're having friends over. And then there's another floor on top of that, and there's a restaurant where you can order food and drinks." I keep my focus on Addie.

"Is your building taller than the CN Tower? I've been to the CN Tower but I was like, five, and Dad was so freaked out that he made me freak out. He hates heights."

"You hate heights?" I say, now turning to Will. "You never said anything when you were over. Or at Hotel 6ix."

"It's no big deal." He shrugs. "Catering events in condo party rooms on the top of buildings is a big part of my business. I have to deal. And you"—he points at Addie again, but he's grinning. "Can you stop making me look like such a doofus?"

She rolls her eyes and pretends to ignore him, asking me for all the details on my building. I tell her about the bowling alley and the basketball court—places I've never actually been but I don't let on because she seems to think I'm the coolest person she's ever met, and selfishly, it's a nice feeling. Will's phone buzzes and he excuses himself. And so Addie and I chatter on for a few more minutes. When I look up, Will's back, and he's just watching us, a smile across his face.

I know that look. "Gotta go," I say, standing.

"See you tomorrow, right?" he says.

"Right," I call over my shoulder, my heart pounding. I pick up my pace, not letting myself turn around.

#

"It's purely professional," I say to Izzy later that day. "I have absolutely no interest in things going any further with Will. And he knows that."

We're sitting on the balcony of her apartment, which overlooks the water. It's a gorgeous, sunny day, and while I'm happy to be hanging out with Izzy I can't help wondering what Will's up to this afternoon.

"Uh-huh." She lives in a building that's the complete opposite of mine—the building is really old, and so are the tenants.

But the units are massive—they have three bedrooms *and* three bathrooms—and Izzy and her husband, Roddy, love the space, and the fact that the only real controversy among the tenants is whether the gym on the twenty-fourth floor should get an elliptical machine. Roddy's out on a friend's sailboat and she's invited me over to help her put together goodie bags for the Olympigs, the weekend festival of pig festivities she runs to raise money for a charity close to her heart. Right now, I'm stuffing the bags with PopSockets that have her new Instagram account—@Instaham.

Izzy always inspires me with her own child-free life. Where being child-free is often associated with being lazy or selfish, Izzy is neither. In fact, she might be one of the busiest *and* most selfless people I know.

"And you *have* to work with him?" Izzy teases me.

"We both signed contracts. We're legally *bound*. That's why we're working together. And anyway, he's the best chef I know."

"Name another."

"What?"

"Chef."

"Gordon Ramsay."

"Who lives in Toronto."

"Susur Lee."

"A stranger. This Will is the only chef you *know*," she corrects me, smiling.

"Well, good reason to work with him, then."

"I don't see what the big deal is. You seem to be justifying him to me, when I'm not asking you to." She stands.

"Where are you going?" I call after her.

"To get more wine. I assume we're going to need it. We still have another five hundred bags to go."

My phone buzzes. Dad's name shows up on the screen.

"Hey, Dad. What's up?" I say, hoping that everything's OK. Dad lives in the country, in an old farmhouse he and Mom bought when they first married. He's lived alone ever since we left home—my sister first, then me a few years later. I often worry that he's lonely, especially in the winter, when the touristy town gets sleepy, and with a bad snowfall, he can be shut in for days. But despite multiple attempts to get him to move closer to us, he always insists he likes his life and that he's not lonely, though every time I visit he seems to have added more fish to the aquarium or a new aquarium to another room. It must mean something—but what?

"I was wondering . . . do you know how to make meringue?" he's asking me now.

"Meringue?" I repeat. "As in the stuff on a lemon meringue pie, or the other kind that you eat by itself?" I ask, as though it makes any difference. I haven't got a clue how to make either.

"Well that's the thing. I'm not sure. I saw a picture of meringues with a raspberry sauce drizzled overtop but now I can't find where I saw it, and I found a recipe in one of your mother's cookbooks but I've just made them and they turned out like the top of a pie, and that doesn't seem right."

"You know this is Kit, right?" I joke. Will would know the difference in a heartbeat. "But I'm at Izzy's—want me to put her on?"

"Ahh, great. I already left a message for your sister earlier. She didn't answer her phone."

"Alright, well, I'll ask her and call you back."

"When do you think that'll be?" he says. "No rush, of course," he adds, which makes me think there *is* a rush.

"Why are you making meringues, Dad?" I say suspiciously, and he clears his throat.

"Oh, no reason, just trying to stretch my skills. Use it or lose it, they say." What is it he thinks he's going to lose—an egg white? I wonder after hanging up. Maybe he's entering a town contest or something. Although not likely. He lives in an actual small town, not an episode of *Gilmore Girls*.

I tell my sister about Dad's call and she gives me a funny look and rattles on about the ins and outs of meringues, but my mind wanders. My sister either paid more attention when our mother was in the kitchen or got her genes, while I got my father's culinary hopelessness. For years now Dad has gotten by on simple meals like pasta or rice and pre-roasted chickens, which he breaks into meal-size portions, freezing them in small containers and then taking one out each night. I don't like to think of it, because it feels like such a sad existence.

Now, I can't help wondering: am I destined for the same life? Will I one day be taking my own dinner out of a Tupperware container I've stored in the freezer?

Of course not, I tell myself. There's always going to be a million takeout and delivery options here in the city. Even if I do live alone for the rest of my life.

nine

Sunday morning lazy lie-ins in my @silkinsheets paja-mas. They're so comfy, it needs to be a really good brunch offer to get me out of bed. PS. Instagram vs. Reality: Swipe ➡ to see how I "actually" woke up. 😊 #ad #Iwokeuplikethis

"Change of plans," Will says when I answer my phone on Sunday morning. He's cancelling? Disappointment rushes through me, despite all my efforts to push him away. Even though I'd love a screen-free day, I was looking forward to seeing him. Plus, even though most of my friends are child-free, too, they have partners, and default to hanging with them. I don't blame them—I used to do the same thing when things were good with Eric and me. I'm definitely happier being single than I was when things were rough with Eric, and I like the freedom to do whatever I want, whenever I want, but sometimes, from time to time, I still get a bit lonely, when I want to hang out with someone and no one's free.

"I was looking over the contract, and it says we should be showing how easy Fresh Food Fast is to take on a picnic, so then I was thinking, let's head to the island. I'll even bring a photographer."

"Oh, great. But . . . the *island*?" I'm shaking my head vehemently, which is not effective over the phone. Though part of me's relieved he isn't coming over—it'll be much easier to keep things professional if we're in public. Still . . . the island? "No. Besides, you can't just change the plan because you feel like it."

"I can if I want to follow the contract to a T. And I do, because I want to deliver what the client asked for—I'm just that kinda guy. So you wanna tell me what the real issue is with changing the plan? You're worried you can't get me in the sack if we're out in public?" His voice is hushed.

"You wish. I told you, we're not having sex again anyway. It was a one-time thing."

"So what is it, then?"

"I'm *not* island people, that's all."

"You're not *island people*?" Will laughs.

"That's right. No thanks. Nuh-uh. How about High Park?"

"You're acting like I'm suggesting going to the island in *Lost*. It's just Centre Island. Everyone loves the island."

"Not me. I hate it. Hate everything about it."

"Tough. It's a beautiful day, and being over at the island is ten times better than any park in the city. Meet you at the ferry docks at eleven." He hangs up. There's something about how Will just assumes that if he has an idea, it's a go—like what I say makes no difference—that irritates me to no end. Obviously this is a clue as to why he's divorced—maybe he treated his wife as though she were also a child.

I don't *have* to go. I could stand him up. That'd show him that I'm not the kind of woman who just goes along with some new plan I never agreed to. But we have to make the next Fresh Food Fast box by tomorrow morning. This is exactly the reason I like working alone on campaigns. And yet—do I really want to have to deal with cooking the meals alone, and risk them being able to tell Will wasn't in on it?

It *is* a beautiful day, an outdoor cooking pic is a good idea, and I've got a new red check blanket that would look great in photos.

Fine. I'll concede. This one time. I pack my things and head out.

Will's waiting by the ticket booth when I arrive—he's wearing a ball cap and another T-shirt that hugs his arms. His face is unshaven, and while I usually hate that look, on Will, it makes him even more attractive.

"Hi, Kit!" Addie rushes over to me, a camera slung across her body. What is she doing here? I look around nonchalantly to see if anyone's looking our way. It's not like I can't be seen with kids, but if someone were to snap a pic of Will and Addie and me together and post it . . . I'm always so paranoid, but I know from experience how much time it sucks to do damage control on a bad pic. And I would never want to mislead the women I've worked so hard to reach out to, with my book, my talks, my meetup groups. Social media makes it so much easier to quickly reach people, but it means that it's also so easy for things to go wrong, so quickly. And if I were to catch sight of the three of us, walking toward the ferry, on a gorgeous Sunday, I would most definitely not think this was any kind of work event.

"Surprise!" Will says, walking toward me. "Our own personal photographer."

Couldn't he have left her with her mom for the day? This feels like something he should've told me, instead of implying that he'd hired the next Ansel Adams. Addie beams. I give her my best fake Instagram smile, then immediately feel bad. She seems genuinely happy to see me—which is nice, I suppose. And realistically, what are the odds anyone's going to recognize me and think we're on a date? So why am I so annoyed? Am I jealous that I'm having to share Will's attention?

"Hey, Sweetie," I say. Then turn to Will. "I wish you'd cleared this with me. I take work pretty seriously and if the pics aren't good we're going to have to redo this whole thing."

"Relax, Boss." He grins. I want to smack him—or kiss him.

He puts the Fresh Food Fast box down and takes my camera and tripod bags from me, easily throwing them over his shoulder. Normally I'd refuse but the straps were digging into my shoulder and now my hands are free to create some Instagram stories on my phone. It's kind of nice having someone else to work with. He bends back down to pick up the food box.

"I'm really good," Addie pipes up. "I took a photography course last summer in Kensington Market. We walked around for hours. It was so tiring but we got all these cool shots in Graffiti Alley and stuff, and then we learned how to develop film in a darkroom and everything. But I brought my digital camera for this cuz Dad says you need it for Instagram."

"She's really good," Will says, smiling.

"Well, I have my own camera and tripod and timer." I point to the bags that Will's now carrying. "I'm kind of a control freak so I'll probably still take my own pics, too"—Addie's face falls. I sigh. "I mean, it would be nice to have the help. Why don't we just see how it goes?"

"Great. And that's the point of digital, right? If you don't like it I can just do it again."

"Uh-huh," I say, then nod toward Will, who's a few paces ahead of us. "Let's get on before all the shady seats are taken."

But we're too late and have to settle for seats along the outer railing. Will unloads our stuff, pushing it under the bench, then holds his ball cap out to me. "Want this?" he offers, but I shake my head.

"And get hat head?" I joke. Even though the thought of putting anything that's been touching Will's body on my own makes my heart skip a beat. Even a dirty ball cap.

Will asks us if we want anything to drink, then says that he's going to get a ginger ale. "Preventative measures. I get seasick."

"Are you kidding? But this was your idea. Why are we on a boat if you get seasick?"

He shrugs. "It's the only way to get to there. And Addie loves going to the island. So it makes up for the fact that I'm working on the weekend."

I nod. I get it. It's a source of stress I've heard over and over from friends with kids—how to balance work and parenting. You're either stressed out because you can't get the amount of work done that you used to because of your kids, or you're feeling guilty for working instead of spending time with them. Plus, even when you're working you're thinking about them. And yet, as Will walks toward the snack bar I can't help admiring him for figuring out a way to make today work—without letting me know it was an issue. And Addie seems really happy to be tagging along, which makes me feel bad for being so negative. And she's not making a stink that her dad's working on the weekend instead of giving her all his attention, so why am I being so possessive?

Addie calls to me and I turn to see her standing on the bench, leaning over the railing. She's making me nervous, but I can't decide whether to step in to offer responsible advice or mind my own business.

"Hey, come and sit down beside me," I say, and thankfully she listens, jumping down from the bench and sitting beside me. "So Dad says your job is on Instagram," she says. "Like, do you work there? And they pay you to take pictures?"

"Not exactly. But kind of." I flip the app open and show her my feed. "I talk about brands I like, to get people excited to try something they haven't. Like the Good Food Fast box. Only I'm a terrible cook, that's why your dad's now working with me." I scroll down to the latest Good Food Fast post, tilting my phone toward her, but she's looking at me.

"Do you wear false lashes when you're taking your photos?"

I shake my head and laugh. "No. I think I'm too lazy for falsies, but I know a lot of influencers do."

"I'm probably going to get false eyelashes and dye my hair purple when I'm older." I put my phone away and study her.

"I don't think you need false lashes. You have lovely lashes. And those things—I don't know, you can get pretty caught up in how you look." I smooth my hair, remembering my "hat head" comment earlier. "But the purple—that sounds fun," I say.

"Tell that to Dad."

"Hmm. Well, how old are you?"

"Eight," she says. I try to think back to when I was eight. Did I even know about makeup at that age? It seems wrong that she should be concerned with her appearance or what others think of her, when she'll inevitably have to deal with that later in life. Why am I even giving so much thought to this girl I just met, anyway?

"So, do you live by yourself?"

"Yep," I say lightly, looking around for Will. A few feet away, on the same bench, an elderly couple is holding hands, their heads bowed toward each other, talking quietly. I feel a stab of envy. I'm happy being single—and much happier than I was when Eric and I were fighting all the time—but sometimes I wonder if, when I'm older and I'm still single and everyone is old and gray with kids and grandkids to take care of them, I'll feel the same way.

"But why don't you have any kids? Are you married?"

Seriously? It's not even noon.

I sigh. "I'm happy with my life the way it is," I say. "I've got a great job and great friends and I don't think I could also fit kids into that. And the world is overpopulated as it is, so I think it's better for those who just *have* to have kids, the people who feel like they've always wanted to be a mom or a dad, to be parents, and if you're not sure, maybe it's better to just be that really cool aunt, or friend, you know?" I wink.

"My piano teacher doesn't have a husband but she had a baby," she says, a bit randomly, then squeals. "And oh my gosh, she's sooooo cute. I love babies. They're so squishy and they smell so good. I'm going to have four kids when I'm a mom."

I force a smile. "Wow. Four? That's a lot."

"It's not *that* many."

"I guess."

"Did your husband die?" she asks, and I just stare back at her wide eyes, wanting this conversation to end. I'm about to tell her that I don't have a husband, that I've never had a husband, that just because I'm in my thirties doesn't mean I have to be married, but then she continues. "My mom died, so I get it. Death and all that."

And her words hit me like a deep punch to the gut. It goes right to that place that I hate, and I feel frozen in time and space. She is motherless, like me. I just assumed Will was divorced—that he was only caring for Addie half the time. I never even considered he was solo parenting. She seems so well adjusted, happy, even, and I feel faint. "Oh Honey, I had no idea," I say, thinking she could probably use a hug, but I barely know her. Should I try to hug her? The idea paralyzes me, and then the moment is gone. It would be awkward, surely, for one of us, if not both. I always feel like my own mother was taken away from me way too soon, when I was too young to be motherless. How unfair it all was. But I was ten, and Addie's only eight.

"When did it happen?" I ask gently.

"When I was three. I don't really remember her that much."

Of course she doesn't. What *do* you remember at three? Much less than what you remember at ten, I suppose. I have the garage memories with Mom. What does Addie have? I look out to the lake and try to block out the city so all I can see is blue against blue. Sky melting into water. Or water melting into sky.

"Everyone thinks Dad is divorced," she's saying and I pull away from my trance and turn to her. "Most kids have divorced parents, I guess. Like my friend Millie. Her parents are divorced, and she stays with her mom one week and her dad the other. Her mom has a house with a pool but her dad has this cool loft-place. Millie still hates that her parents are divorced, and she talks about it all the time. But her parents are always fighting—like, whenever they see each other, so I don't see why she would want them to still be married. Plus, I'm pretty sure her mom likes my dad." Now Addie's looking out into the blue. "And when she complains, I always think, well at least she has a mom."

I wonder if Addie gets stuck in the loop, too. Like I do. *If Mom were alive I could ask her how to make this.* And *If Mom were alive I would know how to do this.* And lately, it's been bigger questions, like: *If Mom were alive, would I feel differently about motherhood? If Mom were alive would I be more willing to risk everything for my dreams?* I want to take Addie's hand, but Will returns and everything falls back into place. The spell is broken and the loop is lost. For now. And I tell myself that's a good thing. The more distance I can keep between Addie and me, the better. I can't be a role model for her, I don't want to be in her life. No ties. Too much risk of things turning out badly. Too messy. And things are already feeling messy, as it is.

Will returns with drinks and sits down on the other side of Addie. "Look!" Addie points toward the shoreline. "We're almost at the island."

Will nods, taking a sip of his ginger ale. "What should we do first—get bikes and ride to find a picnic spot or grab a snack so we don't kill each other?"

I shake my head and grumble that we don't need bikes for the picnic. "Can't we just choose a spot by the ferry dock and eat sooner?"

"We *always* rent bikes," Addie protests. "Dad, tell her. We always get bikes."

"We always get bikes," Will shrugs. "Plus, we want to find a spot where people aren't going to trample us."

I sigh. "Fine."

"Wow, you really don't like the island, huh?" Will teases, poking me in the side. Electricity shoots through me and I feel bad about being such a grump. I grab my camera and tripod while he grabs the large box of supplies.

Once we're off the boat, Will puts the box down again, opens his backpack and starts pulling out snacks like some sort of culinary magician. "Cheese stick? Granola bar? Yogurt drink?"

We are never going to *actually* get this picnic over with. And yet, I choose a granola bar with rainbow sprinkles because I'm starving. "I'm surprised you don't make these yourself."

He raises an eyebrow as he hands Addie a cheese stick. "I'm a chef, not a martyr. Also I'm so busy making boxed meals for somebody, I don't have as much time on my hands."

I can't help smiling.

Will leads us to the bike rental place a few minutes' walk away, and Addie begs us to get one of those four-wheeled bikes, the kind with two rows of bench seating that look more like open-air cars than bikes. "Dad never lets us get one when it's just us because he thinks I won't pedal hard enough to keep it going. But with you here we can do it. Please? Pretty pretty please? If you say yes Dad has to agree." Her hands are together, clasped in prayer.

"Fine by me," I say, thinking how much easier it will be to lug all this stuff around if we can dump it onto the floor of the bike-car. Addie squeals and it makes me feel so good to make her happy, even if this job is turning into an all-day affair. It's a weird feeling—that something I don't really want to do, but that makes someone else happy, is causing me joy. I'm not sure what to make of it.

Riding around on this ridiculous contraption, we pass an ice cream stand and Addie asks if we can stop. "Sure," I say, hoping for another hit of that feeling, but Will's saying no, and we look at each other. "We haven't even had lunch," he says, but I roll my eyes.

"Oh, come on."

He gives in. "You're a bad influence."

He has no idea.

We park the bike by the side of the building and Addie loops her arm through mine. "Dad is so strict about sugar," she says, but her voice is teasing and she's looking back at Will for a reaction. He just shakes his head and laughs.

Addie orders Blue Bubblegum and I order Lavender then look around for a good place to get a shot of my ice cream. I hold my cone out in front of the green wall of the bathroom door and snap a pic. For a split second I'm actually happy to be on the island—since I never come, I'm seeing the opportunity for fresh content.

"Let me try," Addie says, lifting her camera up. She snaps away then asks if I'll take a pic of her ice cream cone the same way. I do and show it to her.

"I like how you just got my arm there."

"I like to think about three things when I'm taking a picture: my surroundings, colors, and something of myself in it," I say. Addie nods, licking her ice cream.

"Taste for taste?" Addie asks and I pause. I do not want to share ice cream with this kid. She has dirt under her nails. But I wasn't planning on eating the ice cream anyway, so I hold it out to her. She takes a lick and makes a face. "It tastes like soap."

"I know. It's disgusting. But it's so pretty in photos, so . . ." I shrug and look around for Will.

"So you got a flavor you don't like just because it looks good?" I feel sheepish and I don't like it. Why do I care what this eight-year-old thinks? I offer my ice cream to Will. "Only because I don't want you throwing it out in front of Addie," he whispers, taking a lick then making a face at the taste. "Oh, forget it." He looks around for a garbage bin. "You're not going to post pics of Addie, right?"

"I wasn't planning to," I say.

"Good. I want to put off social media as long as I can."

"Of course," I say lightly. Obviously I had no intention of posting pics of Addie on my grid today. Even though I meant what I said to the No Kidding group about the need to debunk the myth that child-free women dislike children, my Instagram business is a bit different. There are millions of mommy bloggers out there who flood their feeds with carefully curated, sophistically styled squares of their impeccably dressed children (usually in matching outfits). The key to success is knowing your niche. On the 'gram, mine is to show the chic, child-free life. No exceptions.

We finally agree on the perfect spot to document the picnic. Will starts unpacking the food, and I notice he's done most of the prep work already—all the veggies for the cold tacos are pre-cut into tiny cubes and he's even brought small white ramekins for presentation. "Looks great," I say as I set up my blanket between a few large oak trees. I hand my camera to Addie. "So what's the vibe we're going for here?" Addie says as though she's eighteen, not eight. "Do we need other people in the photo as though it's a big picnic, or is it supposed to be just the two of you?"

"Just the two of us, Kiddo," Will says. He winks at me.

Addie looks around and hops onto a nearby picnic table. "Always shoot from above, right?" And she starts snapping away while Will and I spoon the taco ingredients into the ramekins. Once everything's arranged on the blanket, Will and I sit down.

"You don't *look* like you're on a romantic picnic," Addie says. "Shouldn't you be sitting closer or something?"

Who said anything about it being romantic? It can't be romantic. Except, the thought of an excuse to shimmy a little closer to Will makes all the little hairs on my body stand on end.

"How would *you* know?" Will says, raising an eyebrow.

"YouTube."

He shakes his head but moves closer to me, his hand grazing my knee. Tingles shoot up my leg. "Aren't people going to wonder about the good-looking guy who keeps popping up in your photos?" Will says, his green eyes on mine. He's teasing, challenging me to be seen with him. I want to look around, see if anyone can see us, but I can't tear my eyes away from his. There's just something about him . . . And even though Will's not on Instagram, at some point someone who knows him is going to recognize him in my photos. And then how long will it take for them to put two and two together and recognize that there's more than a work contract going on between us? Which is why there can't be.

"Don't get your dad's face in it," I call to Addie, as Will moves closer, his face inches away from mine. "How's this?" he breathes, and shivers run through my entire body.

He puts a hand on my cheek and tilts my face ever so slightly toward his. His touch is electric. And I can't help meeting his eyes. And then, I'm kissing him. His lips are warm and it feels so good.

"Gross," Addie yells at us. We break apart. My pulse is pounding in my lips as I wipe my mouth with the back of my hand and

Will laughs. Addie holds my camera out to me then plops down on the blanket. "Can we eat now? I'm starving."

"Let me just grab a few more flat lays," I say, snapping pics of the taco ingredients, seven-bean salad and cucumber-pomegranate coleslaw from above. Then I flip through the photos, stopping on one of Will and me. My breath catches in my throat. We look so happy and natural together—like we *fit*. If I had amnesia and saw these photos I would assume this was my boyfriend. Except, I've never dated anyone as good-looking as Will. This is torture.

I turn the camera off and toss it on the blanket.

"That's it?" Will asks. "How do they look?"

"They're fine. Thanks, Addie."

"No problem. Can I go get a hot dog? This food looks disgusting. No offense, Dad."

Will concedes, handing her money and telling her to stay where she can see us. "If you can't see me, I can't see you."

I make myself a taco, but only take a few bites before pushing my plate aside. "Wanna pack up?" I say, impatiently.

"What's the rush? Lie down with me." He pushes the food aside to make enough space on the blanket for the two of us. He stretches out, and reluctantly, I lie down too, and look up at the sky that's filled with white, fluffy clouds. Will shifts his head so it's touching mine.

"I always wanted to have a picnic here on the island, but it always seemed like a lot of work," he says.

"It was a lot of work. Though I didn't do much. Still, I think Addie has the right idea. She's getting her lunch in under a minute, and she didn't have to chop any veggies at home beforehand or do any set up or clean up."

"Yeah, but it was worth it. It gave us a reason to slow down." His hand brushes against mine. I consider saying something now, telling him why this will never work, but Addie will be back any minute. And it's *not* like we're dating. We're just working together. With a random kiss thrown in for the camera. It's acting, nothing more.

I pull my book out of my bag and open it. Will looks over at me. "Always with a book, huh?"

"Yep."

He reaches into his bag and pulls one out too. "Me too. I'm happy to stay for a bit if you are."

I exhale then nod. "Yeah, sure," I say lightly, thinking, *This is nice. Really nice.*

A while later, Addie returns and asks if we can go to Centreville. "Just one turn on the Scrambler?"

"No," Will says, immediately sitting up.

"You always say no," she whines. "Just because you hate rides."

"You hate rides too?" I say to him, sitting up. "I thought kids were supposed to make you young at heart."

"I like to have fun, but those rides are manufactured fun. And technically, I don't hate them, they hate me. It's the motion sickness thing."

"Come on," I say to Addie. "I'll take you while your dad cleans up the mess." I wink and Will looks at me, mouth open, then shakes his head. But he doesn't protest, instead saying he'll meet us by the gates in half an hour.

As Addie and I walk over to the mini–amusement park, I wonder why I agreed to this, when we could've been on the next ferry home. I'm hot and tired and don't really feel like standing in a lineup. But Addie is so excited, and despite my best efforts to have a horrible time, I'm enjoying the afternoon. It's nothing like the times Eric and I tried to come to the island together. The disagreements, the dysfunction. As soon as we enter the park and get our tickets, Addie's immediately leading me to a large wooden-clad building. There's no lineup and we head inside, where it's pitch black, disco lights shooting flashes of light throughout the place, 80s music blasting through the speakers. "Scrambler!" she screams. A moment later, we're hopping into a rattly old car, and I'm praying the seatbelt still works. Then the ride starts, and as we get whipped around, Addie is squished into me. She's laughing and I'm laughing. I pull out my phone and snap a few pics of us before we get off the ride. "Ooh can I see?" she says, leaning close.

"I'll send them to your dad for you." She grins and skips to keep up with me as we walk to the gates to meet Will.

Back on the ferry, Will thanks me. "You didn't have to do that, you know."

"I know. But it was actually really fun." I mean it.

"See? Told you everyone likes the island. You just didn't know what you were doing those other times. Or you weren't here with the right guy."

He bumps shoulders with me. He's teasing, of course, but his words sink in. I walk over to the railing, my face to the wind, and close my eyes. When the boat docks at the mainland, we file off the boat and Will turns to Addie. "Alright, Kiddo, we should get going. We're having dinner at Gillian's and I think we could both use a shower." He ruffles her hair and I feel a pang of jealousy. Who's Gillian? Surely not an aunt, or he would've said 'Aunt Gillian.' And if she has a husband why not mention him, too? *We're having dinner at Gillian and Frank's. Gillian and Enrique's. Gillian and Jamil's.* Why do I even care?

"Kit?" I recognize the voice before seeing his face. My chest clenches. I turn.

And there he is, standing in line to file onto the ferry. Eric. In a blue polo shirt, crisp khakis and leather sneakers that probably cost more than my entire outfit. He's grown a beard.

"Eric."

He looks from me to Will to Addie and back to me. "Hi," I say, my voice an octave too high, feeling like I've been caught, that I owe him an explanation.

"Were you . . . at the island?" he says, surprised, pointing to the ferry, then turning back to me.

I nod. "Yep."

"But you hate the island," he says.

"So do you," I retort immediately.

He shrugs. "Change of heart."

"Kit tried to tell me she hated the island, but I convinced her otherwise," Will says, sticking out his hand and I look from Eric to Will. "Will MacGregor. And this is my daughter, Addie."

Eric's brow furrows. He takes Will's hand and shakes it—firmly. "Eric Uxton." He shoves his hands in his pockets. "I'm checking out that new restaurant that just opened. Did you try it?"

I shake my head and try to act nonchalant when I say: "We brought our own meal."

"You *did*?" He looks like I just admitted to murdering a flock of seagulls. He frowns. "Alright, well, I want to catch this ferry before it goes. Nice to meet you," he says to Will. And then his eyes are on mine. And they stay there. "See you later, Kit." Then he turns and heads toward the ferry. I watch Eric walk away until he's lost in the crowd. I slowly turn back to Will, who's staring at me.

"I have to go," I say, although I have nowhere to go, nowhere to be.

#

On the streetcar home, I scroll through the photos on my camera, trying to push thoughts of Eric out of my mind. Even though I no longer have feelings for him, seeing him still put a damper on what was otherwise a really lovely day. Addie took some great shots, but it's the ones I took on my phone, the ones with Addie at the amusement park, that give me pause. That's the real story of the day, not the staged photos that'll hit my Instagram grid. And there's nothing I can do with them—except text them to Will, as promised to Addie. I wait to see if he'll text back, but he doesn't. Then I look at the picture I took of my book against the picnic blanket, and post it to my Bookstagram account, @BookKit. The one no one knows about. And smile to myself.

Once home, I load all the images from my camera into my computer for editing, choosing ones where Will's face is slightly obscured, just to make sure no one recognizes him, and send them off to Feloise, who will send them to Lucy who will send them to the client for approval. The photos are great and I know the client will be happy, but as I scroll through them mindlessly, I wish there were more of Will, where his face was actually in focus. But then I'd just be wasting time fantasizing about what can never be—because it's not a life I want. Like Will said, they were heading off to dinner and after that I'm sure it would be time for him to read bedtime stories and Addie would probably throw a tantrum about something or wake up because of a nightmare and then it'd be tomorrow and there'd be breakfast to make and some sort of activity to get her to—because that's what life with kids is all about. Being selfless and having zero time to yourself.

No, things are definitely better this way.

ten

A few nights later, I'm out for dinner with Gloria and Xiu at a new Moroccan place that just opened in the west end. We're on our second round of cocktails but haven't ordered dinner yet. We're too busy covering everything from my cousin Lena's upcoming baby shower—which we're all invited to, since Gloria and Xiu know Lena from the year we all did bootcamp together—to Gloria's latest house sale, to Xiu's update on her relationship with Jed. "I've been thinking a lot about it," I say to her. "Can I offer you advice?"

"You know you can," Xiu says, leaning forward.

"There's that saying—and you know I'm not one to live my life by an inspo quote on Facebook, but I got this from John Lennon, so give me a sec," I say before they can tease me. "*Life is what happens to you when you're busy making other plans.* What if you remind Jed that right now, he's married to you. That's his reality. And if you two aren't having kids, you need to make the best decision for that plan, not the one he may have in the future."

Xiu nods. "Yeah, you're right."

Gloria claps her hands together. "Excellent, well now that we have all that out of the way, can we finally get down to what we all want to discuss? The hot chef," Gloria says, as my phone rings and Will's name shows up on the screen. My heart skips a beat, and for a second, I wonder if he's calling to see if I'm free.

"Hey," I say, picking up.

"Hey." He sounds panicked, rambling on about a last-minute request to cater an engagement party that was too good to pass up, which he therefore took, and now he needs to be out the door but the babysitter didn't show up, his sister-in-law isn't answering her phone and Addie's best friend's mother, Gillian, his go-to, is out of town. "It'll only be a few hours," he insists. "Please? I'm desperate."

It takes me a second to even register what he's asking of me. He wants me to watch Addie? Is he *joking*? We spend one afternoon together on the island and suddenly he's put me into the babysitter rotation? No way.

"I'm out with friends," I say, making sure not to apologize—normally my default.

"Oh, right, of course, is—is it important?"

I nearly hang up. It doesn't matter if it's important or not. It's what I'm doing. And I know what he's thinking, that *of course* I'm out with friends, because that's what single people do. I'm annoyed, and, anyway, I'm also underqualified—I never even babysat as a kid, so why would I start now? And yet, I don't hang up, because there's this small part of me that's flattered I came to mind.

"Are you still there?" he asks.

"Yes."

"I'll make it up to you," he adds, his voice low and gravelly.

"I promise." And the thought of *how* he might make it up to me . . .

"You could even just tell me where you are and I'll bring Addie to you," Will is saying. "You don't have to leave."

"No!" I practically shout, then lower my voice as a woman at the table beside us turns and gives me a look. "I'll meet you at my place in ten minutes."

I hang up and gulp the rest of my wine as Gloria and Xiu look at me expectantly.

"Just, uh . . . something with my sister," I say, and Gloria shakes her head.

"Nice try, Kit. Was that the guy?"

"There's no guy."

"There's definitely a guy. I don't know why you're hiding it from us. We're supposed to be your friends. Spill it."

"Yeah, why are you being so weird?" Xiu's brow is furrowed, as though she's trying to figure out who exactly the guy is. I haven't posted the pic of Will and me from the island, but once I do, she's going to be onto me. I don't want to lie to either of them, but the fact they're not just my friends, but also child-free by choice, and part of my No Kidding group, makes it complicated. And because I know what they'll say: *Don't get involved with someone who has kids. It's easy. Break it off before it can begin.* But I can't think about that right now. I grab my purse and slap a twenty on the table before rushing out the door.

At my condo I find Will and Addie waiting for me in the lobby. Addie's looking around, wide-eyed, like she's in Disneyland. "I'll make this up to you, I swear," he whispers in my ear.

"You already said that," I tell him, wondering what exactly he would've done if I'd refused to bail on my girls' night.

"Yeah, well, I guess that's all I can think about." He clears his throat and then turns to Addie. "Be good for Kit, OK? No messing up her apartment. Love you, Kiddo."

He hands me a bag and tells me that her pajamas and toothbrush are inside. "She can fall asleep, and I'll come pick her up as soon as this thing's done. Don't let her get overtired," he adds in a lowered voice, then kisses Addie and he's out the door.

"This is going to be so fun," Addie says on the elevator ride up, but there's this pit in my stomach. Is it going to be fun? I'm not prepared to have a child in my tidy, white apartment. I open the door and Addie pushes through, running over to the floor-to-ceiling windows, leaning up against them, her hands on the glass. She breathes on the glass, then draws a heart and turns around. "This place is so cool. Is that candy?" she says, eyeing the dish on the coffee table. "This is exactly how I want my apartment to look when I'm older. Well, maybe not exactly. I would have more twinkle lights. I have a Pinterest board for inspo." The lid to the candy jar clanks as she slams it on the glass coffee table. I wince. I move her shoes and bag to the corner of the apartment from the middle of the floor where she dropped them.

"Want to make cheese quesadillas for dinner?" Addie asks, her mouth full of jujubes. She's already lifting the lid on the jar again, but this time, the lid slips and shatters as it hits the coffee table, sending shards of glass skittering across the hardwood floor.

She yelps and my initial reaction is annoyance. I sigh—loudly, then realize I should be making sure she's OK.

"I'm *so* sorry, Kit," she says, and I force a tight smile and tell her it's OK. "Come and sit here so you don't step on any glass," I say, pulling out a bar stool. She tiptoes over and bounds, a little too forcefully for my liking, onto the stool, but I grab the back of it before it teeters over.

"Whoa, careful," I say, still feeling annoyed.

"Do you have any more candy in your cupboards?" she asks. "I guess we can't eat those ones now."

"No," I say tersely, then retrieve the broom from the space beside the stacked washer and dryer.

"When I sleep at Millie's, Gillian always lets us make our own cheese quesadillas." She's rambling. I get the glass cleaned up and I'm about to tell her that I'm not Gillian when I think better of it. But why am I so irritated at the mention of Gillian, a woman I've never even met?

"I really hadn't given it any thought, but I can tell you we're definitely *not* making cheese quesadillas. Let's order in. Do you like pizza?"

"Pizza?!" She claps her hands together. "Yes! Dad *never* lets us order pizza. He always makes it himself and puts *broccoli* on it. Pizza isn't supposed to have broccoli."

"I actually like broccoli on my pizza," I say. "With feta and sun-dried tomatoes. It's so good."

Her face falls.

"It's fine. We'll just order two pizzas. You get what you like and I'll get what I like."

Her eyes widen. "Really? Our own pizzas?"

I laugh. "Yeah. Then we have leftovers and I don't have to order in tomorrow. See? You're doing me a favor. So what would you like on yours?" I grab my phone.

"Cheese. And tomato sauce."

"Cheese and tomato sauce it is," I say, punching in the number for my go-to pizza place on the corner. "Alright," I say, once

I've placed the order. "Nail time. Come with me." I motion for her to come into the kitchen. I pull open the drawer where I keep the nail polish.

"Aren't you supposed to have spoons and stuff in here?"

I shrug. "Says who?" And Addie smiles.

"Are these the piggy ones?" she says, looking at the small bottles in my drawer.

"Piggy ones?"

"The nail polish that doesn't have any chemicals. You know, cuz I'm a kid."

Nail polish without chemicals? Then how on earth does it stay on your nails? I sigh.

"Aunt Margot only lets me use that kind. The rest is really bad for you. Cancer, you know."

And I feel bad for being irritated, because she has a point, and I do know. I used to be so afraid of getting cancer when I was a kid. Because of Mom. I was convinced that everything would give me cancer—even though now, I can see that it was irrational, because it wasn't anything Mom did, or didn't do, in particular that caused her cancer.

The worst for me was fruit. Dad would have to wash each piece of fruit—with soap—before I could be forced to put it in my mouth. I'd done a project on pesticides at school and I was sure that the pesticides went much deeper than the skin and that the entire fruit was contaminated regardless of how hard he scrubbed an apple. Some nights I would lie in bed and wonder if a twinge here, a tickle there was the cancer growing inside of me. I'd poke around my body, looking for lumps or bumps or anything that felt like it could be a tumor. Finally, when I was fifteen or so, I got over it, but sometimes I still hold my breath before taking my first bite of any fruit. And now I've gone the other way—choosing to believe that while nearly everything *could* give you cancer, I'm not going to live my life wondering whether it'll be red Smarties or nail polish. But I'm thirty-three. Addie's eight.

"You know what?" I say. "I have some nail decals. Let's use those instead."

Addie nods with enthusiasm. A few minutes later we're set up at the bar and I've laid out sheets of stars and moons and butterfly decals and she seems happy. And I can't help but remember the first time Izzy did my nails after Mom died. She was babysitting me, trying to make things fun. When she finished, I cried. "What's wrong?" Izzy had asked. And for some reason I couldn't tell her that her painting my nails made me miss Mom, because she was the only one who'd ever painted my nails for me until that moment.

I refocus on Addie, who's telling me about gymnastics and school as I apply the decals.

"So who's Gillian again?" I ask, trying to act nonchalant.

"Millie's mom. Millie's my best friend. I told you about her. How her parents are divorced . . ."

"Ahh, right," I say, remembering our conversation on the ferry. "So your dad and her are just . . . friends? Because you two are friends? Is your dad friends with Millie's dad too?"

She shakes her head. "Not really. We mostly only hang out when Millie's with her mom."

"Uh-huh," I say, focusing on the star between my forefinger and thumb. Once I apply it Addie fans her hands to admire them.

"Can we take a picture with your phone?"

"Sure," I say, handing her my phone.

"Do you have Snapchat?" she asks. "I want to send a pic to Millie."

"No. I think I'm way too old for Snapchat," I laugh. "I don't understand it."

"But it's so fun. And if you don't use it you'll just seem even older," she says like she's the wise woman of social media. "Like my dad. He doesn't have any apps on his phone. Except the weather. He's really into the weather. He's always telling me the temperature, as if I care. Here, I'll show you how to use Snapchat." She disappears for a second and returns with an iPad in a Hello Kitty case. A second later she's snapping photos of herself.

"You just can't tell my dad about this."

"He doesn't know you have Snapchat on there?"

"Or Instagram. Or TikTok. He's so overprotective about that kind of stuff." She rolls her eyes.

Although I can't help but feel flattered that she's letting me in on her secret, I'm pretty sure I'm breaking some sort of parenting code. Am I *her* friend—or Will's? Can I be both? And this—this headspace that parenting takes up—is just another reason I want no part in the club.

"Here, let's take a pic with our nails." She tilts her head to mine and snaps the pic.

"Alright, ready to watch a movie?" I suggest, getting two sodas out of the fridge as the pizza arrives.

"Yeah!" She bounds over to the couch, suddenly an eight-year-old again.

"Uh-uh," I say, "we are definitely not sitting on my white couch with pizza and pop."

She stares at me. "Well then, where are we going to sit?"

"The floor." I disappear into the bedroom and return with an armful of pillows and blankets and arrange them on the floor, then bring over the food and drinks. It's raining lightly outside, the drops pattering softly on the windows. "It's the perfect night for a movie," I say as we settle in. Halfway through the movie, Addie snuggles into me. I pause, noticing that there's dried pizza sauce on the blanket she's been using, then remind myself that I can wash the blanket and should be glad it's not on my white couch. And what's more important—this little girl or a blanket? And so, slowly, and a bit uncomfortably, I put my arm around her. I feel wooden, like I'm doing it all wrong, and I expect her to pull away at my touch, but she snuggles in even closer. And it feels nice. Really nice. I relax. Even though I love my friends and my sister, it's not like I would ever snuggle up to them during a movie. And with any guy, there's always that undertone of sexual tension. It's never purely platonic.

But as a clap of thunder shocks us both, Addie bolts upright. The rain falls hard against the window and then there's more thunder, lightning too. I pull her down close and keep my arm around her. "It's OK. It's just weather, right?" I joke, but she's twisted herself around to look out the massive windows.

"I'm scared," she says, her eyes wide with genuine fear. "Can we go in your bedroom?"

"I've been through millions of these," I say with a laugh, trying to lighten the mood. Am I really going to let her sleep in my bed? There's pizza sauce on her face.

"Please?" She looks so scared, and I break.

"Come on."

We move into my bedroom and I tuck her into the sheets, trying not to think about how weird this is—having a kid in my bed. I flip on the fan in the corner and it nearly drowns out the rain. She's pulled the covers to her chin, and still looks freaked out.

Don't let her get overtired, I hear Will saying.

"How about I read to you?" I suggest and go to the closet, where I keep the kids' books. I scan the spines, then pull out a book of fairy tales and climb into bed beside her.

"Do you like fairy tales?" I say, hoping it doesn't seem too infantile.

She nods. "Sure."

I run my finger down the table of contents then turn to page 41 and begin to read "Hansel and Gretel." Although I've probably read the story a dozen or more times in my life, it's never dawned on me that the whole premise of the story is that a widower has married a woman who wants to get rid of his children.

"You know what? Let's read a different story." I flip to "Cinderella," because who doesn't love a good underdog story? But it's only once I've begun reading that I'm reminded the story is less about the heroine defying expectations than it is about her being poorly treated by her evil stepmother. Why am I so rattled by tales of stepmothers? It doesn't even have to do with me, I tell myself. This has to do with Addie. Whoever Will ends up with one day will not want to be competing with these vivid images of evil stepmothers.

But another loud crack of thunder makes even me jump, and I turn to see Addie gripping the covers. She starts to cry. "I want to go home," she says, sounding panicked. "I want my dad. Can you call my dad? Please." Her eyes are wide. I try to comfort her but she shimmies away from me, sitting up and hugging her knees to her chest.

I'm not sure what to do. If Will's in the middle of the event he can't exactly leave, and while I could take her home, I don't have a key. "Come on, let's just try another book," I say, but my heart isn't in it. What if Addie tells Will that I wouldn't let her call her own father when she was frightened? Perhaps if I'd ever been a babysitter, I'd know what to do. I could reference some sort of manual that explains exactly what to do in this situation. But I never was. And I don't want to be one now, either.

I grab my phone and call Will. If he answers, he can talk, if he doesn't then he can't. It goes straight through to voice mail. I try once more.

"Aunt Margot," Addie says. "Call Aunt Margot. She'll come get me."

"OK, sure. Do you know her number?"

I consider letting Addie call herself but I decide to take charge of the situation.

"Margot," I say when she answers. "This is Kit Kidding." I explain the situation so it sounds like I've got it all under control—even though, of course, I don't, not at all.

"It's nearly ten o'clock. What on earth is she doing awake?" she *tsk tsk*s into the phone.

I pass the phone over to Addie, feeling like a failure.

"It's so scary here," she whimpers into the phone. "We're so high up, like on the fiftieth floor, and the thunder is so loud."

"Thirty-ninth," I correct her.

"I want to go home," she says, practically in tears. I look out the window. The storm is passing. The thunder is far away, the lightning infrequent.

I want Margot to say no, that because it's late she should just stay put, but Addie's nodding and then she passes the phone back to me. I reluctantly tell Margot where I live.

Twenty minutes later an impossibly tall blond woman with very pale skin who looks absolutely nothing like Will is standing at my door, peering down at me, and it dawns on me that perhaps she's not Will's sister, but his sister-*in-law*. His wife's sister. While she stares at me, her Husky-blue eyes cold, I can't help wondering if Will's wife looked like her. I'm suddenly very aware of my wrinkled pajamas and hair pulled up in a topknot. Addie rushes over to her, and Margot wraps her long, lean arms around her, runs her slender fingers through her hair. "Oh Sweetie, I'm here." She finally acknowledges me. "Who *are* you? I just don't understand how Will let this happen . . ." She peers around my apartment, as though I'm a kidnapper, holding Addie ransom.

"Will and I are friends," I mumble, but she's not listening. She's steering Addie out of the apartment, taking her backpack and holding her hand, shaking her head. I watch them walk down the hall and wait for them to disappear into the elevator before closing the door, trying to shut the entire night out of my mind. But even as I sit in bed, sipping a glass of wine, telling myself that it doesn't matter, that I had nothing to prove and that Addie's leaving was for the best anyway, so that Will never asks me to babysit again, I can't help feeling like I've let Addie down, and somehow, let myself down, too.

eleven

The next morning I'm washing the pizza-stained blankets and tidying up when I spot a small notebook tucked under the corner of my bed. I pick it up and flip it open. The creamy pages are filled with bubbly figures. Some in dresses, others in flared pants. Several of the pics feature a small girl with long hair and a large man with wavy hair, doing various activities: biking, sledding, reading. The words *Dad* and *Addie* written on many pages. I close the book and put it in my purse to remind myself to give it back to Will when he texts.

Thx for last night. Addie says she had a blast.

I assume he's just being polite, but instead of making me feel better, it makes me feel worse. I don't respond. Instead, I shove my phone in my purse, abandon my half-finished cleaning job, and head outside to clear my head.

A few hours later, I'm coming out of a boutique I borrow clothes from in exchange for posts when I nearly smack into someone running along the sidewalk. He swerves, we meet eyes and I realize it's Thom from the coffee shop. He's wearing running tights and a tank top, ears plugged with AirPods. "Kit, Kit, Kit!" He pulls me in for a sweaty hug, his long hair swinging forward to brush my shoulders. "I've been thinking about you," he says. When he sees the surprised look on my face, he laughs. "Not like that. I get that we weren't on the same page. I mean, you just popped into my head and I wondered if you had tackled that big project you mentioned. The one you wouldn't actually tell me about? How's that going?"

I feel disappointed in myself. "Oh, um . . . I guess, it's not, really. Work's just crazy . . ." The thing is, when *won't* work be crazy, if I continue to take on as much as I keep taking on? Why am I unable to say no to things that don't matter to me, instead of saying yes to something that does?

But I know why. If Mom were here, she'd be pushing me, or encouraging me, or guiding me. And without her, I'm not sure I'll ever truly be able to tackle it alone. Not that I'm about to share all *that* with Thom. "How about you?" I keep my voice light, detached.

He claps his hands together and beams even more broadly. "You won't believe it. Remember that crazy idea I had, to host a massive swap of all that stuff we all have? At City Hall?" I nod, remembering that one of the millions of ideas he regaled me with on our date was to bring people and their used items together, for a community swap, rather than filling our landfills with unwanted stuff. "Well, I'm doing it."

"Wow, that's great," I say, a bit amazed. It's only been a few weeks since Thom and I had that date.

"It *is* great. It felt like this massive *thing* that would take so much planning, but I realized, don't let the perfect be the enemy of the good"—he claps his hands, louder this time—"just do it.

So it's happening—two Saturdays from now. Check it out if you're free. I'm calling it the Be Free Swap. We're all going to *be free* of our stuff, all that stuff that's weighing us down, burying us. Anyway, I'm pumped, dude. It reminded me that doing good doesn't have to be hard. Anyway, I gotta jet. Give me a call if you wanna hang sometime." He bounds down the street. I watch him go, envy bubbling within me.

I call Feloise and ask her if she'll meet me for a drink. She does, and I'm grateful she always makes me a priority. Half an hour later, we're sitting at the wine bar inside Eataly, sipping rosé. "You know I know you work hard for me," I start.

"You're damn right I do."

"And a huge part of the reason I started working with you was because you were known as *the* speaking agent. The one everyone wants. And you've been incredible. I mean, the access you've given me to inspire women and help them pursue their passion . . ."

"Are you firing me?" Feloise slams her hand on the table and I immediately put my hand overtop of hers.

"No. Not at all. Can I go on?"

She nods. I take a sip of wine and continue. "You know I love the speaking engagements, and my groups and the conventions. But it feels like lately, my time has been pretty heavily skewed toward the social media stuff. And some of it isn't even really related to my platform. So I was thinking, what if we scale back on that stuff, which would give me more time to work on some other projects I've been considering—"

"What projects?" she barks. "If you have other projects, you need to tell me what they are. How can I represent you if I don't know what you're working on? And I've told you before, if you're thinking about another project, it should be a book proposal. The publisher keeps asking me if you have anything in the works. Now's the time—"

I sigh. "Feloise, I don't want to talk about another book. And can you please calm down for a second," I say.

She closes her eyes, clasps her hands together, then a moment later, opens her eyes and nods. "Go on."

"These projects have nothing to do with you," I say. "No offense. But I have this idea for a business I want to run out of a garage—"

"What business? What garage?"

"Well, I don't *have* the garage yet because I barely have time to even house hunt. I used to be able to schedule my time—to know when I had an event or interview or book signing, but now it feels like all of my unscheduled time is eaten up by social media, because these posts are taking more and more of my time and—"

"Kit," Feloise interrupts. Once she has my attention, she takes a slow sip of her wine, then places the glass on the table and leans toward me. "The reason I book you for so many social campaigns is because social campaigns are where the money is. And why would we say no when we can say yes?"

I realize that this conversation is pointless. If I want to stop doing so much social media and focus on my business idea for a book garage I need to do it, and let Feloise know after the fact. Thankfully, Feloise checks her phone and tells me she's got to run. I pay the bill, we say goodbye, and I walk home, Thom's questions and Feloise's objections crowding my headspace.

"You could at least say no," a voice barks and I jump, then turn to see a lineup of women standing against a brick wall, smoking. One of them is glaring at me, and I realize she must have asked me something, but I have no idea what.

"Sorry?" I say, noticing the women's shelter for the first time, even though I've walked this area a thousand times.

"Forget it," she spits.

I turn and continue walking, feeling out of sorts.

#

"Feloise says we need to host a dinner party," I tell Will a few days later after getting off the phone with Feloise. It's like nothing I said to her sank in. Hosting a dinner party is rivalling the island picnic in terms of time commitment, and yet, in some other universe where Will doesn't have a daughter, the idea of co-hosting a dinner party with him fills me with wistfulness. "We could use the party room at my place. There's a full kitchen." I'm thinking about which friends I could invite who wouldn't completely see through my act and know I have a schoolgirl crush on Will, but Will's already suggesting his place for the dinner.

"We have a family dinner the last Friday of every month and it's my turn to host. Timing's perfect. You can meet Margot and Ari."

"Margot? Oh right, Aunt Margot. I already met her, remember? When I failed so spectacularly at taking care of your daughter." My voice is light, but the words are heavy.

"Oh come on. Addie's known Margot her whole life. And I should've really emphasized that Addie had to go to sleep early. Especially since she was in a strange place. Like, there's not much even I can do to reason with her when she gets too tired.

You've just basically got to get her to sleep. Anyway, Margot's not that bad. I promise."

"Fine," I concede. "Your place it is."

#

Will's place is in Seaton Village, a row house with painted black brick and a red door and as I walk up the stone path, the sound of kids screaming nearly makes me stop and turn around to leave. I just assumed because I said "dinner party" that Will would realize I meant adults-only. I knock loudly, but when no one answers I turn the knob and push the door open a bit. There have to be at least a dozen kids running around, screaming. I stand, paralyzed, on the mat and take a deep breath. OK, so on closer count it looks like there's only five kids, and one of them is Addie, who's spotted me and is skipping toward me. "Kit!" she says, and flings her arms around me and I feel relieved that she doesn't seem to feel any differently toward me since my failed attempt at babysitting her.

"You forgot this at my place," I say, pulling her notebook out of my purse and handing it to her as another kid slams into me. "Geez," I say, but he's already halfway up the stairs, totally oblivious. "I noticed it was full, and I thought you might want a new one. I love notebooks and pens, so I always have too many." I hand her the second notebook, this one with flowers on the cover, and a pack of sparkly pens.

"Wow, thanks," she says, giving me a hug. She heads into the kitchen to show Will, who looks down the hall, wiping his hands on a towel as he walks toward me. Despite the noise, his house feels warm and cozy, with worn couches and throws, and the walls are covered in a mix of what is likely Addie's hand-drawn art and framed photographs—mostly pics of him and Addie. It has a relaxed vibe, but the constant screaming from the hordes of children is a bit unnerving. Will hollers at the kids to go to the basement but everyone ignores him. My head is pounding but Will just laughs and shrugs, then leans in to kiss me on the cheek, and for that split second, my skin tingles. "Welcome to a typical MacGregor dinner party," he says. "Where we're just one tent short of a circus."

I know my expression is pained, which I hope gets across the point that I am not OK with the situation. "Please tell me you hired Mary Poppins and she'll be here any minute to whisk all the children away?" I hand him a bottle of wine.

He laughs, as though he's enjoying this chaos. "Can I get you a glass?" he asks. "You're probably gonna need it."

I raise my eyebrows. "You've seen me cook. Wine's not going to help my skills." And yet, there's nothing I want more right now than a glass of wine, to calm my shattered nerves.

"True, but it'll help your sanity. It's either that or noise-cancelling headphones, and then how will you hear me barking instructions at you?" Will walks toward the kitchen, but I spot an interesting book on the shelf in his living room and pause to briefly glance at it, then follow him, gingerly stepping to avoid the dozens of toys scattered on the hardwood floor. Will introduces me to his sister-in-law, Margot, and her husband, Ari, who are sitting at the bar. Margot smiles wanly at me, her eyes narrow, like a hyena. Like I'm prey. "We've met," Margot says, sticking out a limp hand.

I grip it a bit too tightly and smile brighter. "We have. Nice to see you again, Margot." Ari gives a boisterous laugh. "You're quite brave coming over here. *I'm* afraid—and I own eighty percent of the rug rats in this place."

"Ari actually owns your building, too," Will says. "Kit's the woman I was telling you about."

"Ah yes," Ari nods, and asks me if I like the building. I tell him I do and Will hands me a plastic glass of wine. People are going to look at my Instagram pic and wonder why I'm drinking out of plastic when at an indoor dinner. But I don't say anything. Instead, I take a sip and remind myself to stop being such a snob.

I exhale. "So where do you two live?" I ask, trying to make conversation, but it's so loud I have to repeat myself to be heard.

"Just outside of the city," Margot says. "Lots of space for the children to run around and play. The way kids are meant to grow up." She gives Will a look. "I keep trying to convince Will to move closer. So Addie can be near her cousins. Hint, hint, my love."

"Not a chance," says Will. "I love this neighborhood."

"You know, I've almost convinced Gillian on moving out near us." She looks at me. "Have you met Gillian? She and Will are . . ." She tilts her head from side to side.

"Friends," Will says, looking uncomfortable. "With daughters who've been best friends since birth."

"Right." Margot rolls her eyes. "Gillian's my oldest, dearest friend. It just makes so much sense for all of us to live closer to each other. But Will just doesn't want to leave this house. It's the home he and Sophie bought together. It's sentimental."

Sophie. Somehow, hearing her name makes her feel so much more real. I want to know more about her, and nothing at all.

"You know that's not the only reason," Will says.

"Oh, right," Margot says tersely. "It's because you're sowing your wild oats before you settle down again and that's much easier to do downtown than in the 'burbs." *Sowing his wild oats?* Who says that? But is this true? I suppose I did have sex with Will in a hotel—even if he *was* only there for work. But I just assumed maybe, possibly, he was so mesmerized by my charm that it was a one-time thing, not a regular occurrence.

"Margot," Ari says, putting a hand on Margot's. Margot reaches for her wine glass and swallows a generous mouthful.

Instead of defending himself, though, Will ignores Margot and looks at the children in the other room, asking one of the boys about the video game he's playing. Suddenly, it doesn't feel loud enough in here. I take a deep breath and look around. Could I just get up and leave? I didn't sign up for this. And yet, just glancing back at Will makes me want to stay. Then Ari claps his hands together. "So Kit, tell us more about this dinner we're having. I'm quite intrigued by this whole food kit delivery thing. It's certainly a booming business, isn't it?"

My emotions feel so jumbled right now that I can barely think straight, but I rattle off a bunch of random details about Fresh Food Fast, trying to find the confidence I always seem to muster when I'm in work mode. Ari nods enthusiastically until Will puts a hand on my back and I turn to him, wrapping up whatever I was rambling on about.

"Let's get to it," Will says as two boys, about five or six, race through the kitchen, knocking a full glass—*plastic!*—of wine onto the floor. I might as well ask for a serving of crow for dinner. "Boys! Outside!" Will excuses himself to finally herd all the kids into the backyard, leaving me alone with Ari and Margot. I grip my glass of wine and prepare for the worst.

"Did you know this house was one of Ari's very first sales?" Margot asks me.

How on earth would I know that? I shake my head.

"Sophie and Will were just married and pregnant with Addie. They were looking for a starter home, a two-bedroom, maybe even a large condo, but it was a good time to buy, back before the market got outrageous, and Ari just knew most people would get priced out of the market within five to ten years. So he convinced them to get this place. They knew they were going to have a ton of kids so it just made sense to get the bigger house so they could settle in . . ." Margot empties her glass and reaches for the bottle. I imagine Sophie—young, pregnant and in love. And likely a less bitchy version of Margot.

"That *is* why Will doesn't want to move. Too many memories of Sophie," Margot continues. "He's still holding on to the hope that he'll get his large family and fill this house." Her words hang in the air between us. Of course. Just because his wife died doesn't mean that Will's done building a family. He's in that transitional period—dating until he finds *the one*. Maybe not someone to replace Sophie, but to be second best. To be a stepmother to Addie, and mother to more children. I feel silly for not realizing this sooner—not that it makes any difference anyway. He has a plan, I have a plan, and just like with Eric, our plans don't line up.

Will returns and we begin preparing the meal. As I pour the arborio rice into the pan, Margot tells us how Sophie just loved risotto.

"Remember Sophie's risotto, Will?"

"I do," Will says politely, then he grabs my camera and snaps a pic of me stirring the risotto in the pan. While I continue to stir rice, Will rubs a mix of spices on a pork tenderloin, then sears it in a frying pan. After popping the pan into the oven—you can *do* that?—he grabs an armful of plates and begins setting the table. And I realize that he's setting it for nine—me and Will, Margot and Ari, and all the kids.

"We should really feed the kids first," I say. "Fresh Food Fast has never wanted kids in my pics. I really think they wanted a nice, calm, *adult* dinner party."

I can feel Margot's eyes on us. "But there are only four of us," she says. "That's not much of a dinner party. And we *always* eat with the children. We're a family."

Will runs his hand through his hair. "Kit's right," he says. "The client never mentioned kids. Though these boxes are great if you have kids. Maybe we should suggest it." He catches my eye, though, and gets it. Laughing, he says, "OK, let's not pitch that angle this minute. If you make the salad I'll make the kids pizza."

"Pizza!" one of the kids screams, running through the kitchen, swinging a lightsaber. I duck and it barely misses me, but sends another glass flying. The plastic bounces off the ground. Will mops up the spilled liquid and then tosses the damp cloth into the sink.

Once I've mixed all the salad ingredients into a large bowl, I walk back to the front door to grab my ring light and tripod. There's a big part of me that wants to just scrap this whole shoot, and yet, as I watch Will through the lens of my camera, I can almost forget for a moment that there's anyone else here. I take another sip of wine and let Margot and Ari dominate the conversation as I start cooking.

Will works beside me, asking me about my week and telling me about a lunch 'n' learn he catered in the financial district today. "They wanted an old-school brown-bag lunch," he says, grating cheese over the pizzas, "so I suggested a twist on PB&J sandwiches but with homemade cashew nut butter and a raspberry coulis. Some of my finest work, but I got up at three this morning to get them done. I'm *bagged.*" I laugh. And he elbows me. "I can always win you over with a good pun."

I want to ask him who organized the event, to tell him this is exactly the kind of event I want to be speaking at, empowering women to set their goals and achieve them. But instead, I give the risotto a few final stirs as it looks like it's done, as he pops the pizzas in the oven. Addie comes through the kitchen, eyes the pizza in Will's hand and then turns to me. "Told you he always puts broccoli on the pizza."

"What?" Will says as we laugh. He pulls the tenderloin out of the oven and tells me it needs to rest for a few minutes before he slices it, but that I can begin plating the rest of the meal.

"You want me to take some pics for you?" Addie asks, looking up at me in such an unfamiliar, adoring way, that I can't say no. Margot and Ari have moved into the living room and are sitting on the couch.

"That'd be great," I say, and she grabs my camera from the tripod, climbs up on a stool, and begins shooting as I artfully arrange the vegetables on the four plates. Will herds all the other kids into the backyard for what feels like the seven hundredth time, telling them he'll bring the pizzas out in three minutes, and Addie hands my camera back to me. I check the pics she's taken and realize that she must have knocked the shutter speed by accident, because all the pictures are blurry. I let out a frustrated groan and quickly get a few more shots of the food at the table while Will takes the pizzas outside. Then I set the camera back on the tripod to film a time lapse while we're eating.

"You look like you need this," Will says, grabbing an open bottle of wine off the counter. As he tops up my wine glass, his hand on my back, I realize I didn't put out real wine glasses to shoot the table setting. Margot and Ari sit on one side of the table and I sit across from Ari on the other, and put my cloth napkin on my lap. Will's just sitting down when the back door opens and two of the boys come flying through the house, naked.

"Avid's stuck in the tree!" one of them hollers.

"Why are you naked?" Ari asks with interest, though he doesn't seem that disturbed.

"We didn't want to wear clothes!" one of them screams, flailing his arms and knocking my tripod over, my camera smashing to the ground. I let out a scream and leap up, racing over to my camera as Will comes after me.

"Is it broken?"

"I don't know!" I yell at him, unlocking the camera from the tripod and inspecting it. It seems fine—thankfully.

Another kid rushes past us and into the living room. I wipe pizza sauce off my arm and stand.

"I'll handle this," Ari says, finally standing and placing his napkin on the table. "Start without me."

Will puts his arm around me and leads me back to the table, though spending any more time here, at this dinner, is the last thing I want to do. My chest feels tight, and it's hard to get a full breath. I've wasted more than two hours here now, I don't have anything to show for it, I'm starving and frustrated. And all

I want is to be at home, in my quiet, calm, clean apartment, by myself. "I've got to go," I say. Will turns me toward him.

"Hey, hey, hey." He pulls me close.

"It's too much," I say, shaking my head, but he holds me even tighter. I let him, even though it's completely breaking our façade of only being colleagues.

"I know, it's nuts. But, it's also kind of fun, in a crazy way, don't you think?"

I pull away and look at him. "Are *you* crazy?"

He laughs and pulls out my chair. "C'mon." He refills my wine glass and then his own, and raises it up as Margot studies us. "Here's to crazy dinner parties."

I don't even bother forcing a smile. I take a sip of wine, then focus on my plate, trying to figure out how much longer I need to be here. This isn't worth it. There's absolutely no way I need to be here, in this chaos, just for a few pictures of a dinner party. If I had hosted the dinner, it would've been calm, fun even. This is cold, hostile. A nightmare. "Dinner looks really good," Will says to me, putting a hand on my leg. His touch is electrifying but also somehow calming. I inhale, taking in Will's signature sandalwood scent that sends tingles all over my body. This feeling I get when I'm around him is the reason I'm still here. *He's* why I'm still here. Damn you, Will MacGregor.

"What do you think?" Will's saying to Margot. She takes a small bite of the risotto, as though I might be poisoning her, and then rinses it down with water. "Mmm," she says, disingenuously. "I think it might be overdone. But, it's all about the photos anyway, right?"

Ari rejoins us, assuring us that the children are now fully clothed. "More importantly, they're locked outside." I laugh, because his words somehow endear him to me, as though I'm not the only one who thinks this whole night feels like a shitshow. Maybe it's not usual? He sits down and digs into his risotto, then turns to me. "Kit, this is excellent."

I smile, feeling grateful, if even for a moment.

Throughout the entire dinner, though, Margot is determined to show me that I don't fit in. It's Sophie this and Sophie that, the importance of family and keeping the cousins close. When she brings up a family reunion where "significant others" are not welcome, it's enough to make me want to get up and go. She's trying so hard to make sure I know that I will never have a shot with Will—as though she knows there's something between us, even though it's not as though we're broadcasting it. Which shouldn't bother me. I've already told myself that a thousand times, anyway—that things will never work out with Will, long-term—and yet I still feel offended and annoyed by her. I have to remind myself that Will isn't a competition to win. But this dinner feels like one. Sure, this is their family dinner, but Will invited me, and this is my work, and I'm not going to leave and let Margot feel like she trod all over me when I have done absolutely nothing to deserve it. When everyone is finally done eating, I silently help clean up, though I'm expecting Margot to tell me how great Sophie was at loading a dishwasher. When the table's cleared, I tell Will I'm going to go.

"You don't have to," he says. "I like having you here."

"It's all . . . a bit much," I admit quietly.

His face clouds over and he nods. "Yeah, I would leave too, if I could," he jokes, and walks me to the door. But I get the sense he actually loves the chaos of it all. And I can't decide if it's completely off-putting, or charming.

"Listen, don't worry about Margot. She gets better with time. Like red wine. Or a pain in the neck. You get used to her."

"I heard that," Margot says, coming to the door.

"You were meant to," Will says. He turns back to me. "Send me the pics from tonight—I want to see how they turned out. Margot, you should follow Kit on Instagram. Kit, you could tag Margot. Maybe she can share your account with some of her friends. Not that you need it or anything. Kit's a big deal on Instagram," he says, smiling. Almost proudly. "I wouldn't know, but that's what I hear." Margot looks from him to me, her hyena eyes boring into mine.

"Yes, I know," she says slowly, and the next part happens in slow motion. "I already follow Kit on Instagram. That's why I thought it was so fascinating that she would agree to a dinner party with children." She turns to Will. "Her handle is @KitwithoutKids. The woman who brainwashes other women into not having children. Because having kids is—how would you put it, exactly?" She turns back to me, her eyes cold. "A death sentence? Or just, a huge waste of time when you could be . . . I don't know, sitting on a pristine white couch or, posting another selfie to Instagram, I guess?"

Hearing her describe me in this way is awful, and yet, it's true. When did I become this superficial woman who's seen as a shallow influencer rather than a supporter of independent women? I reach for the door handle, and without waiting for Will's reaction, I pull the door open and rush out. Down the steps, onto the sidewalk, down the street. Away from Will, away from them all. Into the cool, dark night.

#

I expect Will to cancel on our next cooking session, to come up with some excuse why he can't finish out the Fresh Food Fast contract, but he shows up, as planned, the following Friday. We haven't spoken all week. Not even a text. I'm not surprised by the lack of communication, per se, but given that we haven't spoken, I just assumed he wouldn't show. But as usual, he's got his box of tools, though he looks unkempt, his hair messy, his face unshaven. "Rough night?" I say, trying to break the ice.

"Addie had a nightmare. I've been up since four."

"Is she OK?"

"She's fine. Let's just cut the chitchat and get this over with. OK?"

My hands shaking, I fumble with the lid on the food box, then begin unpacking the items onto the counter.

"I don't get it," he finally says, slamming a frying pan on the stove. "Why deliberately lead me on?"

"I *never* led you on," I say. "We had sex once. And once I found out you had a kid, I made sure we didn't hook up again. I told you I wasn't interested."

"You sure did," Will says bitterly, fiddling with a pair of tongs. "Coming to dinner with my sister-in-law and brother-in-law? I was *really* acting like you were *just* a co-worker."

"How you act is not my problem, and how do I know what you deem friendly versus sexual? It's not like we were making out. You didn't even kiss me."

"Oh, come on. You know I'm into you." A warm rush fills my body. I want him to say more, and yet, I need to shut this down. I know I've been misleading him. But I don't want to admit it.

"You know, I don't keep my career a secret. I'm an Instagram influencer. You know that. You could've gone on Instagram and known in five seconds flat what I'm all about. Or Google—ever heard of it? The book, the articles, the groups I've started, the talks I've given . . . It's all out there for everyone to see. I'm not hiding who I am."

Will turns to me. "You know I hate relying on what's written online. I told you that."

"That's your issue, not mine."

"Right. But you just happened to *never* bring it up, what you do, what you stand for, not once, in conversation." His eyes are slits and my stomach turns. I hate that he's so angry with me, and I hate that I even care what he thinks.

I shake my head, exasperated. "OK, did you want me to explain it to you on the picnic? In front of the *photographer* you brought along? Or, would you have rather that I brought it up at dinner, while your sister-in-law had her four kids running around like wild animals?" I angrily open the instructions.

"Oh gimme a break. You had a hundred opportunities to tell me."

"Still, it was irrelevant. We're working together. Nothing more."

"Yeah. You've made that very clear."

"Great. So let's just get this over with."

"Fine."

"Fine." I grab a knife and dive into a potato. But the potato is wet, the knife slips, and slices through my finger. I scream and Will springs toward the oven, grabbing the tea towel that's hanging from the door and wrapping it around my finger.

"Let me see it," Will says but I shake my head, tears streaming down my face.

"No, just get away from me," I say, sinking to the floor. But he catches me on the way down, wrapping me in his arms. I'm crying, and I can't stop myself even though I don't want to be crying in front of him. "Let me look at it, OK?" he says after a minute and holds my hand, unwrapping the towel, just a bit. "I think it's going to be OK. We're not going to have to amputate, which is great because I can't slice a finger off worth shit."

I laugh through my tears and pound his chest with my good hand. "You're such a jerk. I'm in pain and you're making jokes?"

"Uh-huh. Do you have any bandages?"

I tell him to look under the sink in the bathroom and he disappears for a minute before returning with a box. He removes the towel again and wraps my finger with gauze, then secures it with tape. "There, that should do it."

I look at my finger, then up at him. His eyes are on mine. "Thanks," I say softly, and he brushes the tears from my cheek, his hand lingering just a little too long. Then, his eyes still locked with mine, he takes my bandaged hand in his and brings it to his lips. My stomach flip-flops. I start to shake my head, but he's kissing my palm, and then working his way with his lips, to my wrist, and up my arm.

"Will . . . we can't do this. I—" *I like you too much*, I think.

"You can't deny the chemistry between us," he says, but I pull my arm away from him, standing.

"You have to go," I say as he stands. "This"—I gesture to the space between us—"is never going to be anything. And I don't think we should work together, either."

He nods. "You're right."

He walks toward the door. His things are everywhere, but I grab his bag from the floor beside the counter and make my way toward him. "Here," I say—

—"My bag," he says at the same time, turning around so that he's just inches from me. My entire body feels like it's on fire. I know I should take a step back, but instead, I take a step closer to him. He smells like sandalwood, and I know that I shouldn't do what I know I'm about to do, but there's just something about being close to Will that makes me feel so good. I stand on my tiptoes, and then, closing my eyes, I press my lips onto his. He kisses me back, wrapping his arms around my waist. I drop his bag and lean into him, and then lead him to my bedroom.

twelve

Tired of getting ogled on the way to the ladies' room?
What if every room in the office was just for the ladies?
WomenWork, the new female-only co-working space in
the city, is the best way to make your work feel like fun!
Check out my stories for a full tour, then secure your
workspace before they're all gone! #ad #officegossip
#girlsjustwannaworkfun

I'm on my way out of the three-story open concept brick building on Richmond when my phone buzzes. Eric's name appears on the screen, and it throws me back in time. He hasn't called me in over a year and I wonder what he wants. My heart pounds as I slide my finger across the screen to answer it. His voice sounds stiff as he says hello and then asks if I have time to meet him for a drink after work today. "Is everything OK?" I say, but he says he'd rather not get into it on the phone. We agree to meet at the wine bar across the street from the bank where he works. I hang up and try not to worry about why he wants to meet me, but when I can't shake it, I call Will.

"Hey," he says, his voice making me feel like I'm wrapped in a cozy blanket. "So, I know we said we'd just be casual," I say, referring to our not-so-professional "meeting" about what the hell we were going to do about our feelings for each other late last night, while lying naked in bed together. The solution was to be casual. Keep working together. Hookups whenever we wanted, but not be exclusive. With the understanding that I'm never going to be serious about someone who has a child, just like he's never going to be serious about someone who doesn't want kids. And Addie can't know we're anything more than friends. Will was adamant on that one—explaining he never introduced Addie to anyone he was dating unless it was serious, and until this point, that meant she'd only met one woman, a flight attendant he was dating pretty seriously a year ago. "Addie's already met you, so it's not like I can take that back, but I think any non-work stuff should probably happen at your place," he'd said.

"You mean late-night booty calls," I tease.

"Exactly."

"So what's up?" he says now. "You're not going back on our casual agreement, are you? Because you signed a contract," he teases. "I remember it very distinctly. On my back, with your index finger. There's no reneging now."

"I'm not reneging," I laugh. "I was just clarifying that I'm well aware we are *just* casual, and that, by official dating definition, the term 'casual' means that I have absolutely no control over what you do and with whom—"

"And I have no control over what you do, or with whom— but . . . ?"

"But I told Eric I'd meet him for a drink after work. It's not romantic, I really have no feelings for him anymore and I think he's pretty serious with someone else anyway and well," I sigh. "I feel silly right now. I'm not telling you because I think you'd be jealous or anything, more just like, I needed a friend to tell, I guess, and if I told any of my girlfriends they'd chastise me for agreeing. But I figured you'd just listen?"

"OK," Will says.

"OK," I say, feeling embarrassed.

"I'm still jealous."

"I think I like that."

"Want me to come over after you get home and you're all tipsy?" His voice is low.

I feel lightheaded. "Maybe."

#

Eric is sitting at the bar when I arrive, drinking what I assume is still his go-to—a manhattan. When he sees me, he stands and suggests we move to a table. We used to come here all the time, back when we were first dating, when our romance felt exciting and new. He extends an arm for me to walk ahead of him, which seems formal, and I'm reminded of his manners—the kind that impress parents but feel unnecessary and uncomfortable for people in their thirties. He carries his drink with him.

"The beard is . . . different," I say, and I wonder if he's dating someone who's convinced him to grow facial hair.

"Yeah, well, I was having a bit of a midlife crisis. You might have heard, my girlfriend left me."

"Eric," I sigh.

"I'm kidding. It was a joke. It's been more than a year—we can't joke?"

"I think your sense of humor is having a midlife crisis."

A waiter arrives at the table and places a glass of white wine in front of me. I take a sip and recognize what used to be *my* go-to—sauvignon blanc. "Thank you," I say to the waiter, while looking at Eric.

"I figured some things don't change." He raises his glass, then takes a sip. "Listen, I wanted to see you because . . . I'm selling the condo."

I feel a twinge of sadness. Even if the condo had always been his, it still feels like the last remnant of our relationship that still somehow connects us. The sadness passes quickly, because it's not like I would want to live in that condo anyway. Skyrise living has never been my long-term plan, and my apartment now is just a pit stop.

"I need a fresh start," he says. Maybe his earlier comment wasn't as much of a joke as he let on. "I'm thinking of getting a place uptown, closer to the airport. I travel a lot now . . ." and his voice trails off and then he clears his throat. I study his face, trying to decipher his emotions—but it was always hard to tell what was going on behind his words.

"I'm not going to keep anything," he says. When we split up, we were supposed to fairly divide the contents, but I didn't take much—I didn't want any reminders of our failed relationship. Instead, we agreed that he pay me a reasonable price to keep everything. "So I wondered if you would like anything? You could come by sometime. Remind yourself of what you left behind." He stares into the distance then looks back at me. "I guess I've missed you, Kit."

His words surprise me. Our breakup was mutual. I was disappointed he had changed his mind about something we had promised to each other years earlier. And he was upset with me for *not* being willing to give him what he wanted—children.

"I thought you were dating someone."

"I was," he says, looking into his drink. "It didn't work out. She ... she wasn't you. Turns out you're really hard to get over, Kit." He reaches out and puts his hand on mine. It's warm and comforting. Familiar. And yet—my stomach knots. I pull my hand away, and put it under the table.

"Eric, if this is why you asked me here ..." I push my chair back.

"Please don't go."

I study him for a moment, then pull my chair back in a bit. "I don't get it, Eric. There's really nothing between us anymore. Even if the bigger issue of kids wasn't on the table." A flash of Will enters my mind. Will—lying naked beside me this morning, in bed. Will, who I've now gotten myself entangled with, regardless of the kid issue.

Now Eric's eyes meet mine, his gaze unwavering. "Really? Are you sure?"

And then I get it. He's here because of Will. "This is because you saw me with that chef and his daughter, at the ferry docks a few weeks ago ..."

He waits for me to say more.

"I don't owe you an explanation," I say, but he's still waiting, and I give in. Knowing Eric, he could sit there for hours, waiting for me to talk. "We work together. And he happens to have a daughter. That's it." Will, kissing my neck. Will, running his hands through my hair. Will, checking my cut this morning to make sure it wasn't getting infected. "I'm as child-free by choice as ever. Maybe even more so. I gave this talk at a Women in Business conference, and it was such a success that they've asked me to speak at the international conference next month. Here in town. More than ten thousand women have registered. And they all want to hear me remind them why being child-free is the best decision they could ever make." I down the rest of my wine.

Eric raises his eyebrows and tilts his head as he looks at me. "I know you, Kit. You're pretending that I don't, but I once knew you better than anyone. And that day, at the docks, I saw you before you saw me. The way you were looking at that guy, how you were acting around him."

I feel annoyed by Eric, because he knows me so well. And he's right about my feelings for Will, and I hate that. And yet, I shake my head, to convince him he's wrong.

"You can tell me that you're still riding this whole child-free bandwagon, but you're teetering on the edge. I can see it. And if you're changing your mind, even a little bit, come back to me."

I'm stunned. Is he really asking me to try again? But instead of feeling any sort of love or nostalgia for him, I feel nothing for him at all.

"Why start with someone else you don't know, when we could pick up where we left off? We were good together, Kit." His eyes cloud over, his eyebrows sinking.

"I'm sorry, Eric," I say, shaking my head, though I'm not sorry at all.

"You know dating someone with a kid is asking for trouble, right?"

"Eric, I—"

"There's not a single child in history who ever liked their stepmother." Suddenly I remember that Eric has a stepmother— one he despises. So much so, that he used to insist his father come to visit us in the city without her, rather than us making the trip to their house in the country, just to avoid her. "Why would you even consider going down that path?"

"Are you finished?" I say before pushing back my chair. "Actually, don't answer that. I don't care." I stand and slap down a twenty, then head out the door onto the street, the warm air anything but comforting.

thirteen

It's around eight o'clock on Sunday night and Will and I are in his kitchen. I'm unpacking the latest Fresh Food Fast box and he's pouring us both a glass of wine, which I'm hoping will quell my jitters before he notices. He fed Addie before I arrived and she's upstairs watching a movie on her iPad. The house is quiet except for the soft music playing in the background, and the whole vibe feels absolutely nothing like it did when I was last here with Margot and Ari and their kids at that disastrous dinner.

As he passes me a glass of red, I can't help thinking that if I were to witness this scene through a window, I'd think I was watching a couple on a date. And yet, I can't let myself think like that. Because Addie exists. And so does Will's desire to have many more children. Which is why we've got to stick to the agreement to keep this thing casual. Nothing more. Though I wish we'd met at my place, just so that our "casual" time together could be a bit more fun.

"Addie told me you used to sell couches," I say as I open drawers, looking for scissors.

"Yeah, with my dad. MacGregor Home Furnishings. *We'll help you sit in style,*" he adds in a radio announcer voice. "It was OK. I mean—I liked the idea of carrying on the business my dad had with his dad. I didn't love it—but I never really thought about it too much, if that makes sense."

"So what made you leave then?" I ask, cutting through a plastic package of rice.

"For a while after Sophie died, I held it together because I had a toddler to take care of. But then one day it just all became too much. I guess you could say I had a bit of a breakdown."

I stop opening packages and lean against the counter. "I'm sorry. I can't even imagine."

He nods, crossing his arms over his chest. "Yeah, well, the tough side of me hates to admit that," he says wryly. "But it's the truth and I'm OK with admitting it now. Anyway, I took some time off from the shop and started cooking for something to do. It helped a lot. The grief process, but also my role as a parent. No three-year-old should be eating takeout every single night for dinner." He points his spatula at me. "No grown woman should be eating takeout every night either, for the record."

"We weren't talking about me," I smile. "Get back to your story."

"Right. Well, I started cooking, and it turned out I was a pretty good cook. I guess you could kind of say it saved me—in a whole lot of unexpected ways." He sprinkles freshly ground salt and pepper over the chicken.

"I didn't expect that answer," I say softly. "But I'm glad you told me."

The left corner of his mouth turns up slightly. "Thanks for asking. I don't like to get into it with everyone, but . . ." He reaches up and removes a frying pan that's hanging from a wire rack above the counter, then hands it to me. "You aren't just anyone."

My heart pounds, and I try to focus on snipping the ends off the green beans.

Will tells me to put a pat of butter in the frying pan and I scan the counter, distracted. I fiddle with the handle of the pan as I debate how to keep this conversation going before I lose my opportunity, and my nerve.

"When we were going to the island, Addie mentioned her mom had died—I had just assumed . . ."

"That I was a player?" He winks. I find the butter and cut off a chunk, putting it in the pan and then adding the green beans.

"I was going to say divorced." I know he's trying to make light of the situation, but I want to know more about him, and his past.

He puts the chicken in the oven. "Most people think that. It's only natural. There aren't a lot of thirtysomething widowers, I suppose."

"I can't imagine what you must have gone through. You guys must have been so young, and with Addie . . ." I pause. "Was Sophie sick for a long time?"

"About a year, I guess. It felt long, but also so short. What's that saying about parenthood—'The days are long but the years are short'? It felt like that. Like every day I just had to get up and do it all: go to work, be there for Sophie, take care of Addie. I was so in the moment, and then, just like that, it was over. Everything. The whole life plan."

I realize I've been holding my breath and now I let it out. "I can't imagine," I say again. I thought I had my life planned out with Eric, and of course it stung when things ended, but comparatively, my life went on, for the most part, just as planned. But Will—he didn't get to just move on, solo. "It must have been so hard, to suddenly find yourself parenting without a partner, and not by choice."

Will pops a cherry tomato in his mouth. "Yeah, for sure. And every day, seeing Sophie in Addie. Not physically, but little things she'd say or do. And knowing that she was going to outgrow those things eventually. And then, Sophie'd be gone." Will exhales. "Wow. What a downer I am, huh? You might get a kick out of this, actually." He laughs. "We were going to have five kids."

"*Five?*" I shake my head, my eyes wide. I feel like someone just punched me in the gut. I knew he wanted kids, but five feels entirely next-level.

He laughs. "You look shell-shocked."

I am shell-shocked. What I don't get is, if Will knows I don't want kids, why is he even bothering to casually date me—or whatever we're doing? Like, why bother? And why am I bothering to get involved, either?

"We really liked the idea of having a lot of kids. I like kids. They're fun. They make life fun. Crazy, but fun. Kind of like you." He gives me a sly smile. I feel like I'm walking a tightrope of emotions.

"Are you implying that I'm like a child?" I say, keeping my voice light. "Or that I'm crazy?" Somehow, I've got to get this conversation off kids or we're never going to make it through this meal.

He winks at me as he starts peeling carrots. "Maybe a little of both. Most people think kids are so different from adults, but they're really not. They just have all the energy that a lot of adults don't—and a fresh perspective on life. At least that's what I try to tell myself when Addie's being a pain in the ass." He passes me the bag of rice. "Shoot, we should've done this first. You're distracting me." He pulls a clean pot down from the hanging rack and fills it with water, then puts it on the stove, turning the burner on and covering the pot with a lid.

"You know," he says, his tone more serious, "it was Addie who suggested I start cooking for real. Like, as a job. At first, I brushed it off. I mean, what does a five-year-old know about career choices, right?"

I nod, trying to focus on his words, rather than my own thoughts. "But I think she could see how happy it made me. Or how *un*happy selling furniture made me. I love my dad and I know it meant a lot to him to have me take on the family business, but I just couldn't do it anymore. Sophie's death made me realize that life's way too short to live it doing what you think you *should* be doing, or what other people think you should be doing, rather than just doing something you love. And I love cooking. So I decided to give it a shot."

What other people think you should be doing. His words couldn't ring more true. "I get that," I say, thinking about my own plans for the book garage, how I keep pushing them off because they don't fit in with the way I've carved out my career and I can't figure out how I'll ever be able to make time for it.

"So is the plan to open your own restaurant?" I say, to keep the focus on Will. "Be the next hot young chef?"

"Nah. I don't even want to be tied to one restaurant. That's why I turned the Hotel 6ix gig down. It just doesn't work with Addie. I'm a single dad. The hours don't line up. Catering, on the other hand—I can make my own hours, choose the jobs I want.

The pay isn't nearly as good as being the head chef at a hot new restaurant, but . . . we're OK. We've got what we need. And I get to be there for her, whenever she needs me. Mostly. And that's what matters."

The water's boiling and I pour the rice into the pot, then add a dash of salt, thinking about Dad. I want to tell Will about how my dad was a single parent, too. How he couldn't always be there for me the way Will is for Addie, because he didn't have a job that was flexible. His nine-to-five was often more like eight-to-seven, and he had both Izzy and me to worry about. But I never blamed him. He was doing his best—and it probably made Izzy and me closer because we spent so much time together. She was always there for me. She still is. I have a sudden urge to call my sister.

We're plating the food when there's a knock at the front door and then it opens, a woman with long red hair entering. "Yoo-hoo!" she calls, holding a bottle of wine in one hand. She's wearing cropped jeans and a tight sweater. I run a hand over my own ponytail and oversized, off-the-shoulder sweatshirt, suddenly feeling self-conscious.

"Gillian?" Will wipes his hands on a tea towel and looks from her to me.

"Hello, hello, hello . . ." she says as she walks into the kitchen, then stops when she sees me.

"Gill, this is Kit. Kit, Gillian. Gillian is Addie's best friend Millie's mom."

Gillian feigns offence. "I think I'm more than *Millie's mom*." She turns to me. "Don't you hate it when you're defined as someone's mom?" She looks around the kitchen as Will pulls the roast out of the oven. Everything is nearly ready, and I should be snapping pics, so I pick up my camera.

"I wouldn't know. I don't have kids, actually."

"Oh, that's right." She snaps her fingers as though she just remembered something. "Margot was telling me about you. The kid-hater who can't cook. Sounds like you ended up at the wrong dinner party the other night."

I freeze, then meet Gillian's eye.

"Seriously? I said I don't *have* kids, not that I hate kids."

"Is there a difference, really?" Her voice is sickly sweet.

"Yeah, there's a big difference," I say, my hands shaking as I grip my camera. "Not that it's any of your business."

Her eyes are slits. "I think it *is* my business. Will and I have been friends forever and—" But the way she says it makes me think there's a lot more than friendship between her and Will. Which is supposed to be fine. That's what *casual* means. Will can date whoever he wants. And I have to be OK with it. Except, I'm not OK with it.

Will clears his throat. His face is pale, which just confirms my fears. "Gill, did we have plans tonight? I don't remember . . ."

"We always watch *The Sopranos* on Sunday nights." She flips her hair over her shoulder and turns to me. "When my ex-husband has Millie I always impose on Will. And there are a million episodes of *The Sopranos*. We're *so* behind. But that's what happens when you have kids. You lose a decade of TV watching. But we're determined to catch up, aren't we, Will?"

Will looks uncomfortable. "We've only watched a handful of episodes," he says. "Don't make it something it's not, Gill. We'll catch up another time, cool?"

I don't want to stand around while they make plans. I toss the tea towel on the counter and look for my purse then remember

I left it at the door. "You know what?" I say. "I'm actually feeling a bit off. I think we should just scrap this meal."

"What? No!" Will protests, looking genuinely disappointed. "We're all set."

I shake my head. "We're ahead anyway." I make my way toward the front door. "I'm going to go home and get a good night's sleep. I've got an early morning and it sounds like you two have a late night . . ." I'm babbling, and can't seem to stop. I grab my purse and hurry out the front door.

#

At home, I order a pizza and then head straight for the bathroom, stripping down and leaving my clothes in a pile on the floor, before climbing into the shower and letting the steady stream hit my face, mixing with tears that have me wondering if I'm PMSing. But no—my hurt feelings are completely legitimate. Not one, but two of the women in Will's life that I've met—in fact the *only* two women I've met—have both been unnecessarily mean to me. I'm so used to being around women who *want* to boost each other up, it's disturbing to be around women who don't. And yet, these women could be around for . . . well, for a long time if I want Will in my life. So then why did *I* rush off? Why didn't *I* stand my ground and make *Gillian* leave? I was there first. I was the one who'd made plans with Will. I was the one he wanted to be with. Or, more my style: why didn't I try to include Gillian in *our* plans?

As I wash my hair, I consider what would've happened if I'd stayed and Gillian had left. Would I have snuggled up to him on the couch while we watched a movie, or pretended to until we couldn't keep our hands off each other any longer? No, of course not—there's no way that Will does anything above a PG rating with Addie upstairs. And would he have really sent Gillian home so that I could stay with him instead?

I let the water run over my hair, squeezing my eyes shut as the suds run down my face. That fear, that Will would choose the sure thing—the woman who's so clearly interested in him—over me, is what sent me home. I'd always rather remove myself than be rejected. Who wouldn't?

It's better this way, I convince myself. And the sooner I can finish this contract and be done with Will MacGregor, the better.

I add conditioner to my hair and then stand under the hot water until it runs cold, then shut it off. As I wrap a towel around me, there's a knock on the door. Shivering and still damp, I shuffle over to the door, holding my towel tight, and peep through the tiny hole, expecting to see the pizza guy with the pizza I just ordered.

It's not the pizza guy. A warm rush washes over my body. Even though I just finished telling myself I want nothing to do with Will, it's like my heart has put my mind on mute and is going rogue.

"Are you gonna open the door?" he asks. I take a deep breath. I open the door. Will gives me a sly grin and holds out an orange cactus. "I felt like this situation deserved flowers, but there don't seem to be any florists open on Sunday nights," he says. "The convenience store on the corner only had carnations and aren't they supposed to symbolize death? So, cactus it is." He pushes the cactus toward me and I take it with one hand, holding my towel firm with the other. I focus on the prickly plant and remind myself why I left. This will never work.

"It sort of looks like a penis," he laughs. I can't help laughing, too. "That's not why I bought it. I just felt like I needed to bring you something. The dinner we just finished making probably would've been the better choice. I'm starving, are you starving?"

It's no use. I want to be mad at him, but there's something about him that makes me feel like the sun is shining down on me, my entire body filled with dopamine. *Pull it together, Kit.*

"What happened to *The Sopranos* and . . . Gillian?" I struggle to keep my voice flat.

He shrugs. "It didn't happen."

"So, what, you left Gillian at your place?"

"Yeah. I got Addie to bed and then asked Gill to make herself useful. The corners of his mouth turn up slightly, and I try to picture Gillian sitting alone, on the couch, playing the role of babysitter. I can't help smiling. That was definitely not Gillian's plan.

He smiles too. "Yep. I had more important things to worry about." His green eyes meet mine, but I look away. I can't get hurt. So I can't get sucked back in.

"Listen, you don't owe me anything," I say, trying to sound detached, like I just don't care about Will as anything more than a co-worker. "You can watch TV with *whomever* you want."

"I want to watch TV with you," he says simply, and my heart pounds. He clears his throat. "Really. I want to watch TV with you. And make dinner with you. And eat it with you, rather than you running away. I took a few more pics, by the way," he says. "You forgot this." He hands me my camera. "But I didn't come here to talk about work. I want to talk about other things."

I swallow a lump in my throat. "Like . . . what?"

Will takes a step forward, so he's standing in the doorway. "Like walking. I want to walk with you. Grocery shop with you. Meet your friends. Meet your family. I know we said we'd just be casual, but this"—he waves a hand between us—"doesn't feel casual. Not to me." A door closes behind Will, down the hall, and I look past him to see a guy walking toward the elevator. Will turns too, and all three of us are looking at each other. Will turns back to me. "Can I come in? This is getting awkward."

I push the door open wider with my hip and Will steps inside. I follow him in, and then put the phallic cactus on the counter as Will sits on the couch.

"Hang on," I say. "I just want to put something on." But when I look back, Will's right behind me. He takes a step closer. His hands are on my hips. Mine are still holding my towel in place.

"We don't want the same things," I say sadly. "We can never be more than just casual, and casual is feeling like it's a really bad idea . . ." But his lips are on mine, and I'm kissing him back. And it's soft and tender and . . . somehow very different from before. When we pull apart, he looks into my eyes.

"We're smart people. And I think it's pretty clear we both want each other. We can figure it out." He takes my towel and drops it to the floor, then leads me through my apartment, into the bedroom.

fourteen

"You think the concierge can see us in here?" Will whispers in my ear, his breath hot. It's a late Saturday afternoon in September, and we're in the elevator of my building. We've been out all afternoon—and now we're about to make dinner together. It's been a month since our Fresh Food Fast contract ended, and we're still cooking together. And grocery shopping. We go to movies. He's met Izzy. Margot still strongly dislikes me and Gillian and I tend to keep our distance, but his other friends are pretty cool with me. Though the elephant is still taking up a lot of space in the room—and every time I want to talk to him about kids, I chicken out. Because everything else about us is so, so great. And it's very clear that Will's not interested in anyone else—not even Gillian—which makes me alternately giddy and nervous. All summer, we—or at least, I—convinced myself it was a summer fling. People have summer romances all the time and they naturally fizzle out come fall. But we're definitely not fizzling. Sizzling, yes. Fizzling, not so much.

Now, he presses me against the wall of the elevator and moves his lips from my ear to my neck. "I hope so," he says, in answer to a question I can't even remember asking. The doors open, and we stumble out into the hall and his arms are around me and I'm sort of leading him and not wanting to let go of him. At my door, I fumble for my key in my purse, unlock the door, and then push it open. My toes immediately feel wet. I look down and scream. The entire surface area of my apartment is covered in at least an inch of water, a steady stream raining down from the far corner of the apartment.

"Shit," Will says. "Grab your laptop and your camera," he says, pointing to the island, but all I can think about are the books. I have to get the books. I grab the laundry hamper I keep on top of the washer and set it on the island, then yank open the oven door and begin piling the books into it. It's full within seconds. "We need something else to carry the books!" I say to Will.

"The books?" he says, his arms laden with my camera equipment.

"There's another hamper in my room!" He disappears into the hall and returns, goes into my bedroom and comes out with a white plastic hamper. I start piling books from other cupboards into the second bin, then reach under the sink for large black garbage bags. In the bedroom, I throw open my closet doors, and stare at the books, organized by genre and author, then begin piling them into the bag. I know they're just books, that they're replaceable, but it's not that. These books are the only thing keeping me focused on my future and keeping me tied to Mom. *Do what you love*, she'd said that morning while garage shopping, *and the rest will fall into place.*

My eyes fill with tears, but I swipe them away. The photo albums, I suddenly remember. They're tucked on the top shelf of my closet. All those photos of Mom. Of me. Of Dad and Mom and Izzy and me together. The only family I ever had—the only family I will ever have. I scramble to grab those, too, and put them into the black garbage bag that's now so full I need Will to help me carry it through my apartment and out the front door into the hall. Ivan, the Grumpy Concierge, and two maintenance guys in gray onesie uniforms rush toward my apartment, assess the source of the water and disappear. I hurry back in, determined to get the rest of the books before I'm told to get out. We run out of garbage bags when there are still a handful of books left on the shelves in my room.

"We have to go," Will is saying, has been saying over and over, his arm around me. He doesn't understand. But he doesn't try to stop me, either.

One of the maintenance guys meets us in the hall, explaining that a pipe burst in the apartment over mine. "Unfortunately your unit got the worst of the damage."

I sigh, and drag a garbage bag of books down the hall. Ivan steps off the elevator, and helps me hoist the garbage bags onto a large, flat trolley, telling me I can store anything I need to in a spare storage locker. "I can help you," he offers, with uncharacteristic kindness.

"Thank you," I say, feeling overcome with emotion. He tells me the storage locker number and hands me a key. And that's when I realize I have nowhere to go. It's not like I can move into the storage locker, too.

"Do you have my phone?" I ask Will. "And did you grab that orange box on my desk?"

He looks around the cart, then holds the box up. "This?"

"Yes."

I grab it and start rooting through the plastic cards.

"What are you doing?" Will says.

I look up. "Gift cards. This is where I keep all the gift cards I get when clients don't want to pay real money for promo. Takeout, taxis, spas—anyway, it doesn't matter. I'm sure there's a gift card in here for the Ritz." I know I sound hysterical, and this is *not* a sound plan, but right now it's my only plan. "I'm sure they're going to figure out how to fix my apartment in a few days. This must happen all the time," I'm saying. I have absolutely no idea if this is true, but I've moved into fight mode. Or denial. I've got to believe this is all going to turn out just fine.

"Ms. Kidding," Ivan interrupts. "There's serious damage. We'll need to get a hold of the owner. He'll have to deal with his insurance. That could take days, weeks even. And we'll have to confirm all the work and how it will be paid for. This could be a lengthy process."

My heart is pounding. My fingertips feel tingly but I keep scrabbling through the box. I know there's a hotel stay in here somewhere. Or maybe it's in my email inbox? Suddenly Will's arms are around me. He pulls me close. I resist for a moment. I don't need him—I don't need any man. I can do this myself. But he puts his hand on the back of my head, and I bury my face in his chest as he strokes my hair.

"Stay with me," he says softly.

I look up at him. "What?" My heart races.

"Stay with me." And I know he doesn't mean figuratively, in this moment. He means, *stay* with him. But I can't do that. "If I don't have a free hotel stay I'll stay with one of my single friends or my sister . . ." I say. Even though I know none of them are going to want a long-term houseguest. And I get it. I love my friends, my sister, too, obviously, but we aren't in college anymore.

With Will's arms around me, right now, in this moment, I feel safe. Protected. I want to go with him. I want him to take care of me. But I can't. "No way," I say. "We *just* decided we were going to be casual," I whisper, as one of the maintenance guys comes into view. "I'm not going to live in your house while some other girl booty calls you."

"No other girl is going to be booty calling me," he says. "I'll just . . . meet her at her place. Or a hotel." He grins. I smack him. "I'm kidding," he says.

"It's too crazy."

"No it's not. What's crazy is you living in a hotel or on someone's couch. You need a place to stay and I have a big house." He smiles down at me. "You can even have your own bedroom. And we can bring a bunch of these books so you feel at home."

"I don't know," I say. But I do know.

"Come on." He takes my hand and I let him lead the way.

#

The sun, streaming through the window on the wrong side of my face, wakes me. I open one eye and look around at the walls in confusion, and then remember that I'm at Will's. And I remember the rest of last night. The multiple trips to bring my things to the storage locker and the rest back to his place. How the two of us worked together, side by side, as a team. I turn over but the other half of the bed is empty. I sigh and stretch out, looking around his bedroom in the early-morning light, the sun streaming in, casting a glow on the soft blue walls. At the foot of the bed, floor-to-ceiling bookshelves line the walls. I tilt my head sideways to read some of the titles on the spines, the books a mix of everything from politics to thrillers to children's fairy tales. I reach over to the nightstand to grab my phone, then stand, grab a book off his shelf that I've read, and hold it out in front of the shelves, filling the frame with the colorful spines. I climb back into bed, post the picture to my Bookstagram account, smile at the tiny squares of books, then turn my phone off and put it back on the nightstand just as the door opens and Will comes into his room with a coffee mug. "Morning, beautiful," he says, kissing me on the forehead and placing a steaming mug of coffee on the nightstand. I sit up and take him in. He's dressed and clean-shaven and looks so good.

"Come back to bed," I say, pulling him toward me.

"Nope. Got to go," he says, all business. I'm disappointed. It's not like Addie's even here. If we can't enjoy the empty house now, when will we? "Margot gets irritated if I don't pick Addie up by nine. And she has gymnastics at ten, so I'll take her out for a bagel before that. Oh"—he slaps his head—"and then she has a birthday party at one. So we'll probably be back sometime around four."

I sigh. I envisioned us reading the paper in bed, drinking coffee, having sex. His plan feels so rigid. Unromantic. Not how I envisioned the first morning after moving in with him. But this isn't "moving *in*" moving in. It's just convenience born out of an inconvenience. It's fine. "I have to deal with the apartment anyway. I should call my landlord and my insurance company. Wait, will they be open on a Sunday?" I'm thinking aloud.

"You got this. Oh, and make yourself at home, obviously. One thing: do you mind moving your stuff into the guest room?" He points to his right. "For Addie's sake, I think it probably makes sense to look like that's where you're staying. Not that we can't have conjugal visits when she's asleep." He kisses me on the lips, then leaves.

Sleep in the guest room? Of course it makes sense. And maybe it's better for us anyway, so I have a bit of distance. Still, I feel a bit homeless and lonely. I lie back on my pillow, and try to push through my feelings of disappointment and vulnerability. Will certainly didn't seem disappointed not to be spending the day with me . . . it doesn't mean anything. It's just—life. It goes on, flood or not. I sling my legs over the side of the bed, my feet cold on the hardwood floor. My mind cycles through the nightmare the next few days are going to be as I deal with insurance and replacing everything that's been ruined. It's a good thing I didn't really have that much to begin with. Hopefully my contract with Stay-a-While covers water damage—and at least I already banked a bunch of photos with this month's furniture selection that I can use in the coming weeks. I'm definitely not going to be taking pictures in this house—how on earth would I explain that I went from an apartment with tons of natural light, gleaming white walls, high-end finishes and pristine fixtures to a very lived-in house with bad lighting and toys everywhere?

But then it dawns on me. I have an excuse not to have to create new sponsored content for the next little while. What can I do if I can't possibly shoot in my apartment—and it's not my fault? I'm always saying that if only I had some time, I could devote it to the book garage plan. A sense of relief washes over me.

I take a few sips of coffee then look around for the bag I stuffed with clothes, pulling open the closet doors. And stop. The left side is packed with Will's clothes, the right side is mostly empty, except for a few things—jewelry box, a few pairs of shoes, some shirts. Her things. I look away and close the doors, feeling like I've just read his diary.

I shuffle down the hallway, my feet warmed by the runner on the floor, and drag my things into the room next door. The room has a double bed, a nightstand and a lamp. The walls feature Addie's drawings, and a large framed photo of Addie, Will and an older couple I suspect are his parents. I know nothing about his parents, or where they live, but I wonder now if this is their room, when they visit. I shove my things into the empty closet. In the bathroom, I turn on the faucet, splashing my face with water, then look around for a towel. I open the cupboards under the sink and pull out a white towel. There's an S on it. It takes me a moment to make the connection. Sophie. My hands shake and I grip the towel and slide down to the floor, leaning back against the cold tile on the wall and closing my eyes. My heart pounds.

OK, it's one towel, and the S might not even refer to Sophie. *C'mon, Kit.*

I open my eyes, let go of the towel and reach forward for the handles of the cupboard doors in front of me. I pull them open and rifle through the other towels. Two more S's, and a few W's. Sophie and Will. There's no debating it: these are couple towels. Were they wedding gifts, or something they bought together on a date one Saturday afternoon? Curiosity eats away at me, and yet, at the same time, I long to be oblivious. It's simpler. I don't want my emotions involved, but being here, in Will's house, means I can't avoid it. I refold the towel in my hand and shove it into the cabinet, then find a small gray hand towel at the bottom of the pile and run it under cold water until my hands feel numb. I hold it to my face for several minutes.

Back in the hall, I look around. Even though I've been to Will's dozens of times, I've only been upstairs a handful of those. There's a missing knob on the closet and marker on the wall. The door to Addie's room is slightly ajar. I peek inside. The walls are lavender and there's a mound of stuffed animals in the corner of the room. I take a few steps closer, holding onto her door handle and craning my head to see a framed photo on the wall. Addie's a baby, maybe one or two, and she's in what must be Sophie's arms. Sophie's blond hair is falling around her shoulders. She's tall and lean, with creamy skin, and Will's arm is around her. I lean in a little more, trying not to trespass into Addie's room but also trying to see the three of them more clearly.

The moulding on the door frame is smooth to the touch, and I hang on to it, still looking around. That's when I see another photo in the corner. It's Sophie, pregnant, sitting on the grass under a tree. I've seen hundreds of photos of pregnant women and I've never felt much of anything. But now, looking at Sophie, her face glowing, her hand resting on her swollen abdomen, I feel a stab of jealousy. And wonder. I walk over to Addie's vanity and sit down on the wooden bench and find myself trying to imagine what it would feel like to be pregnant, to have a child growing inside me, to meet that child and see myself in him or her. And then, to get sick, to know I was going to die without seeing my daughter grow up. I cover my face with my hands. I don't want to look at myself in the mirror and see my mother in my face. Or see Sophie in Addie's. I stand and land on something sharp. It's a tiny purple Lego. Holding the bit in my hand, I consider it for a moment before placing it on her dresser and getting out of her room.

After changing back into my clothes from yesterday, I head downstairs. In the kitchen, I refill my coffee mug, then wander around the house, paying attention to details in a way I never do when Will is here. Dirty dishes tower high in the sink, and a series of black marks and dates track Addie's height on the doorframe to the basement. Walls have dings, and pictures are slightly off-kilter. A pile of newspapers sits in the corner of the living room, and there's a half-finished puzzle on the coffee table.

The house feels lived in, and in some ways, you'd never know that it was just Will and Addie. Sophie's touches seem to be everywhere: bright and cheerful knobs on the kitchen cabinets, the owl collection on the living room shelf. Everywhere I look, now that I'm *really* looking, there are reminders of her. They're whimsical and charming and I know Addie and Will must love feeling like she's still with them, but to me, it feels threatening and intimidating. I hate that Sophie had her life so together, so many years ago, when I still really don't, in some ways at least. It makes me hate her even though I don't even know her. I feel like a monster. She didn't do anything wrong. All she did was die, young and beautiful. She was the perfect mom with a perfect husband and a perfect daughter. Everything so fucking perfect and now set, for eternity, in stone.

What am I doing here? I don't belong here. How could I ever belong here, with my messed-up life and flooded apartment? Discouraged, I look out through the sliding glass doors. And that's when I see it. How had I not seen it before? At the end of Will's backyard, leading into the alleyway, is a garage.

#

"What are you going to do?" Izzy asks when I meet her for coffee later in the day. We're at Mug Shot, and the place is packed and noisy, but we managed to get a table on the back patio, in the shade.

"What *can* I do? I'm not going to move just because there's water damage. It's just a temporary inconvenience." I've just heard that the water damage in my apartment is worse than anticipated and they need to knock down one of the walls and rebuild it, so I'm going to be out of my place for much longer than I thought.

"You can always stay with us," she says. "If you change your mind about staying with Will."

I swirl my biscotti in my coffee. "You know, I thought you'd be more alarmed to hear I'm staying with Will," I say. Izzy is usually my voice of reason, the one I can count on to tell me when I'm making bad choices.

"What do you want me to say?" she says. "You're thirty-three. I think it's pretty obvious that you like him. And he obviously likes you, too. He's good, you're good. I think you're good together. I think, perhaps, it could be a bit confusing to Addie, but she's Will's daughter, and I'm sure he's thinking about that. And when your apartment's ready, you move back. Or . . . you don't?"

"That's what I'm worried about. Will it be awkward? I mean, can you ever really go back?" I look at Izzy, waiting for an answer. When she doesn't give me one, I continue. "People aren't like cars. They're more like bikes, only moving forward. Or maybe it's that life is the bike, and we're just the cyclists. We've got to keep peddling or fall off and die."

"You don't always *die* if you fall off your bike," Izzy points out.

"Maybe not, but you get hurt."

Izzy nods. "But you didn't *move*-in move-in," she says, reconfirming what I'd been telling myself. "You're just staying with him.

It's temporary. I think you definitely have an out, if you want one. You're still paying for your place. I wouldn't overthink things."

She's right. It is temporary. So maybe I should just let myself enjoy this *temporary* domestic experience and see how it goes.

"OK. But if Dad asks, let's just say I'm staying with you. Cool?" I sip my coffee.

"Yes, and the offer is always open, if you change your mind and actually want to crash with Roddy and me. I can't promise he'll put the toilet seat down, though, but he will put you to work and make you *really* appreciate your own place when you move back into your apartment."

I laugh lightly. "Can I . . . tell you something else?" She pauses, her biscotti partway to her mouth.

"Of course."

"Do you ever remember Mom talking about opening a bookshop, in a garage?" I say.

Izzy laughs then sees my face. "Oh, you're serious?" She pops the biscotti into her mouth.

I nod. "Yeah," I say slowly, feeling self-conscious.

"No, but, that doesn't mean she didn't. Why do you ask?"

I wrap my hands around my coffee mug, trying to warm them as a chill runs through me. "I have this memory of Mom and me, garage-hunting on Saturdays. She wanted to find the perfect garage, and then convince Dad to move. She wanted to open a bookshop in the garage. She said we could run it together. I'm sure she meant you, too. All of us," I add, hearing how the idea sounds. But Izzy shakes her head.

"I'm not sure about that last part," she teases, as though she knows I added it on so she wouldn't feel excluded. "And that's fine. You two always had a special bond. And you're the readers in our family. Dad and I were the active ones, out bike riding or playing catch, while you and Mom were inside, both your noses in books."

I hang on Izzy's every word, hearing this information, her view of Mom, of me, of Mom and me together, for the first time. "But just because I didn't know anything about it doesn't mean anything." She tilts her head. "I can see you're going through a lot right now, huh?"

I nod. "I guess I am. Maybe it's thinking about how young Mom was when she died, and how I'm almost there. I know you already went through this . . ."

Izzy smiles softly, kindly. "It's not easy. It makes you think. You only live once and all that."

I empty my cup and replace it on the table. "Mm-hmm," I say. "Exactly."

"Well, stick with it. Don't be too quick to brush off your thoughts just because they're scary. Or a hot guy who suddenly comes into your life when you weren't expecting it." She winks, then stands. "You ready to go?"

I stand and follow her out of the café, into the warm late-morning sun.

#

I spend the afternoon at the National Association for Women in Business head office, going through entries for the Women in Business entrepreneur of the year award. In addition to being the keynote speaker this year, I'm also a judge for this award. I think back to a few years ago, when I won the same award, the year I hit fifty No Kidding chapters across North America. It was such an exhilarating feeling, and I can't wait to help another woman feel that same recognition when she wins this award.

I've been at it for hours, and when I finally narrow the entries down to a shortlist of six, I think about calling it a day. I'd love to head back to Will's, curl up on the couch with a glass of wine and my book, but it's only four now, which means Will and Addie will just be getting home. I don't want her to walk in and find me there. Because even though she's only one-third of this equation, she's the most important one at this particular time. And if there's a chance I'll be at Will's for a few weeks, it's important this whole thing gets off on the right foot. I wonder if Will has told her? What if she's already upset about the whole thing? Do I fight to stay or just pack my things and go? My stomach churns.

An hour later, I head back to Will's.

Addie throws open the door as I walk up the steps. "Where have you been?" she says happily and relief washes over my entire body. I drop my bags at the door, realizing how much stress I was holding on to the whole day. "We've been waiting for you!"

As she chatters on about her day and the night, I only half listen, realizing that she's clearly fine with the situation. I think about that glass of wine, my book, the couch, realizing how tired I am. But Addie has other plans for the evening. I once met a woman who told me she ended her work day at two so that she could grab a quick nap before moving into "mom mode" when her young son got home from school. It always sounded a bit lazy to me—but now, as I stand here listening to Addie's game-night plan, I wish I'd stayed at Will's this afternoon, while they were out, and had a nap myself.

I head upstairs to the guest room to put away a few purchases, my purse, my shoes, and I lie down on the bed for a moment, closing my eyes, but don't let myself fall asleep. All I wanted was for Addie to be OK with me being here, and she is, incredibly, and I need to make an effort, too. More of an effort, really. And so, I rally myself to get on board with the evening's activities and be the fun houseguest I know I can be. Will's in the kitchen making pizzas—and I convince him to make hers without broccoli. "Only if you kiss me," he says, and I shake my head, but then kiss him on the neck when Addie's not looking.

"How was your day?" he asks and I tell him about the awards judging. "There are so many great entries. I'm exhausted, though."

"Are a lot of the women child-free?" he asks, and for a second, it throws me. Because even though we both know that my stance is the reason we'll never be serious, we never talk about it. "I'm not sure, to be honest. Some of the entrants definitely talk about juggling motherhood or single parenting and running a business, but it's not supposed to affect our decision."

"It'd be hard not to, though. Trying to juggle both." He spreads tomato sauce on the stretched dough.

"You do it."

"Can you grate cheese?" He hands me a ball of mozzarella and a cheese grater. "Yeah, and it's not easy."

"But just because someone doesn't have kids doesn't mean it's easier. She could be supporting her parents, or paying off debt, or overcoming a disadvantaged upbringing. Maybe she started a business that just took a ton more work than another, struggled through a bad year, had a bad business partner . . . there are so many things we never know about someone. And none of them are more or less important." I shove the chopping block of grated cheese toward him, more forcefully than I intend to, but I'm annoyed. I refill my wine glass and walk over to the couch to sit down. Addie's threading beads on gimp. "Wanna make a bracelet with me?" she asks.

"Sure," I say, glancing back to the kitchen. Will's sliding the pizzas into the oven. I focus on selecting beads from Addie's sparkling pink container.

Will walks over and puts a hand on my shoulder. "Sorry about that. You're right, what you said."

I meet his eyes, and all ability to stay annoyed with him dissipates. "OK."

The corners of his mouth turn up. "OK." He looks over at Addie. "Will you make me one?"

She doesn't look up. "Yep. I'll make it match mine."

#

As we eat dinner Addie rattles on about her day. "You should come watch me at gymnastics next week," she says.

"I'd like that," I tell her. "I tried to do gymnastics when I was a kid. But I was definitely not flexible enough." At this Will raises his eyebrows and I feel myself blush, and have to turn away from him.

"Who wants ice cream sundaes?" I ask and get out the supplies I picked up on the way home. Addie cheers and it gives me a warm feeling all over. "Now she's never going to bed," Will whispers as he loads the dishwasher. But I shrug. "She's so sweet, and sounds like we have a full night ahead of us anyway." When we're finished dessert, Will and I clean up while Addie gets her pajamas on and sets up a game at the kitchen table. I pour myself a glass of wine and listen to the convoluted instructions, but never really get the hang of the game—which suits Addie just fine because it means she wins every round. Eventually Will calls last round and we settle in to watch the movie of her choice, all three of us on the couch, Addie sandwiched between us, a bowl of popcorn on her lap. Maybe this could work out, I think. Maybe I can fit in with the two of them, their traditions, their routines. Occasionally as I reach for popcorn, my hand meets Will's and I get tingles up my arm. It's exciting and very PG all at once—for now, at least.

Addie falls asleep near the end of the movie and Will carries her up the stairs to bed. While he's in her room, I tiptoe up to the guest room and change into the fishnets and lacy corset I bought today. Heels in hand, I slip back downstairs to wait for him on the couch. But ten minutes turns into fifteen and then twenty, and finally I make my way back upstairs, praying that Addie doesn't suddenly get up to use the washroom and run into me. But it's quiet and the door to Addie's room is slightly ajar. I peek inside, hiding behind the doorframe. And there's Will, snuggled with Addie, fast asleep. For a split second I consider waking him up to bring him to bed with me, but I don't because it feels selfish and wrong. And so I go into the guest room, change into pajamas and crawl into the single bed, feeling alone, out of place, and wishing I could be in my own bed instead.

fifteen

The clattering of dishes wakes me up. I roll out of bed and look at the clock. 6:05? Seriously? I shuffle downstairs in my pajamas.

"Hey," Will says, wiping his hands on his jeans and pouring me a cup of coffee. "How'd you sleep?"

"OK," I say, remembering how last night ended and feeling the resentment creep back in. I know I shouldn't be competing with an eight-year-old for his attention. I tell myself to suck it up—for now. I say hi to Addie, who's sitting at the bar, drawing.

"Hey," she mumbles. Will hands me the coffee cup. I take a sip then sit down at the bar and tap on my phone.

"Can you put that away?" he says, a bit testily.

I look up to see what's caught Will's attention. I assume he's looking at Addie, but he's looking at me. "Huh?" I say.

"Your phone. We have a no screens at breakfast rule."

I stare at him. "Oh, um, I always do a few stories in the morning," I say. "They do well. And this is work."

He shakes his head at me. I don't want to make it an issue, but at the same time, I'm bothered. He's not *my* father, and yes, I'm in his house, but he can't tell me what to do.

"If she gets to be on screens, I should get to be on screens," Addie says.

"It's work," I say again.

Will exhales loudly, then asks Addie to set the table, but she looks at him like he has two heads.

"Why are we sitting at the table? We never eat breakfast at the table."

"Because there are only two stools and there are three of us." He places three white plates, cutlery piled on top, in front of her. She doesn't budge.

"So what, we're just going to . . . start eating at the table?"

"Addie, what's the big deal? We always eat at the table whenever we have people over."

"Not for breakfast. We always eat breakfast at the bar."

"And now we're eating at the table," Will interrupts sharply. "Set the table. And not another word out of you."

Addie storms to the dining room and slams the plates onto the table, the cutlery sliding off and clattering to the floor. She comes back to get glasses, making a big production out of reaching for them. I look to Will, unsure what to do. "I'm not much of a big breakfast person," I whisper. "I'm not even that hungry." *Because it's not even 7 a.m.*

But what I could use is more coffee and silence to figure out how I'm going to execute the series of photos I had planned for a new tea client. They'd approved three concepts for shots—one in my tub, one on my couch and one at my marble bar. Showing the Zen life of living alone, having a cup of tea whenever you want. But Will's bathroom is too grimy, his couch is threadbare and his bar is a very well-used butcher's block in front of a chipped blue wall riddled with off-kilter framed photos of him and Addie. The only saving grace is that the wall is the Pantone color of the year. Could I spin that somehow? Unlikely. And how am I supposed to evoke that Zen feeling when I feel completely stressed out?

"Don't leave," he says. "That's the worst thing you could do. She's just hungry."

"I am NOT hungry!" Addie shouts as she enters the kitchen. "I HATE when you say that—and it's not like I can eat because you still haven't finished making breakfast!"

So this is what life with kids is like when you're not eating ice cream sundaes, watching movies or riding the Scrambler. That's the thing—I knew it, I just wasn't prepared to deal with it on a Monday morning at 7 a.m.

#

My cousin Lena calls while I'm rushing to an event for a new dating app, to tell me that she doesn't want a spa gift card for her baby shower gift. While I know I should be happy that she's happy she's about to become a mom, my real emotion is disappointment. Even though she had a tough time last year after her business went bust, I figured once she returned from taking a breather in Cambodia she'd be back to her usual self and back at the No Kidding groups, filling us all in on her latest start-up idea. Now that she's about to become a mom, she feels like somebody that I used to know. The old Lena would never have even told me what gift *not* to give—especially not calling more than six weeks beforehand to do so. But since I have no intention of actually showing up at her shower, I take in her rant as well as the details on where she's registered for items she really needs as a single mother. Which is how, an hour after leaving the dating app event with a code to redeem my free dating credits, I end up taking a thirty-dollar Uber to Babies R Us to get the gift, have it sent to her and remove it from my mind. Now, I'm staring at the seven-page printout of items. I scan the store for someone to help me. Why on earth didn't I do this online?

"Can I help you find something?" A salesclerk has popped out of nowhere.

"Yes. With this." I thrust the papers at her.

"Is this for you or for a friend?"

Do I look pregnant? "A friend," I say, telling myself to stay focused. Stay focused.

"Looks like she's received a lot already," the clerk coos, scanning the list. "OK, let's see what's left and you can pick something out. When is she due?"

"Can you just grab whatever? Just—whatever you think makes a good gift and I'll meet you at the cash? I don't really care what it is." My breathing is shallow. It feels hard to get any air.

But she's not listening. She's walking around the store, pulling items off the shelves, showing me packages big and small, bright colors. My eyes are swimming, and there's a loud ringing in my ears. I can't do this. "How about this breast pump?" she asks. "It's a portable one, for on the go. In a pinch, you might say." It feels like the aisles are closing in on me. Soothers and teethers, socks and bibs. I squeeze my eyes tight, open them, trying to get rid of the spots that are forming, but they're growing larger.

"Are you OK? Ma'am?"

Everything goes black.

I come to and see a bunch of strange faces staring down at me, bright lights behind them. For a split second, I consider that I've died. Am I in heaven? Then I realize I'm still at Babies R Us. So, hell. I sit up, to concerned murmurs. "You fainted," someone says. "Do you have low blood pressure? Diabetes? Are you pregnant?"

So many questions, fired at me.

I tell them all that I'm fine.

"Should we call someone for you?"

I'm not about to call Casey or Xiu or Gloria or Will and tell any of them that I fainted in a Babies R Us. Instead, I call an Uber and head to Izzy's—she'll get a good laugh at my story.

"Do you think that there's something wrong with me?" I say over wine later, on her couch.

"So much." She grins and uses the remote to change the music on her sound system.

"I'm serious." I fold my legs under me on the couch.

"There's nothing wrong with you," she says. "You have a conscience. I think you have a lot going on and your feelings are valid. You're suddenly *living* with this guy you're super into, and his daughter, and realizing, this isn't the life you had planned out for yourself and yet, you don't want to end things with him . . ."

I take a large sip of wine then put my glass on the table and turn toward her.

"It'd be one thing if I were a lawyer or doctor or *any* other job really, but this isn't just my feelings about kids, it's my whole career, my whole life. It feels like I've put so much into all of this, that I can't abandon it all for one guy, regardless of my feelings for him. Even if his daughter is very sweet, and we get along just great. This afternoon must mean something. I can't even go into a baby store without having a panic attack? Clearly it's a sign. A warning."

"Uh-huh."

"What do you mean, uh-huh?"

"Well . . . it could also mean that you're stressed and tired and didn't eat a good lunch. There are all kinds of reasons for fainting. I hardly think you can blame it on a teensy pair of socks or a breast pump."

I sigh. "I don't know, Iz. Don't you ever think it's weird that we never babysat? Like, doesn't every teenage girl babysit? But not us? We never babysat. And we even took that babysitting course at the YMCA. We were fully qualified babysitters yet we never babysat. It's weird."

Izzy laughs. "Are you kidding? We wanted to babysit but couldn't because those stupid twins on Oxford Street got all the families. Remember they had those full-color flyers? And that *jingle*?" Izzy hums a tune that I vaguely recognize.

"Oh yeah. I forgot about that."

"How could you forget? Bitches." Izzy breaks out in song. I laugh, and sing along with her until we're both laughing so hard that my stomach aches.

Did we really never babysit because two other girls got to all the families before us? All this time I thought we didn't babysit because we didn't want to spend time with little kids, because we didn't have the foundation for maternal instincts that all our friends were experiencing around the same time. If Izzy's right, am I wrong? About everything?

#

Feloise opens the large door to her Forest Hill home and lets me in. Her curly hair is wild, and she's wearing a leopard-print jumpsuit that only she could pull off. "Thanks for making the trek over to Never-Neverland," she says as I slip off my shoes.

"I like coming here. This house feels like a hotel." The entrance is grand, with a large round table, a massive bouquet of peonies in the center. A spiral staircase leads to the second floor and multiple doors lead to various other large, empty rooms. Feloise bought the house with her ex, and it always surprises me that she kept it after the divorce. As she leads me to the backyard, the pool is just one of the many reminders that this feels like a house made for a family with children.

"A hotel that's breaking down. The pool heater's leaking, the dishwasher's on the fritz and I'm pretty sure there's mold in the basement. And those are just the issues I'm dealing with this week."

I sit in one of the cushioned chairs and pour myself a glass of water from the carafe on the coffee table. "It sounds like a lot of work for one person," I say sympathetically.

She fans the air with her hand. "Oh woe is me, the barren spinster. I could sell, but I like being the Wild Woman of the West in this neighborhood. The last thing I'm going to do is be a total cliché and live in a waterfront condo," she says. "No offense."

"None taken. I'm not on the water," I say lightly.

"Alright, let's get down to business, shall we?" She flips open her iPad case and rattles through the list of requests she's gotten in the last two weeks—for social media collaborations, videos, brand sponsorships and speaking engagements. "Oh, and the Stay-a-While people said you put the contract on hold? What's with that?"

"Oh," I say, exhaling. "My apartment flooded, so I had to pause."

"What? What do you mean, your apartment flooded?"

I shrug. "It's fine and I should be back in it next month."

"When did this happen and when were you going to tell me? And where are you staying?"

"At a friend's," I say, trying to keep my expression neutral. "I'm just going to use the washroom." Back inside the house, I head toward the large bathroom on the main floor, one that's connected to a guest room. I sit on the edge of the tub and put my head between my knees. It feels wrong that I haven't told Feloise the truth, but she's my agent. And sure, I was there for her when she went through her divorce and she was there for me when Eric and I split, making sure my schedule was packed so I wouldn't have time to feel sorry for myself. But it's not like we tell each other everything, not like best friends would. But at that thought, I feel even worse. Because I don't have a best friend. Sure, Gloria and Xiu and Cascy are my closest, but even they don't know what's going on with me. I didn't call them when my apartment flooded, and now they think I'm staying with Izzy, because that's what I told them. Why am I lying to everyone?

But of course I know why. I'm lying to everyone because, right now, I can barely handle my own truths, or figure out what to do about the fact that I'm falling in love with a single dad and going against everything I believe in. And right now, I don't need anyone else's opinions influencing me.

I check my reflection in the mirror and then head back outside to Feloise. Thankfully, she's moved on from my personal life to goal-setting and has a Q4 spreadsheet on her screen. I focus in on my career and let the other stuff fall away—for now, at least.

#

As the days pass, my relationship with Addie seems to be getting worse, even though I've tried all my tricks: asking her to watch a movie, to paint her nails or to help her hang LED lights in her room. And yet, she tries her best to ignore me as much as possible, focusing all her questions at Will, and pretending that I'm not even there. After dinner one night, Will says he needs to take a call with a client and tells Addie to help me clean up, but as soon as he's out of sight she puts the plate she was clearing from the table on the counter and says she has to go to the bathroom, then runs up the stairs. I stand in the middle of the kitchen in my tank top and jogging pants, annoyed because I know there's no way she's coming back down and now I've got to clean up this mess alone, and figure out why Addie has turned on me. If I were in my apartment, I would've had dinner in peace, in about ten minutes instead of forty-five, and it would've been takeout and now I'd be working or reading a book or watching TV and not worrying about who's mad at me and why. "I didn't sign up for this!" I think as I let out a frustrated scream. It's clear that Addie doesn't want me around. And frankly, I don't want to be in a house where I'm not wanted, either.

Part of me knows that I should go upstairs and talk to her, but I don't want to. I don't want to take this on. It's too much. So, instead, I stick to dishes. And then, after I finish cleaning the kitchen, I walk around the rest of the main floor, tidying up Addie's toys and throwing out bits of garbage, grumbling that I'm spending my free time in this way and yet still preferring to be alone than deal with anyone else and their emotions.

Will comes down the stairs while I'm sitting on the couch, staring at my phone. "Where's Addie?" he asks.

"Upstairs."

"Why?"

I sigh. "I don't know. She's mad at me about something."

"Well, did you ask her what's going on?"

"No because she doesn't want to talk to me," I say, feeling childish. Will calls me out on it. "You're the adult. You have to talk to her."

I sigh. He studies me. "Are you OK?"

I shrug. "I think I need some fresh air. Do you want to come?"

He shakes his head. "Yes, but no. I can't leave Addie alone. She's eight. Plus, I should get her to bed anyway."

Of course.

I slip on my shoes, pull on my jean jacket and head outside. I feel ashamed of myself for leaving the house when I know the right thing to do is to go talk to Addie. And yet, I'm frustrated with Will, but when I try to figure out why, it all feels so immature. That he didn't praise me for tidying his place, when he didn't ask me to? That he didn't jump at the chance to come for a walk with me, when I should've realized he can't leave Addie alone? That my entire night is gone with nothing to show for it? And yet, if I overanalyze the evening, I know that I cleaned his place to avoid talking to Addie, which is the same reason I've left the house for my so-called walk.

After doing a large loop around the neighborhood, I head back to the house, prepared to talk to Addie about how she's feeling.

Inside, the main floor is dark. I take off my shoes and walk up the stairs. I hear Will and Addie chatting in Addie's room.

"I don't get it," I hear Will saying. "I thought you really liked Kit." I stop at the top of the stairs, listening to their conversation.

"As a *friend*," Addie replies. "I thought she was our friend. But now she just, like, lives here with us. And you never even asked me if it was OK. You just told me this was happening. I didn't get any say at all. You always say that it's you and me and that this is our house but then you went and asked her to live here and you didn't even *ask* me what I thought."

My heart pounds. "And Millie said that Gillian said she's trying to be your girlfriend."

"Oh Honey, no. She's not trying—"

"You're supposed to live with your family. She's not our family." Addie is sobbing now.

"Oh, Kiddo." Will's voice is kind. I imagine him reaching over and pulling her close. "I know it's weird to have any other woman here. Someone who isn't Mom."

"She's not even a mom." Addie's voice is getting louder. "She doesn't want kids. She doesn't even like them."

"That's not true," Will says slowly. "She likes you," he says.

"So what? Haven't you looked at Instagram? Gillian says she hates them. And it's true, she's always saying all this stuff about how great her life is without kids."

Shit. When did she see my Instagram? But of course she's seen my Instagram. I *showed* it to her when we were on the ferry, so many weeks ago. And she told me she has her own Instagram account. Why didn't I block her—or explain to her what my account's really about—months ago, before she discovered it on her own? Clearly Will is wondering the same thing because there's silence.

Then he speaks: "You know Instagram isn't real, right? And hers is especially . . . complicated. Don't think of it so much as her, but as a company she works for. And unfortunately that company's kind of awful to work for, but it pays her a lot of money."

Addie sniffs. "Whatever."

I move toward the bathroom, my hands shaking as I open the door and then close it behind me and lock it. I turn on the tap, then slide down to the cold tile, my back against the wall. I grab an S hand towel and wipe away a tear. Two tears. A lot of tears. Addie is right. And so is Will. About all of those things. About me.

#

"I can't do this," I tell Izzy as we're power walking along the boardwalk the following afternoon. I'm finding it hard to keep up. I'm not sure where things stand with Will and me. We've barely spoken since yesterday. He went to bed early, claiming he was tired, and this morning I had to be at the Women in Business office at eight for a meeting. I know I'm avoiding the situation, too, because frankly, I don't know what to do.

"I feel like I'm walking on eggshells. I don't know whether to stay or go, but I know that I hate how this is going," I say. "I wish my apartment would just be finished and I could go home and this could all go back to the way it was."

"So leave," she says, checking her watch, and I wonder what she's keeping track of—distance, heartbeat, calories burned? Or is she secretly checking her texts while I complain about the mess I've got myself into for the second time this week?

"Harsh," I say, sitting down on the bench. Izzy taps at her watch and sits down next to me.

"Maybe, but real," she says. "The thing is, I think you don't want to leave. I think you *want* to be in this relationship with Will, or you wouldn't be staying with him. You could've stayed with Roddy and me, with any of your other friends, or gotten a short-term rental somewhere, an Airbnb, anything. You're not broke and in college. And you're not an idiot, you're not bad to look at—"

"Gee, thanks."

"You could *get* another single guy. Someone without baggage."

"She's not baggage," I say instinctively.

"See?" Izzy stretches her legs out and begins doing triceps dips. "I'm not saying you made the wrong decision," she puffs. "I'm just saying that you're a smart woman who knows what she wants. And I think you want to see where this thing with Will goes. But now you're afraid."

"Of course I'm afraid," I say to her. "I'm a woman who's made a very successful career convincing women to be child-free by choice and now I'm doing *whatever* it is I'm doing with this great guy and . . ."

I take a deep breath, looking out at the water, debating whether to actually say it aloud. "I think I'm falling in love with Will." I pause. "But it's so much more complicated than simply my feelings for him. There's Addie, and she's a person, too. And how my relationship with Will could affect her is just as important as how a relationship with a man and his daughter will affect me. And right now it feels even more complicated because she appears to hate me because, in a nutshell, she thinks I hate her."

"So press Play." Izzy stands and starts walking again.

"*What?*" I get up and jog to catch up to her.

"You're hitting the Pause button. Over and over. I can see it. You're afraid to commit. But I've heard you inspire all these women who hang on your every word, looking up to you for advice. You're the one who's always telling them to own their decisions, that nothing matters except what they think of themselves, and when they want something, to go for it, Michelle Obama–style. So now you have to practice what you preach. Come on." She pumps her arms. "Let's keep going."

As we speed walk the rest of the boardwalk, I look out onto the shoreline as the waves crash in. I once took a surfing lesson in California. After an hour of practicing on the sand, we went out into the water. I thought it would be easy, but each time a wave would come, I'd struggle to stand, fighting the wave as I tried to keep my balance. And failing. Time after time, until I was exhausted and frustrated. The instructor, a lanky blond guy, pulled my board, me lying on top of it, to standing water. "The key," he drawled in his SoCal accent, "is to commit. Hesitation creates instability."

sixteen

The lobby of the Ritz smells like sandalwood, which makes me think of Will's cologne and calms my nerves. I don't know why I'm so nervous—Will said he'd be here. I sit on the navy velvet couch to wait for him to show up. Since I did end up having a credit for the Ritz in my gift-card stash, I figured it was as good an excuse as any for a date with Will.

The revolving door slowly turns and Will walks in. He's gotten a haircut and is wearing an olive shirt that brings out his eyes. He grins when he sees me. "Hey," he says, as I stand and walk toward him. He grabs my hips and pulls me close, his lips on mine. My breath catches and I close my eyes. "Hi," I say softly when we pull apart.

"So what's this mysterious meetup all about?" he says and I take his hand and lead him to the restaurant.

"I thought we could use a date," I say. I give the *maître d'* my name. He leads us to a table by the window and pulls out my chair.

Will leans forward. "Are we really going to waste time on dinner? Tell me you got us a room. Not to be a drag, but I've got to pick Addie up from gymnastics at eight."

"Taken care of," I say.

Will raises his eyebrows. "Gillian?"

I nod.

"Wow, OK then," he says, and then leans back in his chair as the waiter approaches. Will orders a beer and I get a Negroni and exhale, realizing how stressed I've been all day. Will asks about my day and we chitchat idly until our drinks arrive. I take a sip, then shift the conversation to the topic of us. "I like being with you," I say. Will meets my eyes. "I know we didn't really set any boundaries, or define our relationship, but it sort of feels like, maybe we should . . ."

"You want to bring another guy home?" he says, and I let out a nervous laugh, more at his use of the word "home" than at his joke. *Commit, Kit.*

"I'm trying to be serious. I think it's pretty clear I don't want to date anyone else. I really like you. But this has all been so sudden. We went from like, one sorta date, to working together, to living together and I know it's temporary, but I also think that we're blurring the lines with it all. The whole Addie thing. I heard you guys last night in Addie's room and you were weird with me last night. You know I don't hate kids. God, I spent a ton of time and energy trying to figure out how to get that message across to people as it is. I especially don't hate Addie, that's for sure. You know that, and I know that if Addie hears this from someone, it has to be me, but also, all of this . . . is a lot. It feels a bit like I'm being thrown into parenting her."

Will raises an eyebrow.

"I don't—I'm not implying I've been doing anything near what you do, but it feels like I am a lot more involved than I would be if we were just casually dating, and that would be fine except we're pretending, for her, that we're not dating, so it feels a bit unfair and confusing. Like, which is it? And I don't need us to define any of this, but I just wanted you to know why I'm a bit hesitant to have to justify my career to Addie." I'm babbling and none of this sounds as coherent as when I'd tried to rehearse what I wanted to say. I look at Will. Maybe I need to make this more of a conversation, hear what he has to say.

He stares back at me.

"Well? What do you think?"

"What do I think? I think that none of this has anything to do with you and me and everything to do with the fact that a little girl heard that someone who *hates* children is living in her house. It wouldn't matter who it was, if anyone—a friend, a brother, a neighbor, *anyone* was staying with me and this happened—I would ask them to explain themselves and make things right with my daughter." He folds his arms over his chest.

His words hit me—hard. He's right. "And what's more, if you *heard* us discussing all this, why didn't you come in? You had the perfect opportunity to fix things, in the moment."

Tears well in my eyes. *Because I was a coward.*

Will's phone buzzes. I glance at the screen. Gillian. Of course. Now I fold my arms over my chest.

Will pauses, looking from his phone to me. "Listen, I know I've surrounded myself with overprotective women, and they haven't been the most welcoming to you." His phone buzzes again. "But it comes from a good place. They've been in Addie's life since she was a baby. They just want the best for her." He pushes back his chair and stands, holding up his phone. "I really should take this."

He walks quickly toward the door of the restaurant and I pull my eyes away to refocus on my drink, downing half of it. This is not going according to plan—whatever plan that was. That's the thing, I had things I wanted to say, but no real plan. What did I expect Will to say?

Out of the corner of my eye, Will comes into view. "I forgot that Addie was doing her level evaluation at gymnastics today. I really should be there."

Disappointment washes over me. Of course he should be there, but why did it have to be right now? He puts his credit card on the table, and waves to the waiter. "I'm really disappointed not to use the room," he says, his eyes shining.

I nod. "It was comped anyway," I say, my voice cracking.

"And it's not the same, but want to come with me? We could talk more in the car?"

This is Will giving me a chance. It's not the romantic evening I had planned, and yet, I'd rather be with him than without him. "Sure," I say, standing.

"I'm sorry about tonight," he says once we're driving. "It was really nice that you set this up, and I know that I'm not blameless either. I've definitely sent you mixed messages, but this is confusing for me too. My brain is telling me one thing, but the rest of me is trying really hard to ignore it."

"You're right about Addie, though," I say. "And me taking responsibility. I'll talk to her."

"Maybe tomorrow? I have an early breakfast to cater, so I was actually going to ask you if you minded getting her to school? I know, I'm kind of asking a lot of you, but I guess . . . I like having you be the one I can turn to. It can be pretty lonely single parenting, and even though Addie was upset last night, I know she really likes you. That's *why* she was so upset. Because you matter. To her. And to me."

"You're just saying that so I'll do it," I tease.

Will pulls into a large lot beside an industrial-looking building and parks. He shuts the car off and turns to me, putting his hand on my chin and pulling my face close. I close my eyes as his lips meet mine, and lose myself in the moment.

#

The next morning I'm up before my alarm goes off at 5:30 a.m. I still haven't figured out what to say to Addie, but I'm determined to give this morning my best shot.

When I was growing up, one of my favorite memories was waking up to the smell of muffins baking in the oven. Coming downstairs to a warm kitchen and seeing my mother in an apron, oven mitts on, humming to the music in her head made me feel cozy and happy. She would smile as soon as she saw me, give me a hug, and within minutes, have a muffin on a plate in front of me, a pat of butter on the side. She'd ask what one thing I was looking forward to that day. It was our special time together, and after she was gone, I'd envision those mornings, pretending she was giving me advice on university term papers, boyfriends, job drama. The perfect morning to start the day.

Downstairs, I pour myself a cup of coffee, rub my eyes and tell myself I'm not tired. If I'm going to do this, I've got to be awake to do this. On my phone I find a recipe for banana muffins and then pull the ingredients out of the cupboard. Of course I find everything I need, since I'm in a chef's kitchen. The thing about living alone is that I would never have all the ingredients for muffins—or any recipe—in my cupboards and fridge. Maybe it's not only because Will's a chef. I wonder if it's because being a dad, taking care of someone else, forces him to make his house a home. It almost makes me not want to ever go back to my own apartment, even if I'd be getting to sleep in past sunrise.

Once the muffins are in the oven, I fill the sink with soapy water and just as I begin washing the mixing bowls, the stairs start to creak. Addie shuffles into the kitchen.

"Good morning," I say brightly.

"What's that smell?" She yawns and stretches her arms over her head.

"Banana muffins." I smile. "With chocolate chips."

"It's Tuesday."

I'm not sure if we're just spouting random facts, but I nod. "Yep! Anything exciting going on at school today?"

"We always have pancakes on Tuesday," she grumbles. "That's why it's called Pancake Tuesday."

"Isn't that during Lent?"

"I don't know. We're not Jewish."

I bite my tongue.

"Where's Dad? I want him to make the pancakes."

"He had to leave early. To cater a breakfast." I know for a fact she knows this, because Will told her on the car ride home from gymnastics last night. The same silent car ride where she didn't speak to me.

Addie sighs dramatically. "So what, you're, like, my babysitter now, too?"

Now it's my turn to sigh. "I'm not your babysitter. And I'm sorry I didn't know about Pancake Tuesday but ..." The timer goes off and I open drawers, looking for oven mitts. Slipping them on, I take the muffins out of the oven and put them on the top of the stove.

"But what?"

I don't know what else to say.

"Well, are you going to make pancakes, or what?"

"Or what," I say, which is something Dad used to say to me. And I always hated when he did, but now I'm doing it too. "I'm not going to make pancakes because I already made muffins and I don't even like to bake. So I guess if you want pancakes you'll have to make them yourself. I'm going to go upstairs to get ready for work." I throw down the oven mitts and turn toward the stairs.

"Yeah, well I can't make pancakes because I'm not allowed to use the stove without an adult!" she screams after me.

#

I'm just about to bring up the whole Instagram issue as we're walking south on Euclid to Addie's school when she stops dead in her sneakers. "I forgot the tissue!" she says, turning to me wide-eyed. Her hair is matted and her buttons aren't lined up on her shirtdress. I wonder if I should've offered to help her get ready, but this is the first thing she's said to me since blowing up at me about pancakes.

"What tissue?"

"For the pillows," she says turning around. "We have to go back."

"What pillows?" I say, but she's already running back down the sidewalk toward the house. I chase after her, hoisting my bag higher on my shoulder. "What pillows?" I catch her before the street and grab her hand. I expect her to try to pull it away, and for me to have to hold it tighter to make sure she doesn't cross the street without me, but she doesn't tug. Small miracles.

Inside the house, she races around the living room, and then into the kitchen. "Where *is* it?" She reminds me of a wind-up toy. "The bag of used tissue I've been saving up for weeks."

"You've been saving used tissue for weeks? Why on earth would you save used tissue for weeks?" I'm still standing in the doorway, staring at my phone. I'm going to miss my appointment.

"For the pillows we're making! That's what I've been telling you! I've been saving the tissue every time I blow my nose—it's taken me *weeks* because it's not even winter and I don't have a cold!"

The thought that Addie's been blowing her nose and then saving the tissue in a bag is really just too much. I don't know whether to be amused or disgusted. A laugh escapes me.

"Don't laugh!" she says but I can't stop. "I'm sorry, I'm sorry." And then I realize. When I was cleaning up yesterday, I threw a bunch of plastic bags in the garbage. I race out the back doors toward the bins, but it must be garbage day because they're not in the shed. I hurry around the side of the house to the front. A quick glance toward the road tells me Will must have dragged them to the curb before he left this morning. But the bin lids are all flipped open. They're empty inside. It's like the wind's been knocked out of me. I turn back to Addie, who's standing in the doorway.

"They're gone," I say. "I threw them out." I walk toward her. "You *what*?!"

"I didn't realize they weren't garbage. I just assumed."

She turns and goes back into the house, slamming the door behind her. Thankfully, she doesn't lock it and I find her on the couch, her face in her hands. "We can get new tissue," I say, wondering where Will keeps the extra tissue boxes. I open the pantry, scan the shelves, and relieved, I grab two boxes of tissue and turn back to Addie. "Ta da!" I look around for her backpack but she's shaking her head, and throws up her arms. "They can't be *new* tissues! Ughhh, this is the worst. The whole point of the project was to reuse something. We all had to save something that would've been thrown out and filled our landfills. We were going to fill pillows we're making in art class with whatever we saved up. My tissue idea was the best idea—everyone was going to be jealous. My pillow was going to be super fluffy." Her eyes are filling with tears. "Now I have *nothing* to fill my pillow with, and we're filling our pillows today."

I think of all the times I had to muddle through school projects myself. I used to imagine everyone else sitting at the table with their moms, brainstorming, laughing, putting things together. It made me hate school projects. And now not only does Addie not have a mom to work with, she has this other, random, incompetent woman staying in her house, ruining everything.

I have to fix this. Stat.

"I could give you an old sweatshirt I don't wear?" I try. "That's something that would go into a landfill, right?"

"It can't be clothes. It was one of the rules."

I look at the clock over the TV. *Keep thinking!*

"I've got it! Come with me," I say, tossing the tissue boxes on the couch and hurrying toward the door. She follows me and I usher her out onto the sidewalk, and in the opposite direction from school.

"Where are we going?" she says. She sounds excited and hopeful, which is all I need.

"To my place." I flag down a cab. He pulls over and we hop in. I give him my address.

"But isn't your place flooded?"

"You'll see."

While some of the apartment units have upgrades of laundry in-suite, like mine, some of them don't. So there's a laundromat in the basement. And that's exactly where we're going.

Out of the cab, we race into the building and it hits me. This feeling of peace. I miss my apartment. I miss my own space. I miss waking up, having coffee and starting my day in peace—instead of waking up tired, rushing to get Addie to school and now scrambling to find lint for an art project. This life—it's . . . hard.

"To what do we owe this pleasure?" Fionn, the Kind Concierge, says, breaking me out of my thought spiral, and I refocus on Addie. There's no time to wallow in my own pity. Addie is eight and this project is important to her—and the only reason we're racing around trying to solve this issue is because I threw out the tissue in the first place. And so we dash past his desk, through the mail room to a door that leads to a stairwell. I hold the door open for her and she peers down the stairs, then back at me skeptically. "It's fine," I assure her, and we rumble down the stairs. I've actually never been inside the laundromat. I only know it exists because I've seen other tenants carry their laundry in baskets up and down in the elevator. I'm worried—will there be only a handful of dryers? But as we round the corner into a large room, I see we're in luck. The room is massive, with at least twenty machines on either wall, and the dryers are stacked two-high. "Jackpot!" I declare and then race over to the first dryer and pull open the door. Peering inside, I find the latch and pull out the lint screen, surprising myself with my shot of domestic prowess. As I expected, it's packed with lint. I only then realize that I don't have a bag. But Addie immediately grasps what's going on and shrugs off her backpack and unzips it. "In here!" she says, pulling out her lunch bag to make space. With one swift move I sweep the lint into her bag, replace the screen, close the dryer door and move on to the next. And the next and the next and the next. Addie squeals and touches the lint. "It's so soft! And smells so good. And it would've just gone in the garbage! Kit!" She throws her arms around me. "You saved the day!"

I breathe a sigh of relief. A few minutes later, Addie's bag is filled with lint and we're rushing back upstairs as my phone rings. Will's voice is higher than usual and he's speaking in double-time. "The school just called. Did you drop Addie off?"

"Not yet. She's with me. Don't worry. We were figuring something out." I hold the door for her at the top of the stairs with one hand, and cradle the phone between my shoulder and my ear.

"Figuring what out? But you're taking her, right?"

"We're on our way," I say, smiling, as I wave to Fionn and we rush out the glass doors onto the street. I look both ways but there are no cabs in sight. I grab Addie's hand and lead her down the sidewalk. Adrenaline whizzes through me. "I've got to go. I'll tell you all about it when I see you later." I shove my phone in my pocket and flag down a cab. We clamber in and I tell him where to go. Then I lean back against the seat and look over at Addie. She's grinning at me. "This is way more fun than gym class." She pats her backpack and when we roll up in front of her school, we get out and I ask her if I need to go in with her, but she shakes her head. "I can sign in myself." I wait for her to turn, to head up the stairs to the school, but she just stands there.

"I'm sorry about the pancakes," she says. "Your muffins were actually really good. I ate two."

"Well you're probably going to be sick of them because I put two more in your lunch." We both laugh. She starts to walk away and then turns back.

"Hey, Kit?"

My hand is on the cab door. "Yeah?"

"We have a bake sale at Pizza Day tomorrow—would you help me make more muffins after school today? We're trying to raise money to buy a goat for a family in Tanzania."

"Definitely," I say without thinking, then remember I have a completely packed day of events and meetings—but I don't want to disappoint her by saying I don't have time. I'll figure it out later. She rushes back and hugs me and then I watch as she hurries up the steps and into the school.

\#

I somehow make it to the women's shelter at the end of Will's street only twenty minutes late for my appointment. It's not the best first impression, but the director, a woman named Rhoda, with graying blond hair and laugh lines around her eyes, is kind and welcomes me. She leads me down a narrow hallway and through a set of locked doors. She says we'll head to her office so we can have a chat, and as we walk down the hallway we pass a common room. There are tables with chairs, games on shelves, an area that looks like it's set up for doing crafts, but all the women in the room are sitting on a worn sofa, facing the large TV on the wall at the far end of the room.

We keep walking.

"So you were interested in volunteering?" Rhoda says, leading me into a small, windowless room. She motions for me to sit and she goes around to the other side of the desk and faces me.

"Well," I clear my throat. "I was thinking of volunteering my social media, really," I say, realizing that this doesn't sound as generous as I thought it would. But I just need to explain my thinking. That I've been wondering how I can make a real difference, to use my followers for something good. Not that the fight for women to be child-free by choice *isn't* good, I just wanted to do more. Something Thom-like. And the distraught-looking women I see every time I walk to and from Will's haunt me. There has to be something I can do for these women, too.

"Your social media?" She brushes a strand of hair off her face.

"I could post about the shelter and maybe that would prompt people to donate money or time or something. Just bring more awareness. I can get eyes on your message. Use my feed for good instead of selfies, you know?" I smile.

Her brow furrows, and she clears her throat. "I suppose that could help. But what we need are inspiring women to spend some time around here. I was hoping you were offering to speak to these women about empowerment and self-care. I've watched clips of your talks. You're very supportive of women. Women's choices, women's rights. Of course, many of these women have children and have gone through some terrible ordeals. Some of them have had to leave their children behind to come here and get help. Some are counting down the days until they can see them again." And I feel something pinch inside of me. The idea of these women, desperate and forlorn, who are without their kids, but definitely not by choice, makes my heart ache.

"So the whole child-free debate," Rhoda is saying. "That wouldn't be appropriate here. But I still think you could really empower women and help them to feel good about themselves. And these women could use a bit of that. Because they are strong. So strong. The lives they've lived, the decisions they've had to make, would break almost anyone. But not them. They need to see this in themselves though. They deserve some positivity, to feel good about who they are and the steps they've taken to make some serious changes in their lives." Rhoda leans forward, looking into my eyes. "Steps you couldn't even imagine."

I get it. And it moves something inside of me. I understand her point—not to talk about the child-free life, but of course that's the one part of my life I'm proud of. It's certainly not the rentable furniture, the mattress in a box, the food kits they can't even afford. Who *am* I, who have I become?

Hands gripping the chair arms, I push myself to standing. "I think, maybe, this was a mistake."

But Rhoda studies me. Then she says, quietly, but firmly, "Why don't you meet some of them? Sometimes it's best to see for yourself. We'll have to check that the women are OK with it, of course, and it can only be for a few minutes, but sometimes, it can help. Put a face to what I'm talking about."

I don't argue, but instead follow her down the hall to the room we passed earlier. She tells me to wait at the door, while she speaks to a few women. One follows her back over, sitting at a table, looking at me. "Come on, I'll introduce you. Doreen, this is Kit."

Doreen looks me up and down. "You a social worker?" I shake my head.

"No, Kit's interested in volunteering here."

She nods. "You gonna teach us to needlepoint? How 'bout a Fuck Men coaster?"

I laugh nervously.

"We could sell 'em on my Etsy page."

"You're on Etsy?"

"I'm homeless, not an idiot."

She studies my face, pale, I'm sure, and bursts out laughing. "*Homeless people—they're just like us.*" She spreads her hands wide, as though displaying a headline.

"I'll leave you two," Rhoda says, laughing and shaking her head.

"So whaddaya wanna know?" She folds her hands in front of her, leaning forward onto the table.

I shrug. "I guess, I just wanted to meet you. Find out what you . . . *do* here? This is a place to help get back on your feet, get back out there, right?" My voice is an octave higher, filled with positivity. But Doreen's not buying it.

"Ahh, like get a job, all that. Yeah, yeah, yeah." She doesn't sound very convincing. This woman needs a motivational speech. I clear my throat.

"You know"—I start, but she's staring off into space, her face toward the window.

"Is it warm out there?" she asks. "It looks warm."

I follow her gaze, wondering how often she even goes outside. Surely they *can* go outside whenever they want? "Oh, um, it's nice. You don't need a jacket today."

"My husband hated talking about the weather. Drove him mad. I couldn't even wonder if it was raining without him flying off the handle." She turns back to me. "You married?" I shake my head. "You're lucky. Biggest mistake I ever made. You know he locked me in a closet for two days?"

My hands move to my mouth, as though stopping me, making sure I think before I say anything. But what can I say to this? Suddenly all my thoughts seem frivolous, meaningless. That a few minutes ago I was worried what this woman might think about me—and my career choices. Doreen isn't thinking about me. She's thinking about how she's living here, instead of with a man who locked her in a closet. I lean forward in my chair. "Are you . . . OK?" I ask softly.

"I'm alive, aren't I?"

This is the measure of her life—alive or dead?

"That wasn't the worst thing he did," she continues. "At least I was inside that time. Another time he locked me in the shed out back—middle of winter."

I try to imagine this scenario, what could've happened to enrage her husband to the point that he thought locking her in a shed was the solution, but the images don't come. It feels unreal—like a horror movie. I can't find any words to comfort Doreen, and I feel ashamed of myself. This isn't anything close to what I imagined I'd be doing when I walked into this shelter. How could I have been so naïve as to not consider the awful stories that brought these women here?

"Everyone always asks me why I didn't just leave. Like it was so easy. Of course I wanted to leave. So many times. But my daughter . . . I couldn't leave without her, and I couldn't figure out a way to leave with her, either. Not without him killing me. I kept thinking, if he kills me, what'll happen to her? He'd never done anything to her, but I knew I had to stay alive to protect her, which meant staying with him." She lets out a belly laugh.

"And of course he kept telling me it would never happen again. And like a fool, I believed him."

I think about how lucky I am, to have the life I have. To have never come close to being in the position Doreen was put in. "I'm sure he was convincing," I say. "You wanted to believe the best. You had to believe the best."

"What do they say? A zebra doesn't change its stripes? He was one hell of an asshole-zebra."

I'm quiet, letting her speak. But she's quiet, too. Finally, I ask: "So how did you . . . how did you eventually leave?"

When she doesn't respond I wonder if I shouldn't have asked. But then she nods, and begins to speak. She tells me the story— how she and her daughter eventually got away from him, leaving with nothing—no money, no extra clothes. Just the two of them, together. That it was the only way.

My life feels so easy. And yet, I'm always finding things to complain about. I have nothing stopping me from doing whatever I want with my life.

"So you gonna tell me how to get my life back on track? That's what you're here to do?"

I shake my head. "No. It sounds like your life *is* on track, for now, huh?"

She rolls her eyes. "I'll get there. And he's locked up, so when I do get out, he won't be around. But for now, this is OK. Some of the women are crazy, but there are a few good ones here. I've made some friends." I must make a face because she laughs. "Sometimes you have to paddle through shit river to find your island. It's not Tahiti, but it's pretty good, for now." I think about the women in the No Kidding group, how lucky I felt when I found them, these women who felt like me, who didn't make me feel like the ugly duckling, and yet, how our connection seems so vapid compared to what Doreen and the women here are all dealing with. The biggest issue the No Kidding women face is having to spend an afternoon here or there hanging out with women who have kids and having to talk about motherhood? How ridiculous.

If it weren't for being child-free, would Xiu, Gloria, Casey even be my friends? I haven't told any of them about what's going on with Will, because I'm afraid of how they'll react. Will they shun me from the group I founded because I've broken the group's one rule?

Doreen stands, breaking me out of my thoughts. "I've got to go get my girl from school. I guess I'll see you around here?"

I nod. "It was . . . thanks . . ."

She sticks out her hand. "Nice meeting you . . . ?"

"Kit."

"Kit-Kat. See ya later." She saunters out of the room. I follow her, looking for Rhoda, and find her near the entrance, speaking to another woman. As she walks me out, I turn to her. "I . . . I'm not sure what I could really do to help out here," I say. "But I would like to do something, I think." Rhoda presses a code to unlock the door. "Why don't you give it some thought? You know where to find us."

Doreen is on my mind the rest of the day, and when it's time to go to the No Kidding group, I pause before ordering the Uber. I want to share Doreen's story with the women, to suggest we think of a way to support the shelter, but I worry that even bringing up the topic will raise so many emotions and questions, and I won't be able to stop myself from telling them what's really going on. That my wanting to help those women is partly selfless but mostly selfish, because I'm not finding my own career fulfilling anymore. I worry that talking about it will bring up too much, like the real root of the problem: Will. Addie. All of it.

I think about this as I start walking, and slowly, the realization comes to me: that having children isn't a full-time job; it's *more* than a full-time job. And sure, you can do other things, too—you can have a career *and* have kids—but not in the same way. Because it isn't just about the time it takes to physically care for a child, to walk her to school or make her lunch or help her with homework. It's all the *mental* energy it takes, the interest, the worry, the love, the headspace it takes up to think about someone other than yourself, and not in a way that happens when you're dating someone who is self-sufficient. It's different with Addie. It's thinking for her, about what could affect her. I always knew that motherhood would mean less time left to spend on myself, my career. And now, that's exactly what's happening. If I had never met Will or Addie, I wouldn't be thinking about them right now. And yet, I want to know how Addie's pillow turned out today. I agonize that Gillian's dislike for me is going to affect Addie's friendship with Millie. I worry that I won't have time to get my work done tomorrow and show up for Addie's bake sale. Not to mention finding time tonight to bake muffins for the sale. And yet, I don't want to stop thinking about these things.

When it comes down to it, though, I'd rather be *with* Will and Addie than focusing on how great my life is *without* them. So instead of going to the meeting, I walk toward Will's. It's just before six when I turn onto his street, and I'm looking forward to sitting down to dinner with them. When I open the door, though, I see Gillian in the kitchen with Will. They're laughing, there's music playing, Will's cooking and Gillian's drinking wine. I can see through the back glass that Addie and Millie are in the backyard. I stare at the scene in the kitchen as though I'm looking through a two-way mirror. Then I turn and head back down the stairs before anyone can notice me. I feel like a fool.

I end up at Izzy's half an hour later. "Can I stay here?" I say, and when she opens the door wider, I burst into tears.

seventeen

I end up sleeping at Izzy's, not texting Will until eleven, when I know he'll be in bed and won't bother to argue with me to come home.

Lost track of time with girls. Sleeping at Izzy's. Closer to mtg tmrw anyway.

I hit Send before I can overthink it. When I wake up to see that Will hasn't even replied, my stomach turns. Of course he knows it's an excuse—who cares if the meeting is closer to Izzy's? I don't even have any clothes with me. Izzy's much tinier than I am, and unless I want to borrow oversized sweats, there's no chance of raiding her closet. I hurry to throw on yesterday's clothes and go back to the house, arriving around 7:30. The house smells like a mix of sweet and savory, and my stomach grumbles, belying my rule that I don't bother with breakfast. Will's sitting at the bar reading the newspaper, two plates with the remains of whatever they ate in front of him. They ate at the counter, just the two of them, just like before, because I wasn't there. My stomach clenches, my nerves shot. Did they even miss me?

"Hey," I say.

"Hey." He doesn't look up from the paper.

"Sorry about last night."

Now he looks. "You want to fill me in on that?"

I don't answer, trying to figure out how to explain and where to start—how I was feeling, seeing Gillian, not knowing what to think, but I can't think straight. My heart is pounding so loud it's throbbing in my ears.

"I just . . ." I should've prepared what I wanted to say.

"You can sleep at your sister's or wherever else you want, whenever the hell you want, but if that's the way it's going to be, just say so because I was under the impression you were staying with us." I feel like I'm being reprimanded by a parent, not whatever Will is to me. "I guess *I* didn't know you were having dinner guests because you didn't mention it to me either," I say, crossing my arms over my chest. "How late did Gillian stay?"

He folds the paper and pushes it aside. "I'm not sure. I didn't check the time when she left." His voice is even. He doesn't even flinch. He doesn't ask how I knew she was at the house. He doesn't feel caught in the way I want him to feel.

"I saw you," I say a little too loudly. "The two of you. Here, in the kitchen."

He watches me, gaze steady.

"So what, you thought I wasn't coming home for dinner, so you invited her over instead? I thought that whole thing, you know, when you were in my bedroom, after the last time Gillian came over, and you saying *we* were the ones dating, and you and Gillian were just hanging out, I thought you were saying you choose me." I drop my arms to my sides. "But I guess I got that all wrong. I guess I really am just someone staying with you—a houseguest, nothing more. That's why I'm in the guest room, right?"

"Are you finished?"

"Why?"

"Gillian took the girls swimming after school. She was dropping Addie off, it was dinner time, the girls were starving. I was doing what was best for my daughter, because she's my number one priority." He's cold.

"Having her friend and her mom over is what's best for her? Does that help her eat dinner better? That's bullshit. You invited Gillian because *you* wanted Gillian to be here. Don't pretend it was some sort of selfless Dad act."

"So what if I did? Gillian and I have been friends forever, and our daughters are best friends. Having dinner together makes it nicer for everyone. It could've been you here with us, but it wasn't because you were out with your friends, at your child-free group, pretending you're still living a completely child-free life."

"That has nothing to do with it."

"It has *everything* to do with it."

"I didn't even *go* to the group. And you're just as guilty— don't tell me you would've invited her to stay if I'd been here. You invited her to stay because you like the attention. You know she likes you and is jealous of whatever it is we have going on."

"That's exactly the problem, Kit. The 'whatever we have.' I've told you what I want."

"No, you haven't."

"You're staying in my house, Kit."

I shake my head. "In the guest room. You haven't told Addie. And the signal you just sent me is that if I do anything else, go to dinner with friends, sleep at my sister's, *whatever* it is without you, then you're going to go running to Gillian."

"You're being completely irrational. I'm not going to talk about this right now," he says. "And none of this even really matters right now anyway. You owe Addie an apology. You told her that you would make muffins for the bake sale last night and then you just didn't show. I told her that you probably forgot to tell her about the dinner, and that you wouldn't be that late."

Shit.

"I let her wait up until way past her bedtime. She fell asleep waiting for you, Kit. And this morning she looked for you to make them. I had to tell her that you were at Izzy's and you wouldn't be back in time."

I look up at the square clock on the wall behind Will's head. Maybe it's not too late.

"I took care of it. She has to leave for school in twenty minutes."

#

I find Addie in her bedroom, lying face down on her bed, reading a book.

"Hey," I say but she doesn't look up.

I sit down on the edge of her bed. She shimmies over a bit, to get away from me. My heart sinks. But I don't budge. I lean in. Literally. "I'm really, really sorry about letting you down." I run a hand over her hair.

She flips the page.

"I—got completely caught up in myself. And I get that you are mad at me. *I* would be mad at me."

She turns and looks at me. "We had so much fun yesterday and then you just forgot all about the bake sale. I waited for you. And then we went to make the chocolate chip cookies this morning and there weren't enough chocolate chips because you used them in your stupid muffins. So we had to make sugar cookies instead."

I exhale.

"Don't you think chocolate chip cookies are kind of—expected?" I joke. "I bet no one else makes sugar cookies."

She turns and glares at me.

"OK. Not helpful. What can I do? I want to make it up to you."

"Nothing. If you don't like us then don't live here." She turns away from me.

"What do you mean 'don't like you'? Addie, of course I like you." But of course I know what she means. I *still* haven't talked to her about my Instagram. I just hoped she'd forget. But she's eight, not three. I'm learning there's a big difference—not that I have much more experience with three-year-olds.

"Whatever."

She looks like she's going to get up and I gently reach out to her, my hand grazing her arm.

"Can we talk about Instagram?"

She doesn't say anything.

"What if—your school implemented a dress code." I'm not ready for this conversation, but here goes.

"What do you mean?" she asks. "Like, they told us what to wear?"

"Yeah, sort of. Like they told you that you had to wear the white school dress shirt and sweater, but they gave you the option of wearing a gray skirt or gray pants. And all the girls decided to wear the skirts because—"

"That would never happen. We would all choose the pants. They're way more comfortable."

"OK, then you all chose the pants. Except for three girls. Name some of your school friends."

"Chi-chi, Millie and Lauren."

"OK so Chi-chi, Millie and Lauren decide to wear skirts. Every day." I pause for dramatic effect. She turns to me, waiting for me to continue. I've got her attention. "And everyone teases them. All the time. They don't let them skip rope with them at recess . . ."

"No one skips rope at recess! We're not five. Oh my god, this story is so lame."

"OK, so . . . hang out by the . . . *fence*." Surely, they hang out by the fence.

Addie looks at me like I'm killing her slowly. I push on. "They don't get to sit with anyone at lunch, they don't even get invited to birthday parties . . ."

"This is dumb. I doubt Chi-chi would ever choose to wear a skirt but even if she did, we wouldn't *care*," she huffs.

"Right, because she should get to choose whatever she wants to wear and not have to explain why she wants to wear a skirt instead of pants."

"Well, yeah. Because the school said you could wear either. And she isn't hurting anyone by wearing a skirt." She gets up and wanders over to her desk. "Why are we talking about this?" I realize I'm about to lose her.

"I was trying to make a comparison. I promise to get to the point." She picks up a sketchbook and pencil, then returns to the bed, flipping the pad open to a blank page.

"So, in life," I say, "some people think that women have to have children. That they have to *want* to have children, and even if they don't want them, they should have them anyway, because that's what you're supposed to do."

"But no one makes you have children if you don't want to," she says slowly, head down. She's right, of course, and incredibly wise for her age.

"No, but it's expected. Like, it's the default. You get to a certain age, you get married, people think you should have kids." I take a minute to gauge Addie's reaction, but she's focused on the page. So—no clue how this is going. "I don't think it should be like that. Women have all sorts of reasons for not wanting children."

"Like what?" Addie says, not looking up.

I take a deep breath. "Well, maybe they don't want the life-style that having kids can sometimes mean, or maybe they love their career and it's not the kind of career that really works with being a mom, like a pilot or an ER doctor or even a travel writer. Or maybe they just don't think that they'll be able to be the kind of mom a child deserves to have." At this a lump forms in my throat, and I take a moment. "Or," I clear my throat, "maybe there's another reason, and it's private and they don't want to have to explain to people why they don't want children . . . but they feel like they have to. And that's not fair."

I touch her knee and she looks up, her eyes meeting mine for a moment. "I guess the thing is, I've had this career where I decided to defend these women, and in doing so, I've met so many women like this, and I have the opportunity to speak up for them, to show them that it's OK to not want to have children and to help others see that having kids isn't the *only* way."

I swipe at an unexpected tear. "I really like the role I have had for these women. I like supporting them." I pull my phone out. "My Instagram isn't a fair representation of that. It's the 'sassy' side of that, I guess you could say. That message, what I believe in, doesn't totally come out. And I'm sorry that's the side you've seen." Addie's watching me. "Does that make sense?"

"I guess," Addie says. "It's just hard not to think that if you don't like kids then you don't like me."

I nod, discouraged that she *still* thinks I don't like kids. But right now, all that matters is that she knows how I feel about her. "I really like you," I say. "Like, more than I've liked any kid I've ever met." I wipe another tear from the corner of my eye before it falls.

"Does that mean you want to come help at the bake sale?"

"Absolutely," I say, having no idea what I'm getting myself into.

#

When I arrive at Addie's school, there have to be two dozen women lined up outside the front doors, as though it's a sample sale, not a bake sale. Do they really need me, too? But I'm not doing this for me, I'm doing it for Addie. Who knows? Maybe it'll be fun. I spot Gillian near the front of the line, looking at me. I wave, but she turns the other way as the doors open and the women file into the main hallway. I try not to let it get to me—it's not like I *want* to hang out with Gillian anyway. And yet, I feel self-conscious and could use a familiar face— even if it's not friendly. I step inside the building, with its musty smell and tile flooring and I'm transported back to being a kid myself. The smell of pizza wafts toward me and I remember the excitement of Pizza Day. As I follow the women in front of me, I wonder why there are no men helping out. We reach half a dozen tables set up to create one long table stretching half a hallway. As though well trained in this event, women start filing behind the table, grabbing brown paper napkins, paper plates, juice boxes. Someone hands me a wad of papers and Scotch tape and orders me to start hanging the signs. I study them: *Cheese, Pepperoni, Apple, Orange, Chocolate Milk, 2% Milk.* I've just finished taping them to the wall when Gillian rallies us all together for a picture.

"We haven't met before," the woman beside me says. She has long brown hair, pulled back in a messy bun, and lots of bangles on her wrist. She's wearing a black name tag with silver font that reads *Preesha Patil (Saavi's mom).*

"Oh, I'm—"

"She's not a mom," Gillian interjects and I notice she's wearing a similar name tag.

"Just a friend," I say brightly. "Kit."

"Preesha." She smiles. "God, you're a saint. If I didn't have a kid here I would *not* be helping out."

"Oh, come on, Preesha. That's because you wouldn't have time. From here it's dry cleaning drop-off, clean the house, grocery shop, get back here for pickup, after-school activities, make dinner, bedtime, collapse into bed. Until you have kids, you don't *get* everything we do. That's why I'm taking the picture, so I can send it to you later and you can remind yourself how us moms are the reason any of this happens."

"You're always thinking of everything," Preesha says kindly.

"Well, we all know it's not just about showing up for an hour today." She gives me a fake smile.

Thankfully, the conversation is cut short as kids start tearing down the hall like it's the running of the bulls, and another mom turns to me—*Daria Kimble (Tatum's mom)*—and tells me to get into position. I secure a spot at the bake sale section, hoping it'll be less crazy. Kids are dropping pizza on the floor, screaming that they ordered orange juice not apple juice. Most of the moms are expressionless, though, as if they're soldiers on the front line.

"Hello! Excuse me, hi, yoo-hoo," Daria is saying, hitting my arm, and I refocus. "You can't just let them grab the baked goods like that." She swats at a boy who's going in for a chocolate chip cookie. "They have to pay me their quarter and then they can point to the item they want and then you hand it to them with a napkin." She shakes her head at me.

"Oh, OK," I say, handing the kid the cookie he wants.

"Not that one. The big one." I look to Daria but she tsk-tsks him.

"You get what you get, and you don't get upset."

I shrug and hand the kid the cookie. "You heard her."

He slinks off.

Addie shows up a few minutes later. I'm so relieved to see her. "Are there any of my cookies left?" she asks, scanning the table. "Ooh, great," she says, spotting the container. "Can I get one?"

I hand her a cookie and she takes a bite. "They're really good." She hands me another quarter. "You have to try one."

"Thanks," I say, feeling touched. I choose one of her sugar cookies and take a bite.

"No eating while you're working!" someone yells and I look to my right to see a few of the other moms glaring at me. I shove the rest of the cookie into my mouth and suppress a laugh to Addie. "Really good," I mumble with my mouth full. She laughs and waves as she disappears down the hall. I'm watching her walk away, thinking how glad I am that I did this, even if I did have to bail on two events to be here, when someone screams.

I look to where a crowd has gathered. A boy about Addie's age is lying on the ground. "He's in anaphylactic shock!" someone says. A woman pops up and yells to call 911.

"He has an epi-pen. Get his epi-pen. In his pant pocket!" There are shouts in every direction and people moving kids out of the way, moving other adults in, the rest of us watching, not sure what to do. Someone announces that an ambulance is on the way.

Just then a tall man walks over, looking large and in charge. The principal, I'm guessing.

"Ben has a peanut allergy," he says, looking distraught. "Do any of these bake sale items have nuts?" He looks to me and I look down at the table. Nothing is labelled—my guess is as good as anyone's what's in any of the items. A second later Gillian is hovering and pointing at a tin of chocolate balls. "These obviously have nuts—look, you can see them." She glares at me. "Did you give Ben one of these balls?"

I don't know what Ben ate, though I do remember handing the balls to a few kids. "I—I'm not sure."

"Did you *make these*?" Gillian accuses me and I shake my head.

"No, I—I didn't make anything."

"Who let you work the bake table? You have to inspect *everything*. No peanuts are allowed. You would know that if you were actually a parent," she spits, then turns to the man. "She's not even a parent."

He looks preoccupied, but another mom looks over.

"You're not a parent?"

"Who signed you up?"

"Did you do the police check?"

"Did you sign in at the office?"

"Why would you work the bake table if you've never helped out before? Everyone knows you have to be on high alert for nuts."

I feel overwhelmed and out of my element. What made me think I had any right to swoop in here and be one of the moms? I can't just decide to get in on a life like this. These women earned their right to be here. They know what to do. I'm not like them. But then, I give my head a shake. This isn't about me.

"Is the boy—is Ben OK?" I ask the woman beside me.

"He's going to be fine," someone else says. "We've moved him into the nurse's room and his parents are already here."

The principal announces that the bake sale is over, and instructs us to throw all the baked goods out in case they've been contaminated. I silently clean up the table, wiping it down with brown paper napkins. No one speaks to me, but that's OK. Then I grab a garbage bin and haul it outside, tying the bag and tossing it into one of the large dumpsters behind the school. I'm on my way back in when Gillian stops me. "We've got more than enough help. You can go."

I think about fighting her on this, but this is her school, these are her mom friends, not mine. It doesn't matter what I do, I'll never be one of them. I disappear through the closest door, out onto the street.

#

I'm still feeling shaken when Will texts me later in the afternoon and tells me to meet him at the gates to the amphitheater on the water at six, which immediately takes away the

apprehension I'd been feeling all day about our fight this morning. A night alone, with him, is exactly what I need after the
day I've had. This afternoon my landlord called to say it's going
to be another month until I can move home, and I completely
forgot about an influencer event I was being paid to attend, in
addition to the meeting I had to reschedule because of Pizza
Day—but when I see Will standing at the gates, waiting for
me, all of it feels meaningless. He has a large canvas bag over
one shoulder, and as I get closer, he gives me a sly smile that
sends flutters through me. "Hey," he says, leaning in toward me.
"Hey," I say before my lips are on his. I'm about to ask what
we're doing, when I realize what day it is. "You got tickets to the
Meanderers?" I say in disbelief.

He nods.

"How? I tried to get tickets a few weeks ago and it was sold
out." I squeeze him tight and he puts his arm around me, then
we make our way into the lineup to get through the gates. Will
flashes the tickets to the security guards at the gates but when
they ask Will to open his bag, they tell him he can't bring in any
outside food or drink. "Ahh, shit," he says. "How did I not realize
this would be a problem?" "I guess the secret's out that I haven't
been to a concert in years."

We move out of the way and for a moment, neither of us
says anything. Then I tell him to follow me. We walk down the
hill that leads to the parking lot, and along the edge between
the walking path and the water, until we come to a cut through a
set of trees. I bring him up a hill and across the grass to another
area that's hidden behind another set of trees until there's a
clearing overlooking the water.

"Whoa, this is a great spot," he says, looking around.

"I know. I discovered it years ago—no one's ever here when I come."

Will shrugs off his backpack and then begins pulling out items—a bottle of wine, a Tupperware filled with cheese and grapes and salami. Then he pulls out a baguette.

"I'm glad you didn't have to throw this out—this is a spread."

"Yeah well, I like to think I can pull together a good meal." Will pulls out a blanket and lays it on the grass, then hands me two plastic cups. When he goes to open the bottle of wine, he realizes there's a cork.

"Amateur move," he says, then pulls his bike lock key out of his pocket and jams it into the cork and pushes it into the bottle. "Not very classy, but it does the job." He pours the wine. "Cheers," he says. We clink our plastic cups together and then take a sip.

"This is really nice," I say.

"Yeah, well, I'm a really nice guy." He moves in closer to me. "I'm glad you showed up."

"I'm sorry about last night," I say. "I think it's clear I'm jealous of Gillian. Or maybe I would've felt the same way if I'd seen you with any other woman."

He takes my cup, puts it down and then his lips are on mine. The kiss is soft and tender and everything feels so right. He pulls back and looks into my face. "I feel like we're fighting about all this because you feel insecure about your place. Kit, you mean so much to me. Maybe you moving in was a crazy idea, but it felt so natural. And when you weren't there last night, the place felt empty. I want you in my house every day. Morning, night, any time you want."

I laugh nervously. "Be careful what you wish for."

"What do you mean?" He tilts his head.

I give him the flood update. "But insurance is covering me for a short-term rental so . . ." I trail off.

Will's brow furrows. "So, you're just going to move out?"

"Well, I was thinking, it could be fun. We could just date. No domestic obligations. We didn't really *have* that, and that's the most fun part."

"I think it's all been pretty great. You, being around. I don't want you to move out. Just keep crashing with us."

My heart is pounding. Is he asking me to move in—permanently?

I shake my head. "Will—"

"I'm serious. There's no good reason why you shouldn't. You're going to move to one tiny place until you can move back to your tiny place, and be alone again? Don't be stupid."

The way he says it rubs me the wrong way. As though I'm not complete if I'm living alone in a shoebox apartment.

"There's nothing wrong with my apartment, and I like living alone." As soon as the words are out, I feel bad, but also relief, because it's the truth. I miss my apartment. I miss having my own space. I miss the quiet, the ability to control when there *is* quiet.

Will gives me a hard stare.

I try to backtrack. "I don't mean I don't appreciate you letting me stay with you. It's just all a bit quick. The domestic stuff, and I've let a lot of my work slide . . ." This feels unfair to throw in, because frankly, it's been such a relief to have an excuse to bail on some of the contracts that I couldn't shoot in my place. But Will throws up his hands, exasperated, interrupting me before I can continue.

"Kit, I'm thirty-eight. I've been married, I have a kid. I'm not messing around here. That 'domestic stuff' is my life, and it's part of the whole deal. I thought I'd made it pretty clear that I'm only interested in you—if I wanted to date other people, I wouldn't want you staying with me. Sure, maybe the way we've gone about this isn't conventional, but what difference does it make if we end up in the same place?"

My heart is pounding, and my breath is caught in my throat. I have to say something. Anything.

"Can we just, have a nice date? You planned this and I don't want to fight with you."

"This isn't fighting, Kit. This is discussing—our future."

"You know what? You should do this." I wave my hand at the spread. "Picnics. You prepare it, people order it, you could even do adorable picnic baskets. You could get wine glasses with your logo that they could keep, and reuse, and every time they did, they'd think of you, and re-order. Their friends would ask, 'What's this awesome picnic business you're always going on about?'" I pull out my phone and snap a few photos of the spread to show him. But he's just staring at me. I keep rambling.

"See?" I say, scrolling through the photos. "This one is so good. Just let me start an Instagram account for you. You don't have to tell anyone about it, it could just be there, and you could add photos when you want. And then, if you change your mind . . ." I know, as I'm doing this, that I'm being crazy. But I can't stop.

But he's shaking his head. "Kit, what the fuck?" He pauses. Exhales. "I don't want an Instagram account. How many times do I have to tell you that?"

"Right. But you wouldn't have to do anything, I'm saying. I could manage it for you. I could transition my job into managing other people's social media. You could be my first client.

We could call it 'Good Will Cooking.'" I click on the Instagram icon, but my @BookKit account is open. "What's that?" Will asks, leaning closer.

"Oh, it's just . . . something I've been toying with doing." My heart pounds. Why haven't I told Will about this? He, of anyone, would be so supportive of me changing paths.

"Kit, it's me. Tell me."

He's leaning over my shoulder.

"Well, it's this dream I have, I just never make enough time to figure out exactly how to make it happen because . . ." An alert pops up at the top of the page, saying I've been tagged in a photo, on my @KitwithoutKids account. I tap the alert.

"Is that you?" Will says, pointing at the screen.

"Yeah, I guess." I scroll down to the caption.

We'd be nothing without our volunteers. Another successful pizza lunch and bake sale at Alexander the Great elementary school. #school-life #lifewithkids

"Shoot," I say, staring at the picture of us, the large Pizza Stop boxes front and center in the photo.

"What?" Will says, leaning close. "That's awesome that you did that. Addie was really glad you came."

"It's not going to go over well if Napoli Pizzeria sees this. I had a non-compete clause for a month and I just posted for them last week." Pizza Stop isn't exactly the same experience as dining in the chic southern Italian pizzeria-and-wine bar that opened on Ossington last month, but I definitely remember there being a non-compete clause. "I've got to get them to untag me."

"Really, Kit? This wasn't work. It's your life. Your *real* life. Surely the clients understand the difference."

My heart races. I close my eyes for a second, trying to quell my anxiety. "Of course they understand the difference, but it's in my contract *not* to post about competitors. And my account is work."

I stare at the photo, thinking of how ironic it is that Gillian tagged me when she didn't even want me there. "And my persona, @KitwithoutKids, isn't supposed to be hanging out with a bunch of kids, either," I say, "especially not when I bumped a meeting today to be there. It just looks bad. *So* bad."

"Wow," Will says, sounding exasperated, which doesn't make me feel any better. "You really are caught up in yourself. If anything, I'd say it's a bit tacky that whoever posted this did so when it sounds like one of the kids could've died today, from what Addie told me—but you're not even thinking of that. You're so worried what people will think if they see you with kids? News flash. No one cares."

I pull away and look at him to see if he's joking. "You don't understand. My followers will care. It's called authenticity. Being on brand. They look to me for validation that their child-free life is the right choice. They buy my book and come to my talks. It's less than two weeks till I'm going to be standing on a stage in front of ten thousand women who choose to be there, listening to me. Wanting me to inspire them to continue doing what they're doing, being successful in business and in life and in love without children. I can't have them going on Instagram, and—whoops! There I am, volunteering at a pizza lunch for children, with a bunch of other moms. Like, what a fake."

I look down at my phone, and notice there are more than fifty comments, and this photo was only posted a few hours ago. I scroll through them, my hands shaking as I read them all.

Why's the woman who hates kids around our kids?

She doesn't technically hate kids—she just thinks life is way better without them.

Since when do we allow non-parents to volunteer? Seems a bit risky and unnecessary?

Is this someone we want influencing our children? To let them know that life is better without them?

Who can Photoshop her out and make sure she doesn't show up again?

Isn't she the one that almost killed the kid with the nuts?

"I should never have gone." I hold the phone out to Will so he can read the comments. I drop my head into my hands.

He shrugs. "Yeah, they're harsh, but you've probably seen worse. And I can see where they're coming from. They don't know you, they don't know what you're like. But I don't blame them for feeling that way. You know, maybe it's time you think about changing your Instagram account."

"To what? Kit *with* Kids?" I spit, annoyed. "I can't just *change* my account."

"Why not?" He shrugs. "At least it would be more real." He puts my phone down and moves closer to me.

I push him away. "Because Addie isn't my kid. And there are five billion mommyfluencers out there already. That's why I stand out. I'm *not* one of them. This isn't just an account, it's my brand, it's my business. It's who I am. This is how I'm known. I can't stray from this, not one bit, or I lose followers."

I stare at my phone as another comment appears on the post. I click on the photo and a picture of Addie pops up.

"Is that Addie?" Will says, peering at my phone.

Shit.

It's not a bad picture, just a typical tween pic: doe-eyed selfie with a filter. But exactly why he doesn't want her to have an account.

"Does she have an Instagram account?" he asks me.

I look away.

"You *knew* this? Is this how she knew about your account? Fuck. Give me your phone." He holds out his hand and I reluctantly pass the phone over. As he taps on her name and scrolls through her account, his eyes narrow. I lean over his shoulder, looking at her pics, then see the one I took of us at Centre Island. I'm touched she posted it, but realize she must not have tagged me. I should feel relief that there isn't another kid-friendly pic of me out there, but I'm also ashamed. Did she purposely not tag me because she knew I wouldn't want her to?

"This is because of you," Will spits. "I told you I didn't want her exposed to this . . . did you set the account up for her?"

"No!" I practically yell, then look around and lower my voice even though there's no one around us. "No. She already had the account long before I even met her."

"But you knew about it and you didn't tell me?" He's shaking my phone at me.

"I told her I wouldn't. She asked me not to tell you because she knew you'd be angry. I was trying to be a good friend to her." I grab the phone, slamming it face-down on the blanket.

"You're not supposed to be a friend. You're supposed to be a *parent*." A vein is bulging in Will's forehead.

"I'm *not* a parent. *You're* her parent. And if she didn't want you to know then maybe you need to think about that." A tear escapes the corner of my eye and I swipe at it, refusing to let myself feel bad about this situation. This is not my fault, this is *not* my problem.

"Don't tell me how to be a good father. I have to protect her from growing up too fast. She's eight, Kit. She's not a teenager. I told you I didn't want her exposed to this fake world you live in. You knew that. The whole thing is such . . . bullshit."

"Bullshit? Well that *bullshit* is my career. It's my entire life."

"Yeah, where you mislead everyone into believing you're someone you're not. Have you even shown your followers that your apartment is flooded? Do they know you had to move out? If your online life is your entire life, then what—whatever you have with me, with Addie and me, it just . . . doesn't exist?"

"No. But that's not my job. Despite what is happening in my life, my job is my job. My life with you is just one part. And this whole setup is temporary."

"Temporary?" He shakes his head. "That's the thing. You siphon yourself into these various personas, but why can't you just be *you,* all you, one person? It's weird to have all these different pieces. You go from being so great with Addie, to not bothering to come home without letting me know, to being worried about what people will think . . ."

"That's not fair," I say. "It was one night. And I did come home. I just left, because I was jealous." I look down. "Of Gillian."

"Then say that. Tell me you're jealous. Act like an adult. Sometimes I feel like the second your apartment is fixed you're going to be out of here, going right back to your single life. Like you never want to move on because that would mean committing to something, to someone. And you're too afraid to do that."

"I'm not afraid to commit. I was with Eric for five years."

"Yeah, and now you're not. As soon as he wanted something more from you, something serious, something that would bind you forever, you bolted. Just like you're bolting now."

His eyes are fixed on me, daring me to challenge him.

"Let me ask you something—what was the last honest thing you wrote on Instagram?" he says.

I bristle at his question. I have enough people approving my posts, having a say in my persona, criticizing who I am—and they're all involved in my career. Who is Will to question this part of my life, when he's never once shown any interest in it— let alone ever been supportive of it? "I am not dishonest—I'm aspirational. It's curated. It's not inspiring to show people I'm living in a messy house full of marker stains on every surface, dirty dishes in the sink and socks on the couch. Sorry, but it's true. And I don't *force* anyone to follow me on Instagram. I'm not holding a gun to anyone's head."

"But you're leading them to believe that to have a great life they need to be ziplining through the Rockies and at fancy parties every other night. You give the impression that you live in a place with multiple sitting areas, rather than a tiny rented apartment because that's the stage of life you're in." He sounds really angry, and it makes me wonder how long he's been thinking about this. "And I don't even know what you post, but I can sure as hell bet it has nothing to do with us. God forbid someone finds out you're hanging out with some dude and his *kid*. For all I know you're rehashing old photos or pretending you're on vacation while you wait to get back to your place. One foot out the door." He shakes his head.

His words sting, because they're true. Because digging up old photos is exactly what I've been doing, knowing it's deceitful and yet, like a child sneaking an extra cookie, I've been unable to stop. Easier to find beautiful, curated photos than have to work out how to shoot new stuff in his place. I know I should admit this. Let him win the fight. But I won't, because I don't want him thinking he can influence my career. I have spent so many years bringing women up, reminding them they're enough without anyone else, and I'm not going to sit here and let Will think he has any influence over my life, or my career.

The words are there, on the tip of my tongue, and I let them spill out.

"I wouldn't be moving back into my apartment for long anyway, even if I *were* to move back into it. It's temporary. It always has been. Until I buy my own house. That's always been the plan." I say this to make him see that I have a plan. That I'm not the person he's accusing me of being. "That's what I was about to tell you about—the business idea I have."

"You're going to buy a house?" He's staring at me.

"Yes. With a garage. And then—" Just starting to tell him about it makes it feel real. Because if I really make the book garage a business, then I won't *have* to worry about a pizzeria campaign and whether someone tagged me in a photo or not.

He holds up a hand. "You know what? I don't actually need to hear this. You're looking for a house and you're living with me and I have a house and you won't just stay with me? I thought this"—he motions to the space between us—"was going somewhere. Everyone said it was a mistake to get involved with you and I didn't listen. I told them they didn't understand. But they were right. And I was definitely wrong."

"Oh, who was right? Gillian? Margot? Yeah, I guess they knew me *so* well. And yeah, you were wrong about me," I say, standing up. "So there you go. Don't worry about wasting your time on me anymore. You're officially free to go date some other *mom* who can be the co-parent and perfect little housewife you want her to be. I'm done." I turn and walk across the grass, through the trees, and down the hill, not looking back.

eighteen

I wake up with what I think is a hangover, until I remember that I didn't actually drink that much last night. Then the night—all of it—comes rushing back to me. I stare at the stucco ceiling and remember I'm at Izzy's. Again.

It's early and the apartment is quiet, but I creep into the kitchen and make myself a coffee and then crawl back into bed with the book I found on the nightstand in the guest room. My phone buzzes, alerting me to post today's photo, but when I look at the picture—one of me on the beach last year, with a caption about dreaming of a tropical getaway—I think about what Will said. So what if this isn't a picture of something I'm actually doing at this very minute—my pictures aren't fake. I hit Post, and then shut off my phone.

In the afternoon, I join Izzy on the balcony, where she's attacking weeds that are growing between the cracks of paving stones with a knife. "I bet Roddy'll let you stay another night if I tell him what a big help you've been around here." She grins. "There's another set of gloves and a knife in the bucket over there."

I grab the floral gloves and a knife. "I'm going to go visit Dad for a bit," I tell her.

"I was only joking," she says but then straightens to look at me. "What happened?"

I kneel on the hard concrete and run the knife through the crack to loosen a prickly weed. "I should've listened to you. You were right. It would have never worked out. The kids-no-kids thing is a deal breaker. I don't know why I ever thought I could get around it."

"For the record, I think I came around on that too. You two seemed great together. But let me ask you: the kid thing. Do you really think you can't come around on it?"

Izzy, of all people, has never said anything like this to me. And yet, I don't mind that she is asking now. I glance over at her, then shrug. "Look at us. We're Kiddings. We don't have kids. Obviously there's something in us that has made us not want them. Probably because we could never be as good a mom as Mom was. I mean, she was perfect."

Izzy looks at me, her eyes wide, then bursts out laughing. "Perfect?! Mom?!"

When I don't say anything, her voice softens. "Do you really believe that? I mean, Kit, no one is perfect. Don't you remember how she would always overcook pork chops? And she could never fix any of our clothes if a button fell off or the fabric got a rip. And she'd yell at us if we didn't make our beds . . . she wasn't *perfect*, whatever constitutes perfection."

I shake my head. "No, I don't . . . I don't remember that. I barely remember anything."

Izzy stares at me for a moment. "Of course you don't. You were too young."

"I keep trying to bring up those memories—to think about what Mom would've done if I'd had a bake sale or a school project. I'm constantly searching my brain for memories, so I can know how to be with Addie. Like, what was Mom like with me? But I always come up blank. There's nothing there. Or, almost nothing of the mundane everyday stuff. And then she just goes and fucking dies."

Izzy takes off her gloves and wipes her forehead. "What are you talking about?"

I put my head between my knees so I can breathe. "Nothing. Forget it."

"Kit," she says, "Mom loved us so much. I always forget how young you were. How different it must have been for you. Yes, she made our Halloween costumes, she did our hair every morning for school. I remember you used to hate getting your hair done. You'd run around the house and Mom would have to catch you. She'd kind of pin you between her knees and start singing. And you loved her singing so it always worked. But she got cancer, Kit. She was so tired. And everything was hard. She couldn't do anything anymore. If she wasn't throwing up, she was lying down. I remember the last time she did my hair, but I didn't know it was the last time. But I wish I did. She put my hair in French braids, but I'd wanted Dutch ones. So I took them out. Right in front of her. I was going to tell her to redo it, but I saw the look on her face, how tired she was. And I knew. I fucking knew." Izzy's eyes well up with tears and I have to look away. "She was such a good mom," she says. "She really was. But she wasn't perfect. No one is."

"So then why didn't you want to be a mom?"

Izzy stabs at a large weed. "I did. I always wanted kids." At this, I sit down on a patio chair. The weeds can wait.

"Really?"

Izzy nods. "I always pictured myself as a mom. Not with a million kids, but definitely two."

"Then why did you and Roddy always say you never wanted them?"

"We didn't always say that. We tried. Right after we got married. And I couldn't. We didn't want to go through IVF or adoption. We just felt that it would be too much. The waiting, the hoping, the disappointment. You always hear about marriages ending over the turmoil that can cause. So we made a decision. We wouldn't have kids. We told everyone we didn't want them, so that people would stop asking, stop offering advice on what they thought we should do. It was between me and Roddy. That's how we wanted it."

I sit, stunned, as waves of emotions hit me. First, simple shock that this is my sister's truth. Then hurt that I never knew that she wanted children. Then embarrassment that I had no idea she had gone through any of that in private, and that I wasn't there to support her. Then betrayal that she never confided in me that this was a decision they had made.

"You could've talked to me."

"Yeah, I could've. But then we would have spent months, maybe years talking about it, or not talking about it. And it would always be there. As it was, you, Dad and Roddy's family accepted our decision. And life moved on. Our lives became about everything else, not about trying or not trying or kids, kids, kids, kids, kids."

But what if I'd known that my sister wanted kids? What if I'd known they had tried to have them? Or what if she had had children? If she had become a mom, would I have wanted to be one too? Would seeing her with children—with my nieces or nephews—have convinced me that I could do it too? Would it have ignited an instinct that I was sure I didn't have? Instead of me just deciding to shun the whole damn thing?

nineteen

Dad's waiting for me at the train station when I get off, my overnight bag in hand. He grins and gives me a big hug. "Katherine," he says warmly. "What a treat."

"Is it, though? I'm sure you wish I could have driven myself so you didn't have to wait for me here."

"Nonsense. Gets me out of the house."

"Coffee?" I ask as we pull out of the station. Stopping for a coffee and a donut whenever I come home has always been our little ritual.

"I've got something better," he says, and he turns left instead of the usual right heading toward downtown. "A new gourmet donut place just opened on Queen. They're as big as your head, and we won't need to eat again until dinner."

"But how's the coffee?"

"It's OK. But we don't go for the coffee." *We?* I doubt Dad's going for coffee with his mah-jong buddies.

Dad hasn't dated anyone since Mom died. When I was younger I always wanted him to marry our next-door neighbor Mrs. Theroux, or my art teacher Miss Simian. Sometimes I'd even fantasize about him marrying my best friend Julie's mom so we could be sisters, the way we always thought we were meant to be. Now it's been so long that I can't decide if he's still so romantic about Mom that he'd never remarry or if he's just too set in his ways to ever be with anyone else.

With donuts and coffee in hand, Dad and I walk back to the car.

"To what do I owe the pleasure of your trip home?"

I take a bite of my Boston cream at just the right moment to give me a chance to pause before I answer. I shrug and say, "I guess I was just feeling a little homesick."

As he pulls into the driveway, I notice it's been widened, the row of flowering shrubs leading up to the house now gone.

"You widened the driveway? You never told me."

"Oh, you know, most homes have wider driveways nowadays, so you can fit more cars."

He motions to a metal sign at the curb. "They also took away the street parking in the neighborhood."

"But you only have one car," I point out. "Who else needs to park in our driveway?"

"You never know," he says.

Inside, the house is mostly the same as it was when I left home. My friends all have their tales of woe, of their parents turning their bedrooms into workout rooms or sewing rooms, or selling their childhood home altogether to downsize. But Dad has hardly changed anything.

I bring my bag upstairs to my room. Stepping into my room is like stepping back in time. My twin bed, with its pink-and-green quilt overtop, is still pushed up against the wall. Sports trophies sit on my dresser. Nancy Drew books still line my bookcase.

I pull out *The Secret of the Old Clock* and open it. I thumb over my tween-written name on the inside cover.

I think of Addie, and wonder if she's ever read a Nancy Drew book. It makes me sad to think I may never find out.

I slide the book back into place and head back downstairs.

Dad's in the kitchen, arranging wildflowers in a vase. "Pretty," I say, wondering when he started buying fresh flowers.

I pull out my phone and click over to Addie's Instagram, but it's gone. I guess Will made her take it down.

Then I flick over to Gillian's account. And there he is. Will. And Gillian. They're sitting by the side of an indoor pool, while Addie and Millie splash around. Anyone looking at this photo would think they were a family. A nice, happy family. I zoom in to Will's face. He's laughing. Looking at his dimple hurts. Addie's also laughing. Why wouldn't she be? Maybe she'll get the sister–best friend deal. I turn off my phone and toss it into a kitchen catch-all drawer, slamming it shut.

"I've got an idea," Dad says. I look at him, suspecting he didn't just "come up" with whatever idea he's about to propose. "Why don't you help me take down the shed?" Out the window, the shed is the same one we've had in the yard ever since I can remember.

"The *shed*? Why?"

Dad sighs. "It's starting to rot and the mice are getting in. It's time for it to go."

"But what about all the stuff inside?" Pool toys we haven't used in years come to mind.

"A lot of it's junk. Time to toss. And I'll get another shed. A pre-fab one from Home Depot."

"A pre-fab one? From Home Depot?"

But Dad's already gone outside.

If I'm going to tear down a shed, I should probably change out of my silk top. I go upstairs and to his bedroom. After Mom died, Dad kept their room exactly the same for a really long time, even leaving her clothes in the drawers, her jewelry box on the dresser and her perfume bottles on the vanity. Then, slowly, he started to get rid of her things. He'd periodically ask me if I wanted something—a ring, a sweater, an old bottle of perfume. I always said no. I didn't want anything to remind me that she wasn't using her things. That she was gone. Now, the room looks like a bed-and-breakfast. Impersonal, old-fashioned charm. I run my hand over the top of the dresser, the wood smooth under my palm. Was keeping everything as it was for so long the reason he never found anyone new to love? Like how Sophie's imprint is still everywhere at Will's? Did Dad ever meet someone, only to have them quickly realize that they could never compete with a ghost?

I pull open the bottom drawer, find an old T-shirt and meet Dad outside.

He hands me an ax. It's heavier than I expect. "Just give it a whirl."

I study the shed for a moment, then inhale. Finding my balance, I heave the ax over my shoulder and then wail on the shed. The roof collapses instantly.

"See?" Dad says. "Better days."

A few more swings and I find my rhythm. It feels good.

Over the shoulder, heave forward, remove the ax.

Fuck you, Will, for making me feel special.

Fuck you, Addie, for reminding me of love.

Over the shoulder, heave forward, remove the ax.

Fuck you, Gillian, for stealing them from me.

Over the shoulder, heave forward, remove the ax.

Fuck you, Izzy, for wanting babies and not telling me.

And one last time. Over the shoulder, heave forward, remove the ax.

Fuck you, Mom. For dying.

Panting, I lean the ax against the rubble of the shed. For the first time in a long time I feel like I'm finally being honest with myself.

#

"No rush, but maybe, at some point, you could take a look through some of your things in the basement?"

Dad and I are at the kitchen table, iced drinks in front of us.

"My things? Why?"

"To see what you want to take back."

"Take back? I don't even have an apartment right now. What's going on? First the driveway, then the shed and now I have to clear out my things?"

"Oh, Kitty," Dad says leaning forward, taking my hand. "There's something I need tell you. I met someone." He's looking into my face, waiting for my reaction. And of course, I'm shocked, but also, I knew. I had to have known.

"Met someone? Who?" I say.

"A woman. Jeannie. I think you'd really like her. Or not." He chuckles. "Your sister likes her."

"Izzy? Izzy met your girlfriend? When?"

"A few months ago."

I stand and grab the table for support. "A few *months* ago? Why haven't I met her?"

"Well, this reaction, for one. Please, Kitty, sit down."

I do as he says.

"You've always been my little girl," he says, "and I worried how you'd take it. You were so young when your mom died. It hit you so hard. And it probably still affects you. The last thing I want is to make things even harder on you."

"I'm thirty-three, Dad. A grown-up. I can handle it." But without warning, I start to cry. Big heavy tears, and soon I'm sobbing. But the lack of driver's license, not wanting kids, my lifestyle . . . it's all there, mocking me. If Mom were still here, how different would I be?

Dad puts his hand on mine. And it's so full of warmth and love. And sadness. I rest my forehead on it. And I wish I could go back. All the way back. Start all over. Hold on to more. Admit my sadness, admit my loneliness. Admit that I was afraid. But maybe, I'd do it all anyway. I lift my head and rub my face, trying to absorb the tears into my palms.

"Tell me about Jeannie."

He tells me how they met in an aquafit class. How she lives halfway across town but they see each other every day. How they walk, get their groceries together, help each other garden. How they've even joined a bridge group together. How they're talking about maybe moving in together. It doesn't seem to make much sense that the two of them live alone in their own empty houses, Dad says. Living together would be much, much better than living alone. And I can't help but think of Will. But then the image of him happy with Gillian brings on a new wave of tears.

"Oh, Honey," Dad says. "I know it's hard."

And I just nod. Because it *is* hard. Everything. It's all just so damn hard. But is that because I've made it that way?

"So when do I meet her?" I ask, still miffed, once my tears have stopped.

He smiles. "She'll be here for dinner."

#

The doorbell rings at 4:30 and I wonder if the formality is for my benefit. Dad's in the kitchen, so I open the door to a woman in her late fifties with dark skin and even darker hair, and dark eyes that sparkle when she smiles at me. Jeannie. She's holding a bouquet of daisies that she hands to me. "You must be Katherine. I'm Jeannie. I'm so thrilled to finally meet you," she says, trying too hard. I force a smile, gripping the flowers.

"Kit," I say. "No one calls me Katherine but Dad."

She looks taken aback but smiles when she sees Dad come out of the kitchen. "Jeannie!" They hug, then we all go back to the kitchen. After placing the flowers on the counter, I open the top cupboard where we keep the vases.

But Jeannie's right behind me. "Here," she says. And she hands me a vase she's pulled from the bottom shelf of the pantry. "If you put vases on a low level there's less chance of one falling on your head or breaking." She's smiling so sweetly that I only hope I'm not glaring.

During dinner, Jeannie pummels me with questions: about work, my apartment, where I got my shirt, which school I went to when I lived in town. I answer politely while secretly simmering. But because Dad is so taken with her, I take lots of deep breaths, and answer everything the best I can. And I realize that she's just interested in me, that she wants to get to know me. And that she's probably been freaked out that the man she's been dating for several months wouldn't introduce her to one of his two daughters. What did Dad say about me? That I was volatile and difficult to get along with? I want to be the easy-to-get-along-with daughter. I play with my mashed potatoes while mulling this all over, and then turn to Jeannie. "So tell me about you."

And she does: that she was married before—"twice, actually," she adds with a nervous chuckle. "The first was a starter, under a year, I was in my early twenties, it was a bad idea. My second marriage lasted twenty-seven years, until my husband passed away. And now, here I am. I have a few lovely nieces and neph-ews, they're all grown up now, and a wonderful little grandniece who I babysit on Mondays." Her face lights up and I take this all in. But what really resonates is that she doesn't have kids of her own. I want to ask her about this, and yet, it feels too personal a question, so I don't.

After dinner we move to the living room, where Jeannie pours us all cups of mint tea and Dad turns on the TV to *Jeopardy!*. This is their ritual. Jeannie's very good and shouts out most answers, even before I've fully understood the question. She even does it properly, in question form. And I have to admit that I'm impressed.

When the show's over, she gets up and so does Dad. They kiss—a small peck on the lips the way children kiss, then she turns to me and holds out her arms. "It was so lovely meeting you, Kit," she says. I rise and hug her back, breathing in her light floral scent. She smells . . . calming.

"It was nice meeting you, too."

Dad walks her to the door, and I sit back on the couch.

When he returns, he flicks around the channels on the TV, then asks, "So? What did you think?" He's still fiddling with the remote.

"She's great, Dad. But you don't need my approval to live with your girlfriend. Or to be happy."

"You're right," he says. "We would've moved in together whether you liked her or not. But let me tell you, it's much better if you do. Remember when you moved in with that chump without my approval?"

"Eric? You didn't like Eric?" This seems like information that would've been useful five years ago.

"Let's just say he wasn't my cup of mint tea. But I thought, well, he made you happy and you're the one who had to live with him. But if you ask me, he sure acted like he had the biggest cucumber stuck up his asshole."

"Dad!" I put my face in my hands. Then peek at him through my fingers. He's watching me, laughing.

"So I hear there's a new guy."

I slouch into the couch. "Not really. We broke up."

"That was quick. Or maybe Dad just gets the news late. What happened?"

I don't say anything for a moment, the lump in my throat too big to get around. "I don't know," I say. "It was too much, I guess. Too scary. He knows who he is and he challenged me. He made me rethink everything that I do and who I am, and I guess I wasn't ready to rethink everything."

"That doesn't sound so bad," Dad says. "Finding someone who challenges you can be a challenge in itself, but the reward . . ." He nods.

"Does Jeannie challenge you?"

"Nah, she's just really nice."

My mouth hangs open. He laughs. "I'm kidding. Of course she challenges me. That's what's so wonderful about her. You think you get to a certain age and that's it. I've been alone for so long now, and I never really questioned it. I just thought, I loved your mother and she's gone and that's that. And then I met Jeannie, and she made me question it all. At first I thought, Nuh-uh, what's *with* this woman? But then I realized that she was exactly what my life was missing—and not just her but everything she brings to my life and who I am by just being around." Dad leans back in his lounger, hands behind his head, looking up at the ceiling, completely content.

"OK, I get that, and I see how blissed-out you are, but you don't seem like you've changed your values. For me, it feels like this massive domino effect. Like, once I start questioning who I am, what I do for work, my personal life, my family life, it's all just a big ol' mess and it feels like I have nothing . . . and nothing to feel good about."

At this Dad sits up and looks over at me. "You're being way too hard on yourself. You're you—you've always been you. And you're good at everything you do. You lift people up with your talks. And I always want to buy everything in those ads you make for companies," he says. "So if you don't like what you're doing you'll do something else, sell something else. You make people want to like whatever it is you're interested in. That's what you do. You've got a gift. Charm. A *je ne sais quoi*, as the French say. You've got stories in you, and that's what life is about. Stories. People want to hear them, and people want to make their own. So help them do that."

I look out the window to the backyard at the outline of the trees in the night sky, bristling in the breeze, and think about how the trees have to bend with the wind in order not to break. Still staying true to their roots, but also aware of their surroundings. He's right, of course. I have always been who I am, and who I want to be has always been inside me. I just haven't found a way to let it blossom.

But the fact that he thinks I'm essentially an online salesgirl is all I need to hear to know that I've got to make a change in my life.

twenty

In the morning, I email Feloise. I'm a bit afraid to tell her what I need to, and I don't trust myself at this point not to let her convince or guilt me out of my decision. Plus, I don't want to turn my phone on, don't want to get distracted by everything going on back in the real world. For now, I need my country hideaway, my chance to remove all obligations, free myself from thinking about social media posts and who everyone thinks I am and just figure out how to be me. And that especially means cancelling my appearance and guest speaking spot at the International Women in Business conference. Feloise got me the spot, which means it's Feloise I need to let know.

> *Feloise,*
> *I'm sorry but I can't speak at the conference.*
> *I'll explain everything later, but can you please*
> *let the organizers know?*
> *Kit*

I hit Send before I can change my mind. I scroll through my inbox, then realize it was a mistake to think about all the work I should be doing. A second later there's a reply.

WTF??? Are you dying? Is someone else dying? The answer better be YES. Answer your goddamn phone!

I hit Delete, close my laptop and lie down on my childhood bed, waiting for relief to wash over me, but it doesn't come. So I change into my dad's old T-shirt and a pair of shorts and slip on my Vans, which are not great for running, but I don't let myself have that excuse, and set off on a run. I'm always telling my followers that fitness really boosts your mood. Is it even true? I suppose I'll find out.

I haven't run in as long as I can remember and the whole act of running feels uncomfortable. My legs feel stiff. My lungs feel like they're being squeezed. But I head toward the water, and then along the path where I learned to ride my bike when I was younger.

One stride at a time. No selfies, no posts. No phone means no music, either. The only sound is the rustling of the wind in the trees, the leaves gently brushing each other. I run down to the river, through the ravine, paths I haven't taken since I was a child. The wind whips at my face, cleansing me of it all.

#

The next few days pass in a blur. I putter around the house, feeling both like a guest and at home, but in a childlike way.

I help Dad with random projects, bake sourdough bread from Jeannie's starter that I find in the fridge, and read books on the couch. Izzy calls to check in daily. She says she's worried about me, but I tell her not to be. One afternoon, when I'm home alone and Dad and Jeannie are out playing bridge at a friend's house, Izzy tells me that Feloise has been DMing her on Instagram. "I think she's worried you've gone off the deep end. Have you?"

"Yes? No? Maybe so? I'm not sure. I *have* been swimming a lot. It might be a midlife crisis."

"You're a little young."

"Just tell her you're not my lifeguard and to go away."

"That sounds like something I would text, yeah, OK," she kids. "And what's with your phone? Are you ever going to turn it back on?"

"At some point, sure. But for now, the silence is pretty nice. It's like I'm in rehab, it's my social media detox. And the important people know how to get in touch."

"Well, as long as you're OK."

"I'm OK. I've been running, too."

"Did you say *running*?"

"Yeah. Well, only twice. It's a lot more tiring than sitting on the couch."

"Well, good for you."

After we hang up, I decide to go for another run. Three seems like it might make it a habit. I'm pretty sure I've told my followers that, too. Not recently—I haven't posted since being at Dad's. But before, when I would post about running but never actually run.

Twenty minutes later, I find myself on a path that's familiar though I can't figure out why. And then, the black iron gates of the cemetery loom before me.

I haven't been here in years.

When I lived at home, Dad and Izzy and I would go every Sunday after church. Back when Dad used to go to church. Once I left home, I visited Dad less and less often, and when I did, visiting Mom wasn't a priority. Now, I'm not even sure if I can remember the route to her plot.

I slow my run to a walk as I approach the entrance. The road from the gates shoots in various directions, but the one going straight ahead seems right. But at the bridge, it veers left, and turns out to be a dead end. I went the wrong way. Retracing my steps to the gates, I begin again, choosing the other tine of the fork, hopeful that this one is right. A couple standing by a site near the road glance to me and smile as I pass. I smile quickly, then lower my head, praying I won't have to walk past them a third time. The road splits again, and now I'm guessing. Right, then left, then right again. I can barely see the gates from where I stand, and I can't call Dad because I don't have my phone. The rolling green hills are dotted with hundreds of gray tombstones, the winding roads making a never-ending maze. It's hopeless. It doesn't matter that I've chosen to come. The cemetery is too unforgiving. I did my best. Along the bumpy road, I make my way back toward the gates. But when I reach them, I don't leave. I can't leave. A car approaches from behind and I move off to the side. "You alright?" the silver-haired man says, through his open window. I nod, not swiping at my tears, not admitting that they're there. He drives on.

I turn and take in the roads, the grass, the stone markers, the trees. And try again.

This time, my route works. The familiar gray tombstone, nestled between two large evergreens, comes into view. My mother's name is carved in stone. I've found her. Tears of relief bring other tears. Tears that had been buried too deep for too long. Below her name, the day she was born, the day she died.

The evergreens are taller than I remember, but between them are rows of flowers—yellow mums, my mother's favorite, in bloom. The soil is dark; there are no weeds. It's the confirmation I need to know that my father will never forget my mother.

I bend down, resting on my knees. I look around, feeling self-conscious, and then realize it doesn't matter who sees me, who hears me. What matters is that I'm here. With Mom.

#

The run home feels quick, and after kicking off my shoes, I head straight up the stairs to my room. Dad calls out to me, asking if I'm OK, and I tell him I'm fine, that I need to get something done. Rooting around in my desk, I find an old notebook and one of those pens with the four colors. I pop down the blue, but it's out of ink, so I settle on green. And start writing.

I picture all those women in the conference room, staring at me up onstage, waiting to hear what inspiring words I have for them about why the child-free life they've chosen is the best way to go. The goals they'll accomplish with all their time, the relationships they'll have with men who don't expect children, the travel they'll do with their disposable incomes . . . and then I think about Izzy. How she's child-free by choice—but not because it's her first choice. How many other women are out there in one of the No Kidding groups, choosing to tell the world they're child-free, but for reasons that are much more complex than they'll ever let on? And maybe there are women who are too old to have children, who missed their chance and now choose child-free over sorrow for what could've been. And maybe there are women like me—women who always wanted to be child-free, but then something changes. Someone changes them. And they wonder if maybe, the life they thought was the only way might not be the only way. If changing their mind is possible.

It doesn't matter who's in the audience, doesn't matter if I never speak these words aloud. I've got to write what's real. I've got to write the truth. *My* truth. That I changed my mind. That sometimes you can make a decision that's right *at the right time*. And then things change and you realize that maybe you're missing out on something you never thought you wanted—or even really knew existed. Or you get so caught up in the person you think you are, that you're gliding through every day, creating what you know people want, but aren't sure if it's what *you* want. I think about all my posts—cooking and running and going to restaurant openings and store previews for clothes I tried on but never even bought. Trips I only pretended to go on by standing in front of a green screen, or Photoshop techniques I used to make days look brighter, smiles whiter. Do these photos inspire people, or do they just make them feel bad? And do they make me feel better about my own life, because my feed floods with comments about how great I look, what fun I seem to be having, how my friends miss seeing me because I'm so busy living my best life while they're at home, muddling through the mundane details of everyday life? Do I really feel like my life, my *real* life, is just too boring to even share?

I write and write and write, until there's nothing left to say, until, eventually, it's all there, everything I've bottled up, not letting myself feel. And it all just makes sense. I feel calm. I feel relief.

twenty-one

Ten days after arriving at my childhood home, my land-lord calls to tell me my apartment is nearly finished. I can move back in as long as I don't mind workers painting and fix-ing odds and ends for the next week or two. It may be tiny and stark, but it's home, for now, and it's time to go back—to my rented furniture and Bed in a Box; to the city, with its lights and people and energy. I'm not a teenager anymore. I'm starting to see the woman that I'm meant to be and I need to get her back to the city. Back to my life. I miss it.

Dad's in the kitchen making soft-boiled eggs for breakfast. He calls them Toy Soldiers, because he cuts the toast into strips for dipping into the yolk. As we sit at the kitchen table, I tell him I'm going to head home. I feel a bit nervous, as though I'm letting him down, but he grins. "We better get you to the train station early if we're going to fit all those bins in the luggage compartment," he cracks but I just shake my head.

"How 'bout I get them next time?" I smile broadly.

After breakfast, Jeannie asks if I'd like to come with her to her favorite flower shop. We walk there together, and on the way,

I get the courage to ask her about being child-free. "I don't know if Dad told you how it's my *thing*," I say ineloquently. "So I'm just always so curious."

"Honey, your dad didn't have to tell me. I've read your book." She grabs my hand. "So what do you want to know? I never envisioned not having children, I just never envisioned having them. My husband didn't feel strongly either way, so he never put pressure on me. It was definitely against the norm not to have kids, when I was your age. But I always liked to forge my own path. I guess I thought it was a way to define myself. And so, we just never did." We pass a café, the chairs set up Parisian-style, so the patrons can sit facing the street, taking in the passers-by.

"Well, thank you."

"For what?" she says.

"For sharing that with me. It's personal."

"Well, you can ask me anything. Do you want to ask me if I regret my decision?" she says.

I shake my head. "Not really. I hate when people ask that."

"Me too," she says as we reach the flower shop and head inside.

After lunch, Dad and Jeannie drive me to the train station. I hug Dad, then turn to Jeannie. "I'm really glad we've had this time to get to know each other," I say to her, and I can tell that my words are what she needed to hear. She beams and pulls me in for a hug. Then Dad helps me lug three suitcases onto the train. I may not have taken all my childhood possessions as he'd hoped but I filled two big bags with my childhood books.

As the train pulls out of the station, I watch the world zip by for a few minutes, thinking about the days to come, and how

I want them to play out. I think about Mom, and what she would've done. But that's always been the problem—by the time Mom was my age, she was already sick. That overruled all other aspects of her life. But I'm not sick, and I can't use that as an excuse—I don't *need* that as an excuse. I can do anything I want to, and for the first time, I feel lucky about that.

I turn my phone back on. It's time to deal with everything.

A barrage of texts flood the screen. Most are from Feloise, Xiu, Gloria, Casey, and a bunch of people I wouldn't necessarily call friends, but who follow and comment on my Instagram posts daily. But I don't read their texts because before I can click on them, his name steals my attention. Will's sent three messages. One, asking me if we can talk. Another, telling me that he misses me. Another wondering if he should drop off my books. I wonder if he sent these texts before or after his pool date with Gillian. Not that it matters.

And yet, if I had just replied after his first text, or even his second, would we have found a way to make up?

And yet, I don't reply now.

I hesitate for a moment, my finger hovering over the Instagram icon. I haven't posted in weeks, and I know the inactivity will mean that I've lost followers. Brands will be upset and cancel contracts, and while I always maintain that my online paid campaigns have nothing to do with the IRL me, who gives child-free talks at conferences, I know the two are connected. The Kit with hundreds of thousands of followers guarantees more ticket sales, more exposure to an event than another speaker with half the social presence.

I open the app. The first thing I notice is the number of followers—it's higher, not lower. But how? I scan the photos. I'm in them, but there's something off. I recognize them, for sure, but then I realize that I never posted them. I click on the most recent one—a picture of me in a bikini on a beach that I can't place. My hand shaking, I study the details of the photo, realizing it was a picture from Bali, a trip that Eric and I took years ago. It was posted this morning.

Hands still shaking I scroll down to read the caption. It's my voice, I suppose, but the words are not mine. I didn't write this—how I'm on the beach taking a little me-time, and how I got bikini-ready for this trip by working out at an F45 studio for weeks . . . it's all lies. I've never even been to an F45 studio. And it's a paid ad, I realize when I scroll to the hashtags.

But how did this happen? Who wrote this? Who would even have access to my account?

Of course. I flip over to the texts from Feloise, scrolling backward through her rants about where I am, what I'm doing, how I can't just disappear. And then I realize that she made sure I didn't.

I hit Feloise's name in my list of Favorites.

"Look who's alive!" she says.

"Yeah, and not on the beach in Bali," I whisper hoarsely. "What the fuck, Feloise?" The woman across the aisle looks over at me and shakes her head.

"You're welcome," she says sarcastically. "I saved your ass. You disappear for two weeks, and can't be bothered to tell me what's going on? You abandoned four contracts. I don't get paid if you don't get paid and just because you wanted a break doesn't mean you actually get to take one."

"I don't get to run my life? That's what you're saying?"

"That's exactly what I'm saying. It's not your life, it's your business. And so, again, you're welcome. You're lucky that I had the foresight to use the logins *you* gave me to your accounts, to post your scheduled content, and then, when that ran out, to create content for you. And to even get you a new contract. And no, I did not cancel your speech at the conference as you asked me to, because we've worked too hard to build up your brand, your profile, for you to throw it all away with one momentary blip of insanity. I hired a writer for your speech, she was expensive but not the most expensive, and the speech is pretty good. I'll flip it over to you. And the bill."

For a split second I'm speechless. But the fury that's boiling in my belly comes to the surface. "No. Feloise. Just, no. You can't do that. You can't make stuff up about me, you can't write posts in my voice, using my words. You can't pretend I'm in Bali with a picture that's more than five years old. You can't lie and say I worked out at a gym I've never even been to. You can't sign contracts for me. You can't hire people and expect me to pay for it without asking me. Feloise, do you hear yourself? I took a break because I needed a break and you're telling me that I don't matter because I'm not important as a person, I'm purely a brand, a business to you?" The image of Bernie, the titular character in *Weekend at Bernie's*, comes to mind. I'm Bernie, and there's Feloise, keeping me alive. I start to laugh. I'm delirious, and it's all I can do.

"Are you *laughing*?" Feloise screeches.

I take a deep breath. "Yeah, I am. And oh, you're fired." I hang up, shove my phone in my bag and look out the window, leaning my head against the glass, a small smile forming on my lips.

#

Fionn greets me when I walk through the glass doors into the lobby of my apartment building. "Welcome back, stranger." He walks around the massive marble desk and takes my bag from me, walking with me to the elevator bank. "You're gonna love your place. Like new," he says, then laughs. "Actually, I have no idea how it looks but I've been told to tell you that the smell might be a bit strong from the paint, and you should keep the fans on. But that's no big deal—all the better to get that hair-flip like J. Lo for your photos, right?" He laughs a big belly laugh. I've missed him.

Fionn pushes the elevator button for me, waiting with me until the doors open.

Outside the door to my apartment I pause momentarily to let the weight of the moment sink in. Moving out happened so quickly, I didn't really consider what it all meant to leave my place and live with Will. I always knew I'd be back but I didn't really think through the *how*, of what it would mean to be back. Now, it all dawns on me. This apartment first became mine because I failed in my relationship with Eric. Now I'm back because I've failed in my relationship with Will. Failed my audience, my brand, my career.

I grip the door handle, feeling my breath quicken.

Or, I've found myself. And this is me, coming home. To the home I built for myself when I dared to make a change in my life, by leaving the security of a relationship that wasn't working, to be the person I knew I needed to be.

I push the door open and take in my old-yet-new surroundings. The space is empty and reminds me of the day I moved in.

My things are all still in storage, and while at Dad's I arranged to have the rented furniture—the couch, the coffee table, the occasional chair that was in my living room—picked up. I didn't put in a replacement order and now, I'm relieved. Not having furniture means not having to be indebted, not having to post about rented furniture, not having to remind my circle of influencer frenemies to comment about my chair, my couch, my coffee table. No more freebies means I can be free.

Slightly uncomfortable, but free.

And with all the empty space, I can bring my books out of hiding. And so, in the afternoon, after unpacking my bag, remaking my bed and getting a few groceries, I head down to the storage locker and haul the many boxes of books back upstairs. With music playing on my portable speaker and the sun shining through the west-facing windows, I start stacking the books—not in my oven or in cupboards, not under the bed or in the closet, but out in the open. From the floor as high as the stack will go without tipping over. I may not have French doors, but I have floor-to-ceiling windows, and enough books to line the edges of my entire apartment. It takes me hours, and feels like therapy. Finding the right spot for each book, making sure it's the right fit. When I'm done, my place feels magical— like something, well, like something I'd see on Instagram or on Pinterest, but better because it's original, because it's mine. I stand back and snap a picture with my phone. Just one, because it doesn't need to be perfect, and there's no one in the world who needs to approve it. I post it to my @BookKit account. There's really no reason to post the photo to a completely private account without a single follower. But to me, there's every reason in the world.

#

The email comes through as I'm hopping in the shower after having come home from a run. I've never liked running in the city, but somehow, after getting used to running in the country, it feels less like torture and—almost—therapeutic. And exhausting myself means I've been sleeping better, and I've been feeling less anxious, in general. But the email has my stress level skyrocketing within seconds.

It's from the Women in Business convention, with my name, right there in bold letters, headlining the Friday night sessions. How did this happen? This week has been quiet. I've read, gone for runs, and been completely social-media free. Friends have texted to find out why I haven't been posting. Brands have emailed to ask about collaborations. But I've just ignored them all. It's been therapeutic. Now, my bubble is burst. I knew I couldn't ignore real life forever, but I didn't think I'd be jolted back into reality quite like this. I call the publicist in charge of the event, who says she has no record of Feloise cancelling my appearance. "In fact, I just confirmed everything with her yesterday," Salome says. "She said you were absolutely ready to go. Please don't tell me there's a problem. I can't deal with any more problems today."

My mind races. Why didn't Feloise cancel me? Is this her way of getting back at me for firing her? Does she think that, by sending me to the wolves without a speech, she can punish me? It doesn't matter, because on the other end of the line Salome is clearing her throat and asking me if she can expect to see me at 6 p.m. tonight. I have to cancel. To speak as planned would be completely misleading to everyone who's bought a ticket.

Unless I just give up and go back to my brand, to the person people expect me to be. And I can't do that. I can't risk falling back into my old life.

And yet, I blurt out, "I'll be there." Because I know exactly what to do. It may not be what the crowd has come to hear, but it's what I need to say.

I hang up, take a quick shower and then sit down on the bare floor with my laptop resting on my thighs to figure out what the hell I'm going to say to ten thousand women tonight.

twenty-two

The convention center takes up a full city block near the waterfront and inside, the place is abuzz with activity. Thousands of women wearing lanyards carry clipboards, have WIB tote bags slung over their shoulders, sip coffee from paper cups, check signs and cross-reference their schedules with the available options.

I check in at the speakers' desk, pick up my lanyard, badge and gift bag and make my way into Hall B. Eight sets of burgundy doors loom in front of me and I pull one set open and walk into the massive room. My breath catches and adrenaline pulses through my veins. I've never given a talk in a room this large before. I look around, walk to the stage, and wait as women file into the room, finding seats.

Once the room is full and settled, there are opening remarks followed by welcome speeches, and then the president of the Women in Business conference turns to me. "And now, I'd like to introduce you to a woman who really needs no introduction. With a massive social media following, a bestselling book, and a successful career inspiring women around the world to pursue their passion, stand up for what they believe in, be their best selves and make no apologies for who they are—particularly if it's choosing a child-free life—please help me give a massive welcome to Kit Kidding."

As applause fills the room, I walk up the three steps and curl my fingers into my palms to form tight fists. I can do this. I'm ready to do this. On stage, I take the podium and look out into the sea of faces. And then, the lights go out. The room is completely dark. But a moment later the lights flicker as the generator kicks in and they come back to life. But that moment was enough to throw the audience. Everyone comes to life, chattering about what just happened. And to throw me. Should I just stick to the original plan? Do what I've always done? Give the inspirational speech I've given a dozen times, the one everyone's expecting from me?

The crowd quiets down and I look around the room. All eyes turn back to me. Ready. Waiting. So I begin.

"Many of you may have read my book, *Kid-Free Forever.* There's a certain amount of defiance or, perhaps, ignorance, required to write a book on a topic that's controversial. Say, choosing *not* to have children," I say, and the crowd laughs. "But choosing to support someone who has written a book on a controversial subject is brave. It requires that you know who you are without shame. So to all of you who have supported me over the years, I want to thank you." I take a deep breath, then exhale.

"I also want to tell you that I admire you, and that I wish I were more like you, so sure of who you are and what is important to you. I wish I knew who I was with confidence. But the truth is, I don't."

I look around the room, focusing on the walls, rather than faces, to keep my composure. If I see skepticism on anyone's faces,

I'm not sure I'll have the strength to stick to my plan, rather than to revert to my usual style of speech.

"If you've read my book, you'll know that it's an account of how I came to choose a child-free life. And while the book *is* non-fiction, there is a dramatic arc to the book, a storytelling aspect that works. It works for the reader, and it works for sales. Now don't get me wrong; it's all true. I did choose to be child-free. But I can't say that it was a particularly difficult decision." I bite my lip for a moment, then continue.

"My mom died when I was young, my sister never had children, so it felt pretty easy, pretty natural to shun the idea of having a family with children. And when I met Eric, my former partner, who also wanted a child-free life, it all just fell into place. I made being child-free my living. I was able to stand up without really having to fight. Even though I know that for many of you, the fight is very, very real."

A door at the back creaks open and heads turn as a woman slinks to a nearby table. I wait till she is seated, then go on.

"For a long time, it was a life I loved. I had freedom—both of time and money—that most women with children don't get to experience. I've met so many great women because of my beliefs. Each one of you has reminded me why it's so important that we all have the opportunity to be free to live the life we want—free of judgment, or apology, or regret."

I take a sip of water.

"So for as long as I could remember, I found myself living the life I thought I was meant to live. I was fulfilled. I was *happy*. And then, as many of you know, my long-term relationship ended— because my partner decided he wanted to have children after all. And I didn't. They say a breakup is one of the most difficult times in a person's life, but for me, it was a gift. I saw it as an opportunity to hammer home my message. Women shouldn't be in a relationship solely to bear children. If you're with someone who is only interested in being with you to help them have kids, you should rethink that relationship—stat."

I curl my fingers around the edge of the podium.

"Like I did. In fact, I probably jumped a little too quickly at the chance to end things with this man. What I wasn't admitting to myself was that there were many issues with our relationship that I'd been sweeping under the rug. But instead of considering them, or looking to get therapy to repair our relationship, I focused on the deal breaker and moved on. I saw my breakup as a career opportunity—which probably says something about how much, or how little, the relationship really meant to me."

The entire room is quiet—all eyes are on me.

"Newly single, I channeled all my energy into my work. My career was at an all-time high and I was flying. I was me, only better. I had more fun, went out more often, and the brand partnerships skyrocketed. It was awesome. It didn't feel like work *at all*. Sometimes I wondered if I would meet someone new and start a fresh, exciting relationship. But if I did, I was certain that it wouldn't be with just anyone, and certainly not someone who might change their mind about kids somewhere along the line." I take a minute to breathe, to slow down and make sure I don't ramble off course.

"And then, I did meet someone. A few months ago. I didn't think it would work out. In fact, I didn't *want* it to work out. You see, he's a dad. But despite my best efforts, I fell in love with him." I pause. "And with his daughter."

Someone coughs. Out of the corner of my eye, I see a woman stand. A few heads turn, and then someone else stands. Two others follow suit, pushing through the heavy burgundy doors. This is not the talk they came to hear. I know this. They are rebelling—I am a hypocrite and they don't want to hear the rest. But I need to be truthful. I grip the podium and continue.

"I didn't admit any of this to anyone. I kept our relationship secret. I didn't want to let my followers, my friends, my colleagues, *you*"—I motion to the audience—"down. But if I'd dug deeper, I would have seen that it was because I wasn't ready to face what it all meant. I wasn't ready to give up my brand, @KitwithoutKids, my No Kidding groups, being a guest speaker at events like this."

I fan my arm out around the room, being careful not to hit the microphone.

"I wasn't even being honest with myself. My entire life was tied to me being child-free. I couldn't let myself feel what I was feeling, because I couldn't upend my career, my persona, who I am, what I believe, everything."

I know I'm carrying on, but I have to share my thoughts with these women. "We say people don't change, that we are who we are who we are. This is especially true now, when we're seeing the world through a square filter on social media. Everything we do, everything we say, every mistake we make, haunts us forever. Because it's always there. But that's the problem: We don't *let* people change. We're always reminding them of who they are, who they're supposed to be, who we *expect* them to be. By constantly reminding others of who they said they once were, by always holding them up to impossible standards, we never allow them to change."

Someone claps and I get a boost of confidence.

"How many times have you thought, 'I'd like to try that.' Or, 'I wish I could do that.' Only to worry that it won't fit into your narrative? Won't be 'on brand'?" Someone else claps, and there's a "Yes!"

"Even if you aren't on social media, how many times have you thought, I'd like to do that but what if I'm not good at it? What if I fail? Or worse, what if I'm ridiculed? Or shunned?" I pause and look around the room. There are lots of heads nodding and mm-hmms of agreement.

"But what if we're wrong? Maybe people can change. And grow. And evolve. Why can't we try new things? Reimagine ourselves? I'm not trying to justify my actions. I know this is going to be the end of my work as a woman championing a child-free life. Even though I don't have children and things didn't work out with the man and his delightful daughter, it made me wonder what else I've been hiding, pushing down, or not exploring because they didn't fit into my 'brand.'"

I take a deep breath, looking around, which is when I see Feloise, standing at the back of the room. Our eyes meet. She does not look happy—at all. But I won't let her shake me. I continue.

"We get one life. And it can be so hard to figure out who you are and who you want to be. Or maybe that's just me and you guys have it all figured out." There's a bit of laughter, but I can feel the nervous energy, the what-other-bat-shit-crazy-stuff-is-about-to-happen vibe.

"What I'm saying is that I'm still figuring it out. But I know that there are things I want to do, directions I want to take, passion projects I want to pursue that don't quite fit into that child-free, glamorous, Instagrammable life. What I want is choice. I don't want to regret not living the life I want because I'm afraid of what others might think, that followers may unsubscribe, or that you may walk out. I know in saying this I'm no longer the person you thought I was. And I know that some of you may no longer want to support me. And that's OK. Because it's your choice. And I've always stood up for that. Choice."

A few more people walk out of the room. But someone else claps a bit louder for me.

"And I guess, that's what I'm doing now. I'm standing up and I'm making a choice and it's big and it's scary. I almost didn't come tonight because I was worried about not being the person you expected me to be. But I needed to share this with you, I needed you to see me." My hands are in fists, and I'm pumping my arms in a way that I've never done before, and yet which feels completely natural all the same.

"I've always tried to rally you to follow your own beliefs, to do what's right for you, no apologies, no regrets. So this is me, right now, with no apologies or regrets. I was 100 percent sure that who I was, for years, was the person I was meant to be. And now, I'm 100 percent sure that I've changed, and grown, and I need to be 100 percent true to myself, and these feelings, no matter the consequences."

I clasp my hands together, fingers intertwined. "So if you've ever felt the way I've been feeling, that you're stuck in a role from which you want to break free, I want you to know that I'm right there with you. I want you to know that you're not alone."

I clutch the podium and look out to the women in front of me. And take a deep breath, then exhale. I have no idea what they can be thinking. Maybe they think I'm a flake. Or that I have no clue what I'm doing. Maybe a little of both. But several women are clapping. Some are even standing up—and not to leave. More clap and more stand and they're cheering and slowly, I realize that almost everyone in the room is standing with me, regardless of their opinion of me. That I'm not alone.

My body feels so light, like I'm floating in air. I'm free.

#

A crowd of women immediately surrounds me as I leave the stage, and the questions start flying. Everyone wants to know about my career. Instagram. The No Kidding groups. What will happen with my book? Will I write another one? And of course, they want to know about the guy. I field as many questions as quickly as I can, and as the group thins, I make my way to the lineup at the table outside where I'm scheduled to sign copies of my book. I was sure the room was going to be empty by the time I finished speaking, and that no one would even want their copy of my book, let alone have me sign it. So this—seeing everyone being just as supportive as ever, or maybe more so, gives me a surge of confidence and I can't help the huge smile that spreads across my face as I greet each new and old friend.

I knew I was making the right decision for me, but to see that being true to myself, *being me,* has resonated with others, reassures me that I'm on the right path.

After I finish signing copies, I head to the bar, spotting Feloise almost immediately. She's chatting with a group of women, and I walk over to her. She ignores me but when there's a pause in the conversation, I interrupt and pull her aside.

"Listen, I owe you an apology. I wasn't being honest with you. It wasn't fair to you and your business, when so much of it relies on me." Someone bumps me on their way to the bar and I catch my drink before it spills.

Her face is blank, her eyes stony. "You know I'm still getting my commission on this, right?"

I nod. "And to be clear, you're still fired. But I did want to say that I get why you're so upset with me—beyond the unprofessionalism. You need me. Me being child-free by choice helped you to feel child-free by choice too. I get that and I didn't mean to deceive you or betray you."

My throat feels tight. I do feel badly about Feloise. She acts so tough, but I know that she is struggling. "I know you probably want nothing more to do with me," I say, "but if I can offer you any advice, and I know you don't want it, it's that no one can save you from your own truth." I take a deep breath. "You're living in that big house, Feloise, and you can tell yourself and everyone else it's so you can defy some sort of cliché, but if that's not the reason, then do something about it. Change your story. You heard me up there. You only get one chance at each step of your life. Don't . . . don't fuck it up because you're worried about what people will think or because you're worried about getting hurt or whatever it is that's stopping you."

I study her, and for a split second, I think I've gotten through. I don't expect her to throw her arms around me and thank me for my words of wisdom, and I'm not even sure I would want that because I'm still furious with her for her actions, but what I don't expect is for her to just turn, without a word, and walk away. But that's what she does. And I don't stop her.

I take a sip of my drink and look around the crowded room, searching for a familiar face, then spot Xiu. She waves and comes up to me, grinning. "Well that was a bit of a surprise," she says, shaking her head, then laughing. She leans in to hug me. "But I just wanted to say I'm proud of you."

"Thanks," I say when we pull apart.

"I wish you would've told me you were going through all of this, though." She looks genuinely sad and that makes me feel both sad and touched.

"I know. I'm sorry."

She grabs my hand in hers. "I know I'm not one to talk, because I'm so uptight about sharing, but that's just me, and I've got issues. I know that. But you—you always tell us what's going on. It's something I always think about—and I always admire you for it."

I nod.

"That time we were out, and we asked you if there was a guy. Why didn't you just tell us?"

"I was afraid of what you would think." Tears form and I try to blink them away. "That you wouldn't want to be friends with me anymore." Even now, I hate talking about it, knowing I might lose Xiu as a friend.

Xiu's brow furrows. "We're not just friends because we don't have kids. At least I don't think of you like that."

"Really?" I feel relief—even hope.

She sighs. "Of course. We're *friends*. Listen, a bunch of us from the No Kidding group are meeting for dinner, but . . ."

"No, go on." I know what she's thinking. That maybe there's some universe in which I still go out with them, but I know there isn't. Not now, anyway.

"We'll talk, OK? I'll call you tomorrow."

I nod, but a sadness washes over me as she turns and heads out of the room. I look around, finish my drink, and head out of the bar, to head home.

#

Xiu calls the next day, just as she promised, to invite me out for dinner with friends. Not the entire No Kidding group, she warns, but I'm so touched, I don't mind. At seven, I arrive at one of our favorite Mexican places on Queen to find Xiu, Gloria and Casey already at a table. There's one empty chair. A pitcher of margarita sweats in the center of the table and Gloria pours me a glass immediately. I meet their eyes and take a deep breath. "Hi," I say. "So, I'm sorry," I start, but Gloria interrupts.

"Stop apologizing. We get it. We heard the damn speech. Now we want the real deets, so fill us the fuck in." We all start laughing. And so I go back to the beginning, when I met Will—our night together, the contract, Addie, my apartment flooding, moving in with them. How I didn't tell anyone, how I didn't let it show on social media. And then, how we broke up. It's the first time I've laid it all out, and hearing myself talk, it all sounds crazy. I'm ashamed of myself, that I would go to such great lengths to live so duplicitously—and to what end?

They listen and ask questions, but then instead of chastising me, Casey says: "OK, but how are you going to fix this?"

At first, I think she means Instagram. @KitwithoutKids. The No Kidding groups. "I'm not. It's over. That life. I deleted my Instagram account. I guess . . . you guys can just continue with the groups, without me. I guess you'll want to change the name . . ."

Gloria holds her hands up. "We're not idiots. We know all that. She means *Will*. How are you going to get him back?"

"Oh," I say, taken aback. In all that's happened and everything I've been focusing on, I haven't figured out what, if anything, I can do about Will. I've just assumed that it's over.

"You had a fight," Gloria says. "Big deal."

"But it's not that. Every relationship that works has a story. It follows the rules, it's romantic"—I stop talking, because all three women are staring at me, wide-eyed. But also because I've just heard myself tell the story—our story. And sure, my actions were crazy, but they were mine. And Will's were his. And who cares what kind of rules romances are supposed to follow. Rules are made to be broken. And if I've learned anything, it's that I don't need to worry about whether I'm following any rules, period.

"OK, a plan. Right," I say. "I don't have one. So far I've just been feeling sorry for myself, but I think maybe it's time for a new plan."

Xiu leans forward, resting her arms on the table. "You're the one who's always championing us, telling us to take control of our own lives. You helped me get through the whole birth control situation with Jed. You know how to fix broken relationships. You can do this. You've got to get him to meet you and then you've got to talk it out. It's not about who's right and who's wrong. It's not about winning. It's about figuring out how to get through this situation, with all your real emotions, *together*. That's what you told me. Now you have to take your own advice."

"It's not that easy," I protest. "A relationship with Will means having a relationship with Addie. The only possible outcome to that is eventually becoming a stepmom. It's like—the end is there, there's no changing it, there's no shaping my future the way you can when you date someone without kids. And let's face it: being a stepmom to a little girl who doesn't have a mom is basically being a mom." *And I don't know how to be a mom*, I don't add. I think of my own mom, and how, if she were here,

I could ask her *how* to be a mom. That she could help me, without laughing at me. Because who else do I have to turn to? I've let all my other friendships with mothers slip away, and the only moms I've recently met—Margot, Gillian—want nothing to do with me.

"It doesn't have to be that at all. You can make your own rules. You can be as involved or uninvolved as you want. That's your choice. You make your future."

She's right, of course. But is there any chance that Will would ever even consider trying again with me? And how can he—when I would never agree to having children of my own with him? And if I wouldn't do that, why would he want that kind of woman as a role model to his only child?

Any way I look at it, it doesn't work. And yet, the possibility that I'll never see Will again, that Addie is actually out of my life, that it's all truly over, feels so depressing that I know I have to do something.

We finally call it a night hours later, and as I head home, I feel inspired, happy, alive. I don't have a plan, but I have hope. Not even Ivan the Grumpy Concierge, who's on duty, can get me down.

"Boxes," he says. "Ten boxes." He disappears and returns with one large box. "You have to notify us if you're going to be getting large shipments. We're not equipped to store these large deliveries."

"I—I don't know what you're talking about. Sorry," I say, flustered. "I didn't order anything." I lean over, and open the box. My books. From Will. I feel sick—did I miss him while I was out with my friends, once again? Ivan has disappeared and now returns again, with the next box. I open it. More books. I look up at Ivan. "Did . . . was the guy who dropped them off tall with wavy brown hair? Really good-looking?"

"You're asking what the UPS guy looked like?" Ivan calls from the tiny room behind the reception desk.

"Are you sure it was UPS?"

"Unless normal people have just started wearing the brown UPS uniforms and driving around in doorless trucks." I go into the recycling area to get the trolley. "I know, I know, I didn't book the service elevator."

Ivan uses his key to call one of the elevators down to the lobby and then puts it on service. "I'm not saying anything this one time. But one time only."

I load the boxes onto the trolley and into the elevator.

twenty-three

Once I'm in my apartment I look around, then open the first box to unpack it. But then I stop, sit down, and pull out my phone. I text Will, hands quivering, and ask him if I can take him out for a drink, to talk. My stomach in knots, I wait for a reply. It doesn't come. Not even a few minutes later. And despite checking my phone every few minutes, turning it off and back on multiple times, no reply comes. I shove it in my nightstand and grab my book instead. An hour or so later, my phone pings.

I yank open the drawer and grab my phone, staring at the screen.

U there? It's Addie.

I pause. Did she mean to text me? How did she even text me, through her iPad? Or did Will get her a phone after blowing up at me? Who knows? I feel both concerned and happy to see her name, and I realize I've missed her.

Me: *Hi Addie. What's up?*

No reply. I'm about to put my phone back down, thinking that she *did* make a mistake, that she didn't mean to text me after all, when my phone pings again.

Addie: *Can u come get me?*

Get her? I stare at the phone, willing myself to focus. Where is she? I debate calling her, but worry that seems overbearing, not cool. Am I a friend? A parent? How am I supposed to respond? But now's not the time to overanalyze my role. And so I text her back.

Me: *U OK?*

When she doesn't reply, I call her. Screw being uncool. She answers on the first ring.

Her voice sounds weird. Weak. Like she's scared or has been crying. Maybe both.

"Sweetie, what's wrong? Are you OK? What's going on?"

She sniffs but doesn't reply. I stay quiet, waiting, wishing I could see her face. Then she speaks. "I'm at Millie's, and . . . I don't want to be here anymore. Dad's away on a camping trip and I miss him." Her voice cracks. "Can you come get me?"

"Oh Honey," I sigh. I'm about to tell her there's no way her dad would let me come and get her from Gillian's and there's no way Gillian would let me take her either. I'm the evil kid-hater, in their minds at least. If she really needs to leave, she should probably call Margot.

But I don't want to tell her no, not when she's called me. When Addie was at my place, Will told me that when she's overtired, she gets weepy. Maybe all she needs is to get back to sleep, or a hug. And I don't want to tell her that I'm not going to give her what she needs.

"I'm coming," I tell her.

She gives me the address and I immediately order an Uber, then change out of my pj's into a hoodie and jeans, pulling a jacket overtop to combat the cool fall wind. I'm almost out the door when I scour the stacks of books along the walls, miraculously find what I'm looking for, and shove it into my purse. Ten minutes later I'm walking up the steps to Gillian's home, which is around the corner from Will's. I ring the doorbell and wait. A few minutes pass, and I start to wonder if Gillian won't answer the door, won't let Addie see me. But then the door opens and Gillian's looking at me, Addie by her side. Gillian's eyes are narrow and she's shaking her head. "If you think I'm letting Addie leave with you, you're more delusional than I thought." She stares at me, coldly, positioning herself so that Addie can't squeeze by her.

"I'm not taking her anywhere, Gillian. I just wanted to say hi. Check in with her, see if she's OK." I give Addie a small smile. "Come on. It's a nice night. Wanna sit out here on the steps with me for a minute?" I expect Gillian to protest, to remind me that it's nearly midnight, but instead, she moves out of the way, letting Addie pass. She hands us a blanket from the chair by the door. "Here. Just in case. And just for a few minutes."

I wrap my arms around Addie as Gillian gives me a long, hard look, then reluctantly lets the door swing closed, leaving us alone. We sit on the front steps, side by side, looking out onto the street. The streetlamps cast a white glow over the road, making it shift from light to dark every few feet. The night is quiet. I pull Addie close. "I've missed you." She scooches closer to me. And starts to cry. I pull her even closer.

"Wanna tell me what's going on? I've always thought I had rather big ears, and that they're good for listening." She pulls away for a moment to study my ears, then realizes I was joking.

"Can't I just leave with you? I know things didn't work out with you and Dad, but you're not a bad person. Please?"

"Oh Honey," I say, and wonder if she's saying I'm *not* a bad person, did someone tell her otherwise? Her dad? Gillian? Margot? But this isn't about me.

"Sleepovers are supposed to be fun."

"Sleepovers *are* supposed to be fun. So what happened?" I ask softly.

Finally, she speaks. "It's just . . . sometimes, when I'm here, Gillian does this thing," she turns to look behind her, and I let go of her. When she sees the door is firmly shut, she turns back and continues, "where she hangs out with me and Millie. Maybe she's lonely or something, but she does it in this way where they're all mom-daughter besties and it just makes me feel so bad. It reminds me that I don't have a mom." She tucks her hands between her knees. "And I just want to go home, but I can't. And it sucks. And no one gets it because everyone has a mom to call. Everyone but me."

We're both quiet for a moment as two people ride by on bikes. "Tell me your favorite memory of your mom," I say quietly. She leans into me, her head resting on my shoulder.

"I don't know," she mumbles.

I don't say anything, just hold her. Finally she speaks. "Well, she had this really beautiful dress she wore in the summer. It was yellow with flowers all over it. It was so flowy and I would wrap myself in it, like it was a beautiful cape, and I was a beautiful princess." She pauses. "She also always took me to my grandparents' house to go swimming. She never wanted to get her hair wet so she would put it in this bun on the top of her head. And she'd always wear her sunglasses in the pool, too. She liked to horseback ride, but only on vacation. In the mountains. I remember that."

As I imagine Will and Sophie and Addie on vacation in the mountains, Addie adds: "Dad says I can't actually remember that because I was too little. That I've seen the pictures and I think I remember but I don't. I hate it when he says that. Like, maybe I don't even really remember her. Maybe it's all just the pictures." Her voice is shaky.

"That's what photographs are for," I say softly. "I don't think you should worry about whether you remember her without the pictures. What does it matter anyways? Either way, you remember your mom. You think about her. You miss her. That's what matters." I pause, thinking about my own mother.

"I have this memory of my mom and me," I tell her. "We would look for garages—like the detached kind you have at your house. We would go out on Saturday mornings together, hunting for them. Mom said when I was older, we would open a book garage. People could come, hang out, read books, meet friends, make friends. We could host book clubs with tea and cookies. We could invite authors to come read their own books to kids. We had a whole plan, and then she died." I pause. "And the thing is, I felt like us looking for garages was this thing we did, every Saturday morning, for years. But when I really think about those weekends, I always picture us walking the same route, seeing the same houses. We're always wearing the same thing—Mom in light jeans and a sweater, me in flowery overalls and sneakers. So I have to wonder, was this a ritual at all, or just one memory, one Saturday that somehow stuck out in my mind?"

I'm talking aloud, looking out into the sky, the sun setting between the houses across the street. I realize I've probably over-shared and I turn back to Addie. She's looking up at me.

"Your mom died?" she says and I realize that I've never told her.

I nod. "I was a bit older than you," I say. "So I remember a bit more. It's hard to not have a mom, isn't it?"

She nods.

"You're really brave, you know."

"You're really brave, too," she says. I laugh, then wrap my arms around her to hug her.

"And who cares if you only went to look at garages with your mom one time? It sounds like it was a fun time, even if it's kinda weird."

"You're right. Except the weird part. Well, maybe the weird part too." I move her hair off her face, tucking a strand behind her ear. "You should get back inside. I know you don't really want to be here, but your dad'll be back tomorrow, right? So just one more night. You can do one more night, right?"

"One more night. Yeah. Maybe I'll just fake being asleep." She grins.

I reach into my purse. "Maybe this'll help." I pull out *The Secret of the Old Clock*. Addie studies the faded cover. "Have you read a Nancy Drew before?"

She shakes her head.

"Great. Then you're in for a treat. She doesn't have a mom either. She lives with her dad and their housekeeper. And she solves mysteries. She's brave, like you. I think you'll like it."

Addie takes the book, turning it over in her hands. "*The Secret of the Old Clock.*"

"It's a whole series. This is book one. So if you like it, there are about fifty or so more where it came from. Except #24. I'm missing #24, for some reason."

"Thanks." Addie reaches over, and I realize she's looking for a hug. I wrap my arms around her and squeeze her tight. When I let go, she stands. "I think I should go back inside. But thanks a lot for coming." I stand too and wait until the door closes behind her before turning and walking down the steps.

"Kit." I turn. Gillian's standing in the doorway. "Can I have a minute?" *Do I have a choice?* I think, but nod, and walk back up the steps. She steps onto the porch, pulling her thigh-length cream-colored cardigan closed, crossing her arms over her chest. "You can't do this anymore," she says.

"Do what?" I keep the emotion out of my voice.

"This." She raises her eyebrows. "Come back into Addie's life. Into Will's life."

"Gillian, Addie *called* me."

She tilts her head. "Yes, but she didn't need to—and you coming here is disruptive. I care about both of them—a lot. As I'm sure you know. We're part of their lives and they're part of ours. It's been that way for a long time, and it's going to stay that way for a long time and there's nothing that anyone that Will dates can do about that."

"Gillian, I'm not interested in preventing you from being friends with Will," I say. "It feels like a moot point, given I'm not even speaking to Will."

"Right. He's not interested in you anymore." *Anymore.* The word stings. "You had your chance with him, and you blew it by lying to him. Will's a great guy. He didn't deserve that."

I nod, tears filling my eyes. She's right, and as much as that hurts, the truth hurts more. Gillian has clearly had these emotions pent up, because she bulldozes on. "And it's confusing to Addie to even see you. You need to go away and stay away. If you don't make sure of it, I will." She gives me one long stare, and before I say anything in reply, she turns, opens the screen door, walks inside and closes the heavy wood door, the click of the lock echoing in the silence.

#

Back in my apartment, I climb into bed, pulling the covers up to my chin. I'm not tired, just emotionally drained, and yet too worried to sleep. It feels like I did as much as I could for Addie, but that I still didn't do enough. Is she going to be OK? If this is what Will goes through every day, I don't know how he does it. I'm not cut out to think about someone else, to worry about them, and wonder if I'm doing the wrong thing, and second-guess my decisions, and know that I've done all I could, and it still doesn't feel like enough.

My phone pings. *Thanks for coming over.*

My eyes fill with tears.

Go to sleep, I text back. Then add: *Call or text me anytime.*

Then I gather up my duvet and move out to the couch, where I curl up and scroll through Netflix. I'm about to hit Play on *Sleepless in Seattle,* but pause instead, to wonder what a sequel to this movie would've looked like. What would life have been like for Meg Ryan and Tom Hanks's characters—Annie and Sam—once they got married and Annie became the stepmom? Would Jonah be so enamored with her when she was nagging him to tidy his room or clean up his chocolate milk spill on the couch? Was a sequel never in the cards because the writers knew there could be no happy ending to *that* movie—that inevitably little Jonah would end up hating his stepmother, the way every fairy tale ever played out? Surely there's a movie out there that has a stepmother being kind and good, isn't there? I find a list on my phone and then scroll through them: *Ever After*, *Tommy Boy* . . . the list goes on and on. Even in the fairy tales, there are stepmothers without children, like the one in "Hansel and Gretel," which is why she hates them, and the stepmothers who do have children, like in "Cinderella," love their own more. And the Brothers Grimm couldn't really have it wrong, could they? Those tales were passed down for years and years. Household tales. If a kind, happy, loving stepmother existed—wouldn't someone, somewhere, have written the story down?

I need to forget about Will and move on. There are hundreds, thousands, millions of single men without kids in the world. And maybe, even some who have no interest in ever having kids. And it's easy to find them—that's what dating apps are for.

And yet, despite this, I don't want to move on.

I need to talk to Will.

Sunday passes and he still doesn't reply to my messages. I tell myself that he hasn't replied because he is on a camping trip. But even on Sunday night, when I know he's home, there are no texts from him. And he doesn't reply to my text all the following week, either. I check my phone incessantly; I try turning it off for hours at a time. Nothing works. I can't get him out of my mind.

I keep myself busy. I make a business plan for the book garage, which includes reaching out to publishers to figure out how to stock new books in addition to my collection of used books, and half-heartedly look at houses with garages for sale online. I need to move on, I know this, and yet, I don't want to move on without Will. I keep replaying the past few months, what I could've done differently. But ultimately, a lot of it comes down to timing—and me being ready to make a change. I've known for a long time I wasn't totally happy with my career, and I've also been having the idea of the book garage take up more and more space, but I didn't let myself fully explore either because they didn't fit into the career I'd built for myself. But the real truth is that in both cases—Will and the book garage—I'm afraid of failure.

And now that fear is making me feel so alone. I miss Will. I miss Addie. And I have no idea how to get them back in my life.

I try to distract myself with writing—in my journal, and writing book reviews. Without the distraction of social media, I've been reading more than ever. One of the books I read is based on a true story about an orphanage. Jeannie had recommended it to me when I was at Dad's, and my gut reaction was to smile politely, keep the book for an appropriate amount of time and then return it without reading it. It sounded like the kind of book I would never read—it wasn't on-brand to read a book about children, and even if I did, I would never recommend it, or express any opinion about it at all. No one wants to hear a child-free woman's opinion about a book that has to do with children. But Jeannie recommended it so highly that I took it. And I'm so glad I did. It was moving, and even now, days later, I'm still thinking about the story.

I sit down at my laptop and begin to write down those thoughts. I post my review with a photo of the book to my @BookKit Instagram account. Then I scroll down through the dozens and dozens of books I've reviewed over the years. Secretly. No one knew. Now, it's time to share these books, these ideas, this dream with the world. I flip to the Settings tab and scroll down until I find the button to make my account public.

And hit Confirm. All the pictures I've taken of books I've read, the picture of my apartment, the books stacked up against the windows, the bookshelf in Will's bedroom, the book I read on the island when I was with Will and Addie, it's all there now, for everyone to see.

I put on my sweats and running shoes and head out for a run, leaving my phone at home. As I jog, I think through my plan for the books, the book garage. I should call Gloria about actually going to see some of the houses with garages I've been looking at online, so I can begin moving forward with this new plan and what I've always wanted to do. But my thoughts keep coming back to Will. I don't want to put my life on hold for some guy I can't get out of my mind, but there's something inside me, in my gut, telling me that my life would be better with him in it. I slow at the intersection, waiting for the light to change, and I give my head a shake, telling myself that it's over with Will. I lost my chance and I'm not getting another one. We're too different; I need to move on. And then I see the poster, plastered to the lamppost with orange duct tape: FOODIEXPO. I hear Will in my head, telling me that he goes every year—that he could never imagine missing it. And I know I have to go.

twenty-four

What was I thinking? FoodiExpo is massive. A row of life-sized carbon-fiber cows flank a green-carpet entrance to the hall, followed by a massive wheel of cheese for picture-taking. But I haven't even got my ticket yet. The lineup is at least fifty people long and out of the corner of my eye I can see the media booth with not a single person in front. The old me would've walked over to that booth even if I hadn't registered for the event, shown my Instagram account and told the PR rep I must've forgotten to RSVP, but that I'd definitely share the experience with my followers, and then bypassed the line and the ticket price and been inside by now. The new me, however, has to fork over a credit card after a twenty-minute wait.

Once inside, I'm completely overwhelmed. There have to be at least fifty rows of booths and as I make my way down the first aisle, thinking I'll be methodical about this whole thing, I realize I'm an idiot. What did I think would happen? I'd just waltz down an aisle, see Will walking toward me, the lights would dim, blocking everyone else out, spotlights would shine down on us as we locked eyes and fireworks would explode as we rushed toward each other? In reality, the aisles are slammed with people trying to make their way closer to each booth, to see how sharp the samurai knives are, how fast a new quick-dry towel dries dishes, and get a sample of spicy hummus on a broken cracker.

I can barely see two feet in front of me. And even if I saw Will, there would be no way to get to him. Still, I push on. He has to be here. I sample wines and spirits, buy a chopping block I am told I can't live without, and take a break by watching a live demo on how to organize your kitchen cupboards, which I tell myself will be useful now that I've got my books out of them. I try to keep my spirits up—telling myself this is fun. I'm not here for Will, I'm just a gal filling her day at a food expo. But I don't believe my pep talk. I walk some more, doing a double-take every single time I see a tall guy with swoopy brown hair, and whipping around every time I think I hear someone call my name. Turns out a lot of people say "kitchen" at one of these things, which sounds a lot like "Kit."

And then, around eight o'clock, somewhere between my second full glass of wine and watching a sheep-cheese taste-test competition for the second time today, it hits me. He isn't here. He obviously didn't come, or if he did, it wasn't meant for us to find each other. My head is pounding, my shoulder is aching from carrying my butcher's block. I feel discouraged and disappointed in myself for even coming. I look up, searching for the large EXIT sign that leads out of the massive room, when I hear my name. For real this time. Overhead, through the speakers. At first I don't trust myself that the voice was really for me, but then I hear it again: *Kit Kidding.* I freeze, craning to hear more, deciphering that I've won a door prize. A set of non-stick pans that I can pick up at Booth 281.

CHANTEL GUERTIN

It almost feels laughable at this point. What am I going to do with six pans? It's as though a higher being is looking down at me, laughing, rubbing pink Himalayan salt in my wounds. You can't have Will, but you can reflect on what an idiot you were to think this plan would work every time you fry an egg in one of these pans. Well, forget it. I don't need a box of pans. Except, as I walk toward the exit, I realize I have to pass right by the 200s to get out of the hall. And so I make my way, through the crowds, down the 200s aisle, the numbers getting higher and higher. Then I see it: 281. There's a crowd in front of the booth, watching the demo—how easy it is to make omelets without them sticking in these non-stick pans. I wait until the crowd disperses and then make my way to the front.

"I . . . heard my name called. That I won?" I say unsurely, feeling shy. But the guy at the booth, with his goatee, red bandana on his head, fingerless gloves and apron, looks positively delighted. "You are going to absolutely *love* these." He comes around the side of the booth, handing me a massive box. "There are actually seven different pans in here. And if you go to our website you can get tons of recipes to make anything from breakfast burritos to steak. Feel free to give us a shoutout on social media!" I can barely hold the box and it immediately drops to the ground. I bend down, struggling to pick it up again.

"Seriously? You don't even *like* cooking," a voice behind me says. I turn around and look up. It's him, and his green eyes are on me. My heart's beating so loudly I can barely hear myself speak, my hands are trembling and I'm starting to sweat.

"I—I won them," I say nervously to Will. I wait with anticipation for him to speak.

At first, his expression is blank, and I feel discouraged, and consider that me coming here was a huge mistake. That just because I've changed my mind about him doesn't mean he's changed his mind about me.

But then, Will raises an eyebrow, looking amused. My heartbeat slows, my chest swelling. All those feelings I've had for him? Still there, but if they were nicely contained to a pot, the pot would now be overflowing.

"I heard," he says. "Never in a million years did I think I'd find you here. So who's the client?" His tone is cynical. He doesn't think I've changed.

I shake my head. "There's no client." He studies me, his eyes intense on mine.

"Actually, there are no more clients."

"What do you mean?" I can't read his tone. Is it hopeful? Does he get it? Or is it too late—does he not care?

"It's done," I tell him. "My Instagram account. Influencing. The sponsored content. All of it. I actually had to buy my ticket to this thing," I laugh, shaking my head. "First time for everything."

"You bought a ticket?" he says slowly, his brow furrowing.

I look up at him and take a deep breath. "I came to see you." My voice is barely a whisper.

"See me?" He's curious.

I find my voice.

"Will, I wanted to see you," I say assertively. "You said you never miss this event. So I figured I would find you here." I pause and then add, "To convince you why you should give us another chance."

And then everything stops, including my breathing, maybe even my heart. This is it, my last chance. I know it. I've done everything to be true to myself, and I'm taking a chance on an unknown, to make my own way against all the odds. But I'm only half of the equation. What happens next depends on Will's reaction. Seconds feel like an eternity.

And then Will moves. He comes in a bit closer and I hold my breath. Then he bends down to pick up the box. My stomach drops. He doesn't feel the same way. He stands and cocks his head. But I'm not giving up. I came here to talk, and I need him to listen. "Will, I know that—"

He holds the box up, giving a small smile. "Looks like you could use some help carrying this home. Maybe we could chat along the way."

My body feels like it's on fire, but I try to keep my cool.

"Sure. That'd be great."

#

Side by side, Will and I walk out of the convention hall and onto the street. The cold night air hits my cheeks and I inhale deeply.

"So what happened?" he asks, shifting the box in his arms. "Last thing I knew was I was texting you and then you just disappeared."

I tell him about going to Dad's, about seeing the picture of him and Gillian, about shutting my phone off. "I just couldn't do it anymore. Everything was just so confusing. I needed to turn off the noise. I was so tired of constantly worrying about every little thing I was doing and if it was fitting into this 'brand' I had created. It's like I didn't even know who I was anymore."

A couple holding hands walks toward us. I wait until they've passed before I continue.

"I thought I'd miss it, you know? That I'd feel irrelevant without posting what I was up to—or what I wanted people to think I was up to. But it was the opposite. I felt so free. It really was a digital detox. I had all this time to think about what I wanted to do—what I wanted my life to look like." I turn to look at him, that thoughtful look on his face as he looks out onto the street. "Will?"

He turns to look at me.

"What I want is you," I say softly.

He looks away, nodding his head slowly.

"I've really missed you, Kit," he says looking off into the distance. "I mean, you have no idea. I know I didn't respond to your texts. I didn't even thank you for what you did for Addie that night. She told me, you know," he says, turning to look at me again, "about your mom, how you were there for her. And I didn't even have the balls to tell you how much that meant to me. I didn't think I could handle texting you and hearing from you, wanting you, and then not having you. So I did what every good coward does—I shipped your boxes." He shakes his head. "What a coward move, I guess."

"Yeah, it was," I say. "But I get it." I reach over to push the pedestrian crossing button and Will slides his fingers through mine with his free hand. Tingles run through my body.

"I'm just . . . I'm worried," he says. I look into his eyes. I know what's coming. It's what I need to hear, but still, I dread it. He lets go of my hand as the light changes and we cross the street. "I can't be with someone who just runs away when things get hard. And it's not just me, Kit. Addie, too. She needs stability to feel safe, secure and sure of what's going on. You mean so much to her, I can tell, and it's just so confusing when you're in and out.

Of course we're going to disagree, we're going to fight, but we need to be able to resolve things like grown-ups. By talking."

His words sting, because I haven't been much of a grown-up. I know that now.

"Addie needs to see how good relationships work," Will continues. "I'm only going to expose her to a relationship if it's real, and if it's honest and sets the example I want for her."

"Which is . . . ?" I challenge him. "You have to admit, the way we went about things wasn't exactly conventional. You didn't want Addie to know we were dating. How is that honest?" I move away from him as a cyclist zips between us on the sidewalk.

"You're right. But you didn't want to be serious with someone who didn't want kids," Will says.

"And you knew you couldn't be with me unless I changed my mind, so you're at fault too."

Will stops walking. "Basically, I let my overwhelming urge to get you into bed with me overshadow all rational thought." His green eyes meet mine and the corner of his mouth turns up.

"Strange, since you made me sleep in the guest room." My voice is teasing, but my heart is pounding.

"I can see why you'd feel like you were just crashing with us, rather than being in a relationship with me," he says. "That wasn't fair. Sometimes despite *wanting* to think things through, I don't." We pass a bench and he stops, putting the box down.

I look up at the nearly full moon, then turn back to him. "You were right, I am terrified of commitment. I thought being committed meant I was trapped, that I couldn't live the life I wanted. That I would have to change who I was to fit a mold. And I didn't want that." The wind picks up and blows my hair across my face. I push it away, tucking a strand behind my ear.

"But I also didn't like being alone again as much as I thought I would. And it wasn't about being with someone or being alone. It was about missing you two."

Will nods, and I continue. "But it's still scary. I've never wanted kids in my life." I know this is the kind of stuff Will doesn't want to hear, but I need to be able to be true to myself, and tell him where I'm coming from. To be clear about what's changed, and what hasn't.

Will's brow furrows. "Well that's a problem, and one I think you really need to think about. Because you can't flit in and out."

"I know that."

Will looks away, not saying anything for a moment.

"And you know you can't say certain things then, right?" His eyes meet mine. "You can't be with us and then say you don't like kids—"

"I've never said I don't like them," I correct him. "Just that I never saw a life where I had my own."

He crosses his arms over his chest and nods. "OK. It's just—hard to know the difference."

I take a deep breath. "I know. And me saying that I don't see a life with them doesn't help our situation. That's why I gave it all up. I can't be that role model to child-free women and also have a life where I live with a child. It feels hypocritical." I reach for his hands, untangling them from his crossed arms. He lets me, and that fills me with the courage to continue.

"But having you in my life, having Addie in my life—that's more important to me. You're real, and you make me feel alive, and happy and loved and a part of something that's bigger than just me."

I bite my lip.

"And it doesn't change how I feel about motherhood—I still don't think motherhood should be a woman's obligation and I still feel so strongly that every woman should be able to choose what's right for her, without others having any say in her decision. Which, I guess, is the right that I'm allowing myself."

Will studies me.

"But you have to think about the kid thing, too," I say. "How you really feel about your own future. Like, do you really want to be with someone and not have more kids . . ."

"No."

I freeze. Why let me go on this way if there's no chance for us?

"No, I don't want to be with just someone," Will says, taking a step closer to me. He pushes a strand of hair off my face, his fingers lingering behind my ear.

"I want to be with you."

I close my eyes as a warm feeling fills my entire body.

"But you want five kids." I open my eyes and study his face. He rubs the stubble on his chin.

"I wanted five kids with Sophie. Sophie wanted five kids with me. You're not Sophie. And if I wanted Addie to have siblings, then I'd date someone who wants a lot of kids too," Will says. "I'm a big boy. I can make my own decisions. And I'll be honest with you. I've thought about it. A lot. But I keep coming back to one thing." He looks deep into my eyes and this time, I don't close my eyes, because I want to remember every moment of this conversation. "No one else is you, Kit. No one, unfortunately."

I press my lips together, but I can't stop smiling. "Unfortunately."

"Listen, if we can go through everything we've been through these last few weeks and I can still feel this way about you—I just think that's something special. You don't get that every day. And that's life—you never know how it's going to play out. Or with whom." The corners of his mouth turn up.

I reach for his hand, intertwining my fingers with his. "I know I don't always say the right things or do the right things. But neither do you, I just have to say that," I tease him.

Will's mouth hangs open. "Me?"

"Come on," I say laughing. I hit him lightly on the chest. "You're not the most flexible guy." But then I get serious. "I might run when things get tough, but you stiffen. You have a hard time seeing things from other people's perspectives. You didn't agree with my life—my *previous* life—but instead of trying to understand it better, you just instantly dismissed it, made fun of me, reduced me. You weren't willing to come to me and try to fix this. *I* had to come to *you*." I grab his hands in mine. "I know for Addie you have to be this solid guy, but it feels a little like it's your way or no way at all." My heart is pounding in my chest. What if I've just blown it? But I remind myself that if I'm going to be open to change, he has to be, too. And I have to be able to say what I'm thinking, even if it's not what he wants to hear.

"Wow," he says exhaling. My entire body tenses. "That's what I mean," he says. "This. This is good. I need you to be able to talk about things. Hard things. And you need to challenge me back." He squeezes my hands. "And you know what? You're right. I can be pretty rigid and that can be a bit . . . unfair."

I pull a hand away and brush an unexpected tear from my cheek. "I want this," I tell him. "The two of us. We're good together. You challenge me, you make me want to grow. And I want to be there for Addie. I want her to know that she can *always* count on me."

He nods, taking my free hand back and looking deep into my eyes. "I want that, too," he says huskily.

Another tear escapes. "You know it was really hard for me to go to Gillian's that night. Wow, that woman hates me. But I knew it wasn't about me. I had to put aside my own petty feelings so I could just be there for Addie. And you know what? I'd do it again. And again and again and again. Every time she calls, I will be there for her. Because I love her." And it's out there. I look back into Will's green eyes, the anticipation thick in the air between us.

I unlace my fingers from his so that I can reach up and touch his face. His cheeks are smooth and warm against my palms. I take a deep breath, feeling nervous and happy all at once.

"And I love you, too," I whisper softly, then wait for his reaction.

"What did you say?" His voice is teasing, his eyes are twinkling and his lips slowly curl up into a grin. And I know, in that moment, that he feels the same way about me.

I laugh and punch him lightly in the stomach but he puts his arms around my waist and pulls me closer. "Come on, Kit Kidding," he says, his voice low and gravelly. "I'm not sure I heard you correctly."

I hate how much he's enjoying this and yet, I'm happy to say it, again and again and again. "I said I love you, Will MacGregor."

"That's what I thought you said." And he looks so happy I could cry. That my words, my feelings could make him feel that way. He pulls me toward him.

"I don't think I need to tell you that the feeling is mutual," he says, his breath hot on my face, his nose practically touching mine.

"Oh, but you do," I whisper, my lips brushing his.

"Well, then," he says, pulling back just enough to look into my eyes. "I love you, too, Kit Kidding." Then our lips are together, and any trace of the cold night air is gone.

#

"So what's your next move, Kit Without Kids, who's now dating someone with a kid?" Will says lazily. It's the next morning and I'm in Will's arms. We only have a few minutes before he has to go get Addie from Millie's. Dad life never stops, not even when you're in love. But we have these moments and I don't intend on wasting them.

"Funny you should ask," I say, rolling onto my back and looking up at the ceiling. "Remember the Bookstagram account I was starting to tell you about, the night of the Meanderers concert?"

"Mmm. Yeah, but tell me more."

And so I do. "I have a completely unsound business plan, but it's getting there. All I know is that I haven't felt this excited about something in a long, long time."

He pushes himself up onto an elbow, facing me. "I've been thinking about it forever," I say. I roll over so I'm facing him, too. "And maybe it's nostalgia, or a sense of closure on my mom's death, but I just feel like I've got to do it." I laugh nervously because what if it is just a crazy idea? But Will nods.

"Then you've got to do it. Is there anything I can do to help?"

"Actually," I say, biting my lip, "I'm supposed to be looking at a laneway apartment this afternoon with Gloria. It's not exactly what I've been looking for, but it's more affordable than my original plan, which was to buy a house with a garage."

"Right," Will says, his face clouding. He clearly remembers our conversation, which also occurred at the scene of our awful fight.

My stomach tightens. "The thing is, now that I'm in this relationship with you for real, for the long haul, it seems sort of silly to think about buying my own house." My voice is light, gauging his reaction.

"I like the sounds of that," he says, his eyes meeting mine.

"And I'm not saying you've got to re-invite me to live with you. Because I'm kind of enjoying my place now." I look around my room. I just bought an ornate antique dresser at a garage sale last weekend. It felt good—to spend money on something I love, something so completely opposite of the kind of modern, sleek stuff I'd been borrowing from Stay-a-While. Something that may or may not look good in photos, and it doesn't matter, because I love using it. And I love how I'm finally putting my own touches on my own space, treating it as permanent instead of completely temporary, like I was before.

Will runs his fingers through my hair. My whole body tingles with his touch.

"Don't love living here too much," he says.

I run a finger down his chest. "So that's the thing." I feel overcome by nervousness at what I'm about to propose, the morning after getting back together with him, but at the same time, it feels so right.

"So what I'm thinking . . ." I say. "If I'm going to be spending a lot of time working on my new business, and a lot of time with you and Addie . . ." I take a deep breath. "What if you rent me your garage? If I run my business out of your garage, then I'd be at your place pretty much all day, every day." I lean toward him, kissing his chest.

"My garage, huh? You've never even been in my garage. What makes you think it's for rent?" He pulls away and I look up at him but his green eyes are shining.

"I think I can convince you." I shimmy up so my face meets his.

"Oh yeah?" he says.

I plant my lips on his, his stubble rough on my chin, but I don't care. Eventually we break apart, though my entire body is warm and tingly. "I wouldn't want you to think I'm using you for your garage."

He leans in and his mouth is on mine and my body's on fire all over again.

"You can use me for whatever you want."

I pull back. "Really?" I say, feeling excited at the prospect.

"Uh-huh." He nods.

"If we do this," I say, "I want to pay rent. Like, have a contract and everything."

"Contract," he mumbles in my ear. "Rent. You really know how to get me going."

"I'm serious."

"So am I. Let's do it."

I pull back to look at him. My body rushes with adrenaline. "You're sure?"

"I'm sure." He looks at me, and I can hardly believe it. I'm doing it. After all these years, I'm finally going to do it. I squeal, then kiss Will square on the lips, then leap up on the bed in my shorts and tank top, jumping up and down on the bed until I fall down again, and Will wraps his arms around me, pulling me close, alternately laughing with me and kissing me back.

twenty-five

It's Saturday morning in late October and Will's up early and downstairs. Because that's him. I'm feeling lazy this morning and stretch out on the bed. I've been spending more and more time at his place. It just feels natural to go to bed here and wake up here, even if it's usually at 6 a.m. I listen. The house is still quiet, unlike last night, when we hosted the monthly family dinner with Margot and Ari. It was a lot of noise and a lot of life—especially with the boys. Avid got his head stuck in the banister and we were all distraught until Will reminded everyone, including Avid, that if he could get his head in, surely he could get it out. With Will's reassurance, the little boy calmed down, and slid his head back through the railing. They were all banished to the basement until dinner. It was loud and messy but I found myself actually relaxing into the chaos—like, it wasn't perfect, and it didn't need to be. And in that, it felt calming. Seeing Addie with her cousins reminded me how important family can be and how nice it can be to have this built-in support system of people who care for you unconditionally.

But maybe the most surprising of all has been Margot. We're never going to be BFFs, that's for sure, and I don't even know if she'll ever get to really like me, but last night, before leaving, she looked me in the eyes and told me she could see how happy Will and Addie are. She didn't say "because of me" but I know that's what she meant. She was *almost* warm. I thanked her, and meant it.

Now, I roll onto Will's side of the bed and bury my face in his pillow. I take in his scent—that mix of musky deodorant and sweat—and then get out of bed.

"Mornin', Sunshine." Will slides me a coffee across the bar, which I take gladly. Tiny mounds of chopped veggies on a butcher's block beside the stove tell me Will's planning on omelets for breakfast—my favorite. I know he's trying to make the mornings enticing so I'll want to stay over, and I don't mind one bit. "How'd you sleep?"

"Great, actually. I think you tend to change your sheets a lot more than I do. Makes a difference." I take a sip of coffee and the warmth fills me. I smile. "You?"

"Never better." He comes around the bar and runs his fingers up the back of my neck, through my tangled hair, and pulls my face into his. Tingles run down my spine.

"But I haven't brushed my teeth yet," I protest.

"Neither have I." And then his mouth is on mine.

"Eww, it's not even seven."

Will pulls back and I turn around. Addie is standing there in one of Will's old T-shirts and pajama bottoms. "Jeez."

I laugh and pull her in for a hug and Will gets back to the omelets.

"Good morning to you, too," I say.

After washing the breakfast dishes, Will reminds us of our full day. "Gymnastics in a half hour and then Zyata's birthday party this afternoon."

"And we still have to get her gift," Addie reminds him.

"Right." Will turns to me. "What are your plans?"

"I need to get a bit of work done at my place," I tell him. And for a moment, I hate the way that sounds. I think he does, too, because he kind of flinches, but doesn't say anything. "I want to start getting some of the books in order," I say. "I need a system for knowing what I have. But I'll be back around four—and then Addie, how about you and I work on your Halloween costume?"

I know I've let her down before, and maybe there's a part of her that still might not fully believe me, that I'll be back, that I'll actually help her, but I know the only way to really earn her trust is through action. I know I'll be here for her, not just this afternoon, but in the long run. And soon she'll know, too.

"Awesome," Addie says, beaming.

"Oh, and don't forget," I say as Will pops a couple of slices of bread into the toaster. "The Olympigs are next weekend. We have to go there straight from your gymnastics practice, so don't make any other plans. No VR or errands."

"We know," Addie groans, pouring herself a glass of orange juice. "You remind us *every day*."

I laugh. "I know. It's just so important to Izzy," I say. "We can't forget. Also, when I was talking to her yesterday she told me that she has a very special job for you."

"She does?" And Addie's eyes light up. "What is it?"

"There's a smaller 2K run just for kids," I tell her. "Kids sometimes have to get transplants, too." Addie nods, her face serious.

"So she was thinking maybe you could be the one to give the kids their medals when they finish."

She smiles broadly. "Yes, definitely. I'll do a great job—I'll think of a cheer."

Will turns to me. "That's the perfect job for Addie."

I think of how Izzy couldn't have kids and feel warmed that I have a part in bringing Addie into Izzy's life, too.

"Oh, and another thing," I say. "My dad and Jeannie are coming. And I was thinking that we could have them for dinner. With Izzy and Roddy. It won't be as adventurous as your family dinners but—they're my family."

"I dunno. Do they taste good?"

I roll my eyes. "Will. Have them *over* for dinner, dummy. You know what I mean."

"I have to say, I like all these plans you're making for us . . ."

There's a knock at the door but it opens before any of us even attempt to get to it. "Yoo-hoo," Gillian singsongs as she enters. I haven't seen her since the night I went to see Addie. I brace myself. "Brought you a coffee," she says, focused on Will, handing him a takeout cup. She's wearing yoga pants, white sneakers and a hoodie, and her hair is smooth and her makeup perfect, if a bit much for this early on a weekend morning. "I was thinking I could bring both girls this morning," she says as Millie comes into the kitchen behind her. When Gillian finally sees me, she freezes, then turns to face Will. "What the hell is she doing here? Is this why I haven't heard from you lately? Will . . ." She shakes her head.

Millie heads toward Addie, but Gillian puts her arm out, stopping her. "Come on, Millie, we don't need this. Screw you, Will. You're messing up your own life—and Addie's. Millie, say goodbye to Addie because you're not going to be seeing her outside of school and gymnastics—not as long as *she's* around," she says, her eyes focused on me. Millie and Addie both protest, but Gillian tugs her toward the door and then it slams shut. Will, Addie, and I stand in stunned silence.

"Are you serious?" Addie says finally, her eyes wide, her face red. "So now Millie and I can't hang out because of you guys?" She races up the stairs. I take a deep breath and turn to Will. His eyes are equally huge and his face equally angry.

"I knew this was going to blow up eventually."

"You haven't told her about us?" I say slowly. Anger, hurt, disappointment—these feelings all hit me at once.

Will sighs. "I haven't actually seen her since we got back together, and my romantic life is actually none of her business. You know that."

"But does *she* know that?" I ask, putting my hand on his arm, surprising myself with my own ability to feel bad for Gillian. "I think this is going to be really hard for her, and you're doing what you accused me of doing—running away from a problem instead of facing it."

"You're right. I've been avoiding it."

"I know it's not easy to talk to her about something like this," I say softly, trying to put myself in Gillian's position. "She has a huge crush on you and she's hurt. But right now, someone needs to talk to Addie."

Will takes a deep breath. "You're right. We've got to leave for gymnastics anyway, which is the last thing I want to be doing. But I'll talk to Addie on the drive."

He puts peanut butter on the toast and wraps it in paper towel. "And then I'll talk to Gillian."

I put my hand back on Will's arm. "Try to be kind," I say. He just looks at me, shaking his head.

"Kit Kidding," he says, putting his arms around me. "You are simultaneously making my life hell and better by the moment. And I wouldn't have it any other way."

I brush him off, laughing. "Good, cuz you're stuck with me. I'll see you later."

#

I'm staring at the stack of books in my apartment, overwhelmed by decisions. I still haven't figured out how I want to organize the garage. Alphabetically by genre just seems too obvious. I want my space to be special and unique. I want people to know that although the books they can get at the Book Nook are just books—books they could get at any store, at the library, online—there's a reason to come to the Book Nook instead. But what is that reason? Discouraged, I pull out my phone and open Instagram. To my surprise, my @BookKit following has gone up again. I know this is mostly thanks to my true friends—Xiu, Gloria and Casey have been on board from the start and have been sharing the account in their stories. Within days a lot of @KitwithoutKids ladies were following me too. And that's been nice to see, but what I love most about this new account are the comments. It's not just people tapping the first emoji possible—no more 🐦 or 😍 emojis or other superficial comments based purely on the photo without even reading the caption. Now, people are actually reading, *responding* to my posts. Sharing their thoughts on the book reviews I've posted. Sometimes they agree with me and want to add their own take. Sometimes they disagree with me and tell me why. Then other people jump in and comment on others' comments. They start actual conversations. People have even gone back to some of my older posts, from before my page was public, to comment on those posts. I'm starting to feel like I'm even making friends—@bookybookgirl and @readingwarrior are always the first to have something to say when I post, and I'm pretty much the same on their grids when they post, too. I'm building a community again, which was the best part of what I created with the No Kidding groups—bringing like-minded people together. That's why the Book Nook has to be really thought out. I know that some of these readers are going to want to get together so that we can actually *talk* about the books. Last week, I even got my first request from an author asking if I would review her book—and telling me she didn't mind if I gave her a bad review because she just loves what I'm doing and the community I'm creating.

A knock at the door breaks me out of my train of thought. I look through the peephole and nearly do a double take. It's Gillian, and she looks tired. I stand back for a moment, wondering if she's heard me, deciding if I should answer. And then she knocks again.

"Kit?" she says through the door. "Are you there?"

I take a deep breath and open the door, just enough to see her and give her the message that her unexpected visit isn't welcome.

"I hope you don't mind," Gillian says. "I need to talk to you." I stand there, staring at her. "Can I come in?" I have no clue what could possibly be so important that she needs to see me face-to-face for the second time in a day, but she looks sincere, so I step aside and let her in.

Gillian looks around. "Wow," she says. "You sure have a lot of books." I look into my apartment, seeing what she sees. Probably, to the uninitiated, my apartment seems bizarre. Cluttered. Without order. "Have you read them all?"

"No."

"But why do you have them? Why not get rid of the ones you've already read? I never understand people who hang on to books. Also, have you considered built-ins?"

And there's that tone, that Gillian tone that's always a little bitchy and a whole lot judgy. But this time I hear it as someone different. I hear it as someone who's maybe a bit frightened about things she doesn't quite understand. And is trying to bond with me. Too bad I really don't have the patience for her right now.

"What do you want, Gillian?" I ask her, folding my arms across my chest.

"Right, well," she says, shaking her head. "Can we sit?" I motion for her to step in farther. My couch is filled with books so I wave a hand at the stools at the island.

"Nice view," she says, turning to look out the windows. When I don't respond, she turns back to face me. She's wringing her hands together and I exhale, feeling a bit sorry for her. Not a lot, but a bit. "I want to apologize for this morning," she says. "I behaved poorly. Very poorly." When I still don't say anything, she continues. "I put the girls in the middle of this whole thing, too, which," she exhales, "was so awful. They were a shitshow at the gym. And this has nothing to do with them and everything to do with Will and me." Her face is drawn. "I was wrong. How I acted, and about you. I know you don't want to hear this, or probably anything about me, but when Peter left—Peter is my ex-husband—I was a mess. I mean, an absolute *mess*. I didn't know how I was going to survive—financially, as a single mom, without a man. I was a stay-at-home mom. A kept woman. And I prided myself on that little gold star." Gillian looks sheepish. "God, how pathetic does that sound?"

At this, I give her a sympathetic look, though she's really just enforcing why I started the No Kidding group, why I spent so many years supporting women who wanted to support themselves, to break the stereotype that Gillian herself was perpetuating. But now, I nod to encourage her to go on. "Will was there and he filled a void—not all voids, but I guess, I always kept hoping." She's right, I don't want to hear this. But this is her truth, so I let her continue. "Things were really good with us for so long. And then you came along, and I could see that Will was happy. Really happy. And instead of being happy for him, I hated you for it. *I* wanted to be the one to make him happy. Now Will's so pissed at me," she says. "I've never seen him so mad. So's Millie. And Addie. And I deserve it. I fucked everything up. Everyone hates me and now I've lost everything." I soften at her words because I've been there, I've felt what she's felt—but at the same time, it's hard for me to feel too sorry for her when she's done nothing to be kind to me. "That's not why I'm here," she says suddenly. "I don't mean—I'm not trying to fix things with you so Will won't be mad at me. This isn't some sort of ploy."

I take a minute and close my eyes, trying to figure out what tactic to take. I turn back to her and say, "You may have fucked things up, but nobody hates you and you haven't lost everything." I sigh. "That's a bit dramatic, right?" Why I am doing this? Shouldn't I be yelling at her to get out of my apartment and to leave Will and me alone? But I can't bring myself to do it. "You made a mistake," I say. "And God knows, I've made plenty.

And now you've realized it and you're fixing it. I'm sure your coming here is going to mean a lot to Will. And to Addie and to Millie." Gillian looks at me expectantly. "But it means a lot to me, and hopefully that's the real reason you're here." Am I seriously almost forgiving this woman? "I know you're not going to want to hear *this*," I say. "But, I think we're a lot alike, Gillian. You can come off as brash and rude," I say, and at this Gillian purses her lips. "But deep down, I know that you are quite kind." Her shoulders relax. I smile. "I just paid myself a compliment there, too." We both laugh.

"Listen," I continue. "I know how much you love Will and Addie. I love them, too." I meet her eyes and she nods. "I think we both had this idea of who we were, who we thought we wanted to be, and then things changed. You just didn't *want* the change. Maybe your ex-husband totally blindsided you when he left or maybe you knew it was coming but were in denial. Either way, you had to pick up the pieces and put yourself back together. And figure out a new path. I get it. For me, I so badly wanted to change, to be true to myself, to be with Will without secrets, without worrying what people would think, without worrying what it would mean to suddenly have a kid in my life, but just didn't know how to go about it. And then I fucked up and lost a lot too. So here we are, different women from who we once were, just trying to figure it all out. I wish I could tell you that everything's going to be OK. But . . . I can't. You're in love with Will and I get that, but I guess—you're going to have to get over him, in some way or another. Be OK with being just friends with him, seeing me with him. Or maybe you can't be OK with that and you'll need some time away. I can tell you that I hope we can find a way to make things work. Mostly for the girls, but also because

I know Will does like having you in his life. And I don't want to stand in the way. I'm not saying we have to all start hanging out together or anything, but I don't want to be your enemy, Gillian."

Gillian exhales deeply and looks down at her feet, then back at me. "Me neither," she says. "And I promise to try harder to be respectful of you guys, and no more freak-outs." She stands, sighs and walks toward the door. Then turns back. "I want to say you lucked out with Will, but it's not luck. On either side. I hope you guys make it. I think you're probably really good together. And there are plenty of guys out there, right?" She gives a half smile. I walk toward her, and then, before I can overthink it, I hug her.

My gut instinct is to call Will the minute Gillian leaves, but I don't. I'll fill him in later. I get back to my books, thinking through my system. As the sun starts to dip behind the buildings I finish loading all the books into bins and then sit on the couch. It's my favorite time of day—the light casting a golden glow across the sky, streaming into my apartment, casting a halo on everything it touches. I know that I'm going to miss this place. I take out my phone, but not to take a photograph. I text Will.

Be home soon. It's not my home, but being with him, it feels like home.

#

After dinner, Will and I are sitting on his couch, drinking wine, listening to music and chatting about the day. Addie's upstairs changing into the Halloween costume we worked on this afternoon.

"So . . . Gillian stopped by my place today."

"Shit," he says, rubbing his chin. "And you're just telling me now?" He swivels to face me.

"I didn't want to talk about it with Addie around." I take a deep breath. "I'm not going to pretend I know what's best for her, but what happened this morning, that wasn't cool. It was really upsetting, on so many levels."

"I know. I really laid into Gillian when I saw her at the gym," Will says. "I didn't want to bring it up again to you, but I told her it wasn't OK, her barging in here like that, having a massive meltdown, treating you so terribly . . ."

"That's the thing, though, Will. She walks in here because you let her. You know that she's in love with you, and sure, maybe you haven't reciprocated necessarily, but you haven't exactly stopped her from having hope." His face pales, but I continue. "I've spent a lot of years really fighting for women to stand up for themselves, to take care of themselves, and to be heard. And I don't know a lot about Gillian, but I know she had to figure out how to be this single mom, and to go back to work, to support herself." I reposition myself on the couch, tucking a leg underneath me. "And I feel like she's put herself out there, to you, and put herself in a bit of a holding pattern in terms of her personal life, because of you. If you always knew that you weren't interested, you should've told her that, straight up. So she knows when she's watching a show with you, it's as friends. If she's bringing you coffee, it's as friends. You know?" I'm more vehement than I intend, but I don't back down. The old me is back.

It's quiet in the house. Will is looking away from me. I bite my lip, knowing I've probably overstepped, and at the same time, feeling proud of myself for standing up for Gillian, even though it *is* Gillian.

"You're right." He sighs. "I guess my ego likes all the attention. Who wouldn't? I told myself it was totally platonic on both sides, that we were two friends, with girls who were friends. But of course I knew it was more, on her side. Now she knows that there's no chance for her and me, but only because I made it clear to her that I love you; that I'm going to do everything I can to make sure that you and I work out. But I need to apologize to her for leading her on. Because it's the right thing to do and also because I'm a bit afraid of you." He grins. "When you feel strongly about something, you don't back down, huh?"

A small smile forms across my lips and I shake my head, my ponytail swinging over my shoulder. "Nope. So you're really going to do whatever it takes to make us work? Like . . ." I slide my hand up his leg.

"Are you guys ready?" Addie interrupts and I pull my hand away, and turn to look up the stairs at her. She descends and we clap. She's in her costume—a Pegasus, complete with wings and a long pink wig.

"You made that?" Will says, nudging me.

"We made it together." I meet Addie's eyes and she beams. My chest swells with an unfamiliar feeling.

"This is the best costume I've ever had," she says. "If I don't win a prize with this . . . well, actually," she shrugs, "I don't really care if I win anything or not because I love my costume so much." She flips her wig over her shoulder. "Can I FaceTime Millie?" she asks Will.

"You bet." She heads back upstairs and Will turns to me. "Slow clap on that one," he says. "But you know what that means, right? Now that I've seen your skills there's no getting out of it."

"What?"

"You, me, couples costume. So what's it gonna be: Peanut butter and jelly? Fork and knife?"

"Oh, no . . ." I shake my head.

"Yep, yep, yep. This is a side of me you probably didn't know but I have always wanted to do a couples costume. Never have. So now, it's you and me, Boss." Then he makes a face. "Aw, shoot. Does this count as one of those times where I'm just deciding stuff and it's irritating to you? Are you really saying no or are you sort of saying yes?"

I laugh. "In this case, I'm actually flattered that you want to do a corny costume together."

He snaps his fingers. "Corn and butter. Very original. And since we're on the topic of celebrating holidays together, I was thinking we could maybe host Christmas here, together? Invite both our families? We like to do a big Christmas Eve graze all night, sing carols by the fire kind of thing. But what are your traditions? Let's make a new tradition together. And then there's New Year's Eve, and Valentine's Day, of course . . ."

I laugh. "Let's take it one holiday at a time, OK? Although now that you've got me thinking about mistletoe . . ." I lean over and press my lips to his, feeling my entire body melt into him as he wraps his arms around me.

#

I spend the following weeks decluttering and cleaning the garage, only taking breaks to eat, sleep, and spend time with Will and Addie—I've helped her with a book report and to build a replica of Saturn for the science fair, and we've been baking batches and batches of muffins. Even though Will's an excellent cook, he hates to bake—and it turns out I love it. Addie and I are trying to perfect our own special recipe and the latest batch went into the oven an hour ago. Will has been great, especially when I had to haul out most of the contents of the garage—his tools, bins of Addie's old clothes, a bar fridge, a rug—the list felt endless. Will never complained and figured out where to fit everything in the basement. He even got a pre-fab shed, with Dad's advice, for all the outdoor stuff—lawn mower, bikes, shovels. I've spent days hosing down and scrubbing the floors and walls, then more days painting the walls a shade called Skywash, a soft blue that I envisioned making the room look warm and cozy—but now that the paint is dry and I'm really assessing it, the room feels cold and empty. It doesn't help that it's been raining all day and the garage is damp and chilly and that I'm exhausted, and discouraged.

"Lookin' good," Will says as I'm gathering up the drop sheets Saturday afternoon, after doing the final touch-ups in the hard-to-reach spots, which always feels like the hardest work. I shove the folded drop sheets into a large garbage bag and sigh.

"I don't know what you're referring to. I know it's not me—I look like one of those characters from Avatar." I pull at the clump of hair that's come loose from my ponytail. It's covered in blue paint.

Will comes closer, brushing my hair off my face. "Not quite. They didn't have blue hair, only blue bodies."

I sigh and lean into him. His arms fold around me. When we break apart, I wave my hand around the room. "I don't get it. I had this vision of how the garage would look and now it's gone. All I see are oil stains and pipes I can't move . . . maybe this whole thing was just a terrible idea."

"What was a terrible idea?" It's Addie. I turn and she's standing in the door, a plate of muffins in her hands. "Ta-da," she says.

"I took them out of the oven myself." I had completely lost track of time, but she's so proud of herself that I don't feel that bad that I abandoned our baking.

She places the plate on one of the large boxes holding the unbuilt shelves I ordered, then unwraps a muffin and hands it to me. I take a bite. "These are amazing. You think we nailed it?" I try to sound cheerier than I feel.

Addie takes a bite of hers. "Maybe it needs to be blueberries *and* chocolate chips."

I smile and ruffle her hair.

"So what's the terrible idea?" Addie asks again.

"This," I say, sitting down on one of the boxes. Addie sits on one side, Will grabs a muffin and sits on the other. "You know when you build something up in your head for so long and you think it's going to be so great, but then you go to do it and . . ."

"It's not perfect?" Will finishes.

"Yeah."

"No one wants perfect," he says. "You have to forget about perfect. Tell us why you wanted to do this in the first place."

I groan. "You know why."

"Tell us again."

So I do. My vision, the feeling I want to create for people. "To give people a getaway in the middle of the city, where they can go, and be in the most beautiful little retreat, and they can relax, and read and . . ." I sigh. "I'm describing a bookstore. This isn't anything new. It's exactly why bookstores were created. And I've fooled myself into thinking this is something special—"

"It *is* special," Will says, putting his arm around me and pulling me close to him. He smells like sandalwood and I breathe deeply, trying to relax. "It's not *any* bookstore. People can buy a book anywhere. It's the feeling they're going to get when they come in here. It's you, injected into this space, the feeling you had when you came up with this idea. They're going to feel *that*." Will says it so emphatically that I have to believe him.

"Yeah," Addie says, pumping her hand, which is holding a muffin, in the air. I laugh and put my arm around her, so we're all connected.

"You're right. It is special. I guess, I was just really hoping that I'd feel that connection to my mom, by creating this dream she had. And I'm worried I might never have that with her."

"But you have us," Addie says. "And I think this is the coolest thing ever." She stands, clapping her hands together. "Who else has a bookstore *right in their backyard*?" I laugh, feeling better already.

"It's just cold feet," Will whispers, nudging me.

Addie waves her hands to get our attention. "I've got an idea, too."

"What?" I say, smiling.

"You know how most kid sections are alphabetical? What if you don't know what you want to read? I think you should group everything by subject. Like, if you love mermaid books, like I do, then here are all the mermaid books. But it can't be just about books—people buy books on their computers or get them at the library for free. You have to make it so kids want to come and hang out. Make it fun. Like, get beanbag chairs, or drinks—with lids so they don't spill—or maybe even get a hanging chair." That idea seems to thrill her most. "Sorry," she says. "I know this is your project."

"No, I love your ideas," I say, my enthusiasm returning. "I've been trying to figure out how to organize it all, actually."

"Oh and then you have those fairy tale books," she says. "Those could go over here." She walks to the far corner of the garage, and I nod.

"Right." I look to Will. "Have you noticed that most fairy tales have an evil stepmother?"

He grins. "I hadn't, actually."

"Well it's true. I was considering not even selling fairy tales, but then, they're part of history. And history doesn't have to repeat itself."

"I like the sounds of that," he says, taking a step closer to me and nuzzling my ear.

"You guys are so embarrassing."

I clear my throat. "You know, we can even organize some of the adult books the way you're suggesting," I say to Addie. "Not just by author, but by theme. If you like books with strong female characters, they're all here," I say pointing to a section of the wall. "And it can be a mix, romance, non-fiction, historical fiction. Lizzy Bennet can take her place next to Joan of Arc. I love it!" And I'm starting to see it again. My vision, my plan. I look to Addie and my eyes fill with tears.

"Thank you," I say.

"Don't cry," she says. "This is going to be fun. And I can help you. I know you were going to do this with your mom, but maybe now you can do it with me."

"Oh Addie." I put my arms around her and hold her close. "I would love to do this with you."

I sit back down and ask her to sit next to me. I pull my phone out of the front pocket of my sweatshirt. Holding out the phone with one hand, I pull Addie in toward me with my free arm. I grab Will with the other and pull him in too. When we're all in the frame together, I tell them to smile and I snap a picture. We all lean in to look at it. My hair's wild and Addie's laughing, and the top of Will's head is cut off. But we're happy.

I open my Instagram app and write out a caption.

Coming soon . . .

And then I hit Share.

"You're just gonna post it, just like that?" Will asks, teasing. "No editing, no scheduling?"

"Yep." And then I slip my phone back into my pocket. "Just like that."

Addie stands and heads back toward the door that leads through the yard to the house. "Back in a sec," she calls. I watch her go, wondering what she's up to, then turn back to Will as he wraps both arms around me.

"This is it," he says.

"What is?"

He waves an arm around. "This. Us. This is what I've always wanted."

"You always wanted someone to move your tools to the basement and take over your garage?" I tease.

"You know what I mean."

I rest my blue hair on his shoulder and let myself totally relax. "Yeah, I do." I breathe in the scent of this moment, so I can remember it later when things get tough or stressful or just plain tiring. Though one thing I'm learning is that it isn't all or nothing, with Will. Every day, he seems to find ways to make things special, for us to share a laugh, to lighten a stressful moment. I always thought the perfect relationship meant long stretches of romance, but now I see that sure, there are dates, and nights alone, but it's the everyday stuff, the stolen kiss while doing a mundane chore, that feels almost more romantic. Maybe not quite as romantic as an island getaway for two, but it's definitely more real.

A few minutes later Addie returns, holding a brown, rectangular package.

"What's that?" Will asks.

"It's between Kit and me."

"Alright, alright. I can take a hint." Will kisses my forehead and then ruffles Addie's hair on his way out of the garage. Addie hands me the package.

"This is for you. It was supposed to be for the grand opening, but I don't want to wait." She watches me as I unwrap the paper gently, careful not to rip it. I recognize the faded yellow of the book cover immediately. I turn it over and it's a Nancy Drew book. But not just any Nancy Drew book, it's #24: *The Clue in the Old Album.* I bring my hand to my mouth.

"How did you . . . ?"

"What can I say, I guess I'm a super-sleuth." She grins and sits down on the box, next to me. "You like it?" Her eyes are full of hope.

I wrap my arms around her, pulling her close, and kiss her on her head. "How could I not? Now everything's complete."

Acknowledgements

My agent, Samantha Haywood, believed in me and this idea, when it was only a few paragraphs on a page. Thank you—you are such a superstar, and also, my hair idol. Also thanks to Megan Philipp, Laura Cameron, Devon Halliday and the entire team at Transatlantic Agency.

One hopes for an editor who believes in your book. I feel so lucky to have landed a dream team of two smart, savvy, encouraging editors in Bhavna Chauhan at Doubleday/Penguin Random House Canada and Esi Sogah at Kensington. Thank you for falling in love with Kit and her story. I have loved working with both of you. I'm also grateful to the entire Doubleday/Penguin Random House Canada team for your wonderful support, including Kristin Cochrane, Amy Black, Melanie Tutino, Danielle LeSage, Emma Ingram, Val Gow, Kate Panek, Jennifer Griffiths, Melanie Little and Erin Kern. At Kensington, I'm so grateful to Steven Zacharius, Adam Zacharius, Lynn Cully, Jackie Dinas, Kristine Mills, Carly Sommerstein and Jane Nutter. And thank you to my personal publicist, Kathleen Cutter.

This story is loosely based on my own experience of going from single-in-the-city to almost-instant stepmom, so I would be remiss if I didn't give a big shout-out to Tom Best. Founder of Pongapalooza, an annual ping-pong event in support of First Book Canada (a charity that provides books to children in need), Tom unknowingly set the stage for my meeting with my now-husband, Christopher Shulgan.

Janis Leblanc, for walks, talks, texts and emails, for reading and editing this novel in its many forms, and for endless encouragement and friendship. Also to early readers Melanie Dulos and Sarah Hartley, and to Brenda Torrance for proofreading, thank you.

My coven, for friendship, support and motivational mugs: Karma Brown, Kerry Clare, Kate Hilton, Liz Renzetti, Jennifer Robson and Marissa Stapley, who's been there for me, making me laugh and cheering me on, since book one.

Kerry Clare gave me a copy of *The M Word*, an insightful anthology she edited about motherhood, and many of the essays—especially "Babies in a Dangerous Time" by Nicole Dixon and "Doubleness Clarifies" by Kerry Clare—were helpful as I created Kit. The essay "Something Like Motherhood" by Carolyn Megan (as published in *Modern Love: True Stories of Love, Loss, and Redemption*, edited by Daniel Jones) was also insightful.

To my family—the Guertins: Dad and Susan, Danielle, Sarah and Rob, Janet; and the Shulgans: Myron and Nancy, Mark and Jody, Isaac and Julie and all the littles. Thank you for your endless enthusiasm and love.

Finally, to my own instafamily: Myron, Penny and Fitz. You have shown me what I never knew I was missing when I wasn't a mom and stepmom. And to Chris, for getting a babysitter and walking into Spin for the Pongapalooza event—alone!—that warm spring evening all those years ago. For walking me home later that night and asking me out on a real date. For cottage weekends of living and breathing this book with me, but also for all the little things you do every single day so that I can make the time to write, and for being my own personal happy ever after.

Connect with Us

Visit us online at
KensingtonBooks.com
to read more from your favorite authors, see books
by series, view reading group guides, and more.

for sneak peeks, chances to win books and prize packs,
and to share your thoughts with other readers.

facebook.com/kensingtonpublishing
twitter.com/kensingtonbooks

Tell us what you think!

To share your thoughts, submit a review,
or sign up for our eNewsletters, please visit:
KensingtonBooks.com/TellUs.